A Man
With A
Maid

Book Three

Also Published by Grove Press

At your bookstore, or order below.

Grove Press, Inc., 196 West Houston St., New York, N.Y. 10014.

Please mail me the books checked above. I am enclosing $_____
(No COD. Add $1.00 per book for postage and handling.)

Name _____

Address _____

City_____ State_____ Zip_____

A Man
With A
Maid

Book Three

GROVE PRESS, INC., NEW YORK

First Black Cat Edition 1982
First Printing 1982
ISBN: 0-394-17993-5
Library of Congress Catalog Card Number:

Manufactured in the United States of America

GROVE PRESS, INC., 196 West Houston Street, New York, N.Y. 10014

Chapter 1

THE mastering of my beautiful Marion and her maid Kay had left me but momentarily satisfied. I thought of her indeed as "my" Marion, for she had emerged from her sweetly torturous adventures in The Snuggery as a young woman of truly voluptuous temperament, just as had her sister Alice. Both had first responded to me with a proud defiance which I had stripped from them little by little, as surely as I had their clothes.

Whether they would now confide in one another intrigued me, for I meant yet to possess them both together. The very thought filled me with exquisite longings. I had little doubt that the same hesitations, the same blushing protestations and embarrassments would issue from their lips when both were denuded and whipped together as had first occurred. Had they ever kissed one another mouth to mouth and caressed with lingering sighs those very treasures I had unveiled beneath their bodices and between their thighs?

Women are giving to artlessness in all such matters. The possibility was indeed there. Had they not yet done so—had they not yet given way to the frailties of passion in the dark of their beds—then I knew well now that they could be brought to. For there is in all young women a propinquity toward intimacy which in men is thankfully never apparent. I had observed enough before this how two girls will often bathe together, using the same warm water in the bathroom while they freely display their nudity to one another.

I had known of my sisters, cousins, and even the maidservants at my parents' house do this. Listening of occasion by the bathroom door, I had heard their sweet chatter, their laughter and their whispers. Were they not all made so that of occasion at least they would reach out playfully to toy with one another's polished, rounded breasts, or even more daringly dip their fingers beneath and within the warm, moist honeypots between each other's thighs?

The thought frequently quickened me and stirred my cock, for I meant on some future occasion to extract from Alice and Marion every lingering detail of their past dalliances. Yet, unknown to me then, I was about to be diverted from this attractive goal by the most unexpected of events.

I had lunched at the Army and Navy Club, from which I emerged full of such fond thoughts into the bright sunlight of the afternoon. So immersed in dreams which I intended soon enough to realise, I raised my arm at the approach of a hansom cab and was about to approach it as the cabby reined in his horses when a woman of striking aspect all but collided with me.

"Forgive me, but 'twas I who hailed it first," she declared so coolly that I looked at her anew. I judged her to be in her early thirties. The skin of her oval face was flawless. Her large dark eyes, bewitchingly adorned with long black lashes, betokened both passion and a marked feeling of observation. Some five feet seven inches tall, she possessed a slender but superbly rounded figure which her black dress and tricorn bonnet but enhanced.

"Madam, I do beg your pardon," I exclaimed while the cabby sat quite impassive, judging us both by our attire to be passengers who would no doubt be forthcoming with a generous tip. "Permit me—I was but going to Regent Street," I went on, opening the door for her.

She gave a little bow that was as much mocking as grateful. "I, too, pass along that way. Perhaps we could share?" she asked in a softer tone.

The opportunity seemed too good to pass up, and in a moment I was seated beside her while she fussed momentarily with the folds of her skirt in such manner that my eyes were immediately attracted to the splendid lines of her thighs that I judged neither slim nor fat. Several diamond rigns glittered on her fingers, but none which would have betokened marriage. Was she divorced, I wondered. Separated? With some uncanniness she appeared to read my thoughts as the cab wheeled to enter the Haymarket. Again her eyes seemed to mock, and she gave a little lift of her lovely features as if to question me silently.

"You live in town?" I asked. She had a defined air of sophistication which I felt could not have come from rustic living.

"Of occasion," she replied blandly and in such manner that I dearly longed to have her in the same pleading, helpless positions that I had so recently had Alice, Marion, and their two maids. The cab jolted at that moment over some of the rougher cobblestones, bringing her warm hip briefly against mine. The sensation was quite delicious as it always is with unknowns. She went on, "I do not, though, have a small permanent abode here, as you do."

Saying this, to my complete astonishment, she looked out of the farther window and then back at me, as if indeed challenging me to deny her remarkable assertion. Then it occurred to me that she had made but a good guess, no doubt having seen me come out of the Army and Navy Club and mentally adding thereto the cut of my clothes which spoke of Jermyn Street and Savile Row rather than a country tailor.

Intending to respond to her, measure for measure, I merely nodded and waited to see what else she would say. The thought that she might be an adventuress or even an expensive courtesan crossed my mind and yet was instantly dismissed. Her air of quality was undeniable.

"I prefer the country," she said. "The residences there tend to be larger and have a greater seclusion, have they not?"

The gentle accent that she placed on the word "seclusion" struck me forcibly. Moreover, we were about to enter Piccadilly Circus and I would normally be alighting from the cab in but a few minutes.

"You must forgive me for not introducing myself," I began, quite deliberately though I hoped not discourteously.

"Oh, but you are Jack, are you not?" She smiled at my total bewilderment and therewith she waved a gloved hand languidly toward Regent Street, which the cab was turning to enter. "You alight about a hundred yards along, if you are going to what you term 'The Snuggery,' " my mysterious companion went on.

For a moment I sat in frozen astonishment, not being able to bring myself to believe for a moment that I could ever have met this entrancing creature before and forgotten the encounter. It is not normally my way to be dumbfounded by women, however much I may desire them, but here was one who in but a few remarks had managed to turn me topsy-turvy. My expression showed such.

She laughed. "Perhaps it is I who should be forgiven, for I have taken you quite unaware."

"Good heavens, had I but seen you for a thousandth

part of a second before this, I would never have forgotten you," I exclaimed, to be met yet again by that lightly mocking smile.

"Such gallantry!" she declared. "But I expected it of you. In such circumstances as this, that is—though perhaps not in others. Tell the cabman to stop now, for you are almost past your destination."

So coolly were the words said, whilst she smoothed her elbow-length kid gloves, that I leaned out of the window and stopped the cab.

"You must uncover the mystery," I begged, thoroughly aware that I had never in my life begged a woman ere this, save but for the briefest of moments when Alice had jilted me, as I unfolded in the first volume of my memoirs.

"Very well," she responded to my vast relief and got out of the cab with me. Awarding the astonished cabby an entire sovereign in my bemusement, I escorted her through the press of carts and horsemen until, gaining the side street where was my abode of seduction, I led her there in some inner whirl of excitement, not to say a tinge of apprehension. Could she conceivably have come from Lady Betty, her daughter, or Alice or Marion, even? No doubt such temporary botherment showed in my expression, for I could feel her eyes upon me even until we were ensconced.

"I would like tea first—are you capable of making it?" she asked, though lightly enough rather than rudely. I assured her that I was as I bade her be seated. Her glance went immediately to the special chair whose hidden mechanisms had first imprisoned my former victims, for she could see it through the door into The Snuggery which I had unguardedly left open to my sitting room.

"I will take this couch," she declared, unpinning her bonnet and, with a shake of her head, letting down a veritable cascade of glossy dark hair as nestled appealingly about her shoulders that gleamed pure white above the neckline of her gown. "You will not take long?" she asked crisply whilst a little ripple of anger and resentment flowed through me. Even so I could but assure her that I would not, for she held perhaps a secret—one at least—that could undo me socially and therewith all my future plans.

The making of the tea took but a moment. When I returned into the sitting room, she had stretched her long legs upon the sofa and arrayed herself thus elegantly, if not also with a certain boldness. I intended, however, to ask her nothing further. She was, after all, but a woman. The doors were closed and virtually no sound could issue out to the world at large. The curves of her hips were quite delicious, her waist spanning no more than some twenty-two inches, thus giving her torso that divine violin shape which thrusts the bottom into such exquisite prominence.

Taking the cup and saucer, but waving away the sugar tongs, she began smoothly, "I intend not at the moment to divulge to you such knowledge as I have of you, Jack, nor where I obtained it. Be certain of one thing, however—that your secrets are perfectly safe with me. A pity indeed that I was not here to enjoy some of them.

This said with a silvery laugh made me gaze at her almost in awe, though I endeavoured to recover myself sufficiently to look as bland as she.

"Secrets?" I asked ironically. "What secrets could there be? And if there were secrets, how could you possibly know of them?"

The bait was not taken—but I knew her already too well for that. My own tone was slightly mocking now, and another woman might have responded to it with such anger as would have made her speak in haste of that very thing which she had wished to conceal.

"Let us merely say, Jack, that I, too, have a penchant for training young women. Oh, but forgive me. It is I who have not introduced myself. My name is Helen—Helen Hotspur. Quite pleasantly Shakespearian, is it not?"

"And meaningful also, I trust," I smiled, though within me I could scarce yet believe what she had said about young women.

"Indeed so," she responded, this time with a smile upon her beautiful lips that betokened the first real hint of sensuousness I had seen in her. Neither too small nor too large, her mouth was perfectly shaped, as was the aquiline straightness of her nose, whose nostrils flared gently now and then. Thinned by tweezers, her eyebrows were thin and finely arched.

"What form of training do you then indulge in?" I asked, as one who might politely ask a visitor an idle question.

"Oh, Jack, you take the cake—you really do. Let us not beat about the bush, my dear. I have raised many a girl's bottom in my time by whip, strap, birch. Is it not a perfect delight to hear them plead, to listen to the throbbing cries that issue from their throats whilst their hips and bottom cheeks so blatantly twist, offering that which they would prefer to conceal? To uncover the polished gourds of their breasts and see thereupon the delicious nipples that have erected themselves in their untoward excitement, to . . . Oh! Sir! how dare you! No! Back now!"

I need scarcely say that her exclamations were occasioned by the fact that I had risen already from the chair facing her and would have taken her lovely mouth in that very instant, had not a snakelike flickering of her gloved hand whipped so smartly across my face that I started back in total astonishment rather than reaction from the quickly whipping movement of her fingers which, by a ridging of one of her rings through the kid leather, had brought a smear of blood to my lips.

For a long moment, half-risen as I was, I stared at her, her cup and saucer still poised in her other hand and her eyes no less cool and yet languid than they had been.

"One should never draw blood—do you not agree?" she murmured as if otherwise nothing had happened. I mopped my lip with my handkerchief and nodded. That I of all people had been quelled by a woman in this manner was almost too astonishing to contemplate. Such thoughts of revenge swirled in my heated mind as I had not even indulged with Alice or Marion, yet I endeavoured still to regain such composure as I might.

"Indeed not," I answered stiffly.

"Nor should one spill tea," she laughed, observing that I had nudged my cup in the brief melee. "You have not heard a woman speak so before, except perhaps in the after-passion of a moment, and hence I forgive you. There will be time for many things, Jack. Even to whip my white, naked bottom, perhaps? Yes, my dear, I too, indulge, and in all manner of ways. Why else do you think me here. To taunt you? I am well aware that we are alone and that I could find myself bound by your ropes, had you the mind to do so—but where is the pleasure in binding and stripping a woman who wishes you to do so?"

"There would be some," I said with some stiffness not only in my voice but in my cock, which had begun to arouse itself fiercely, as she could clearly see by the increasing bulge in my trousers. Making no attempt to conceal it by drawing my jacket together, I let her eyes rest upon it, which they did not without interest.

"Perhaps a little," she shrugged, "but were there a dozen different girls so to be treated, there would be much greater pleasure in it, would there not?" Putting down her cup and resting her head back in a manner which indicated that she had no fear of me whatever, she continued, "Those of like minds assist one another best, Jack. You must be well aware that I have meant what I said, for what woman would speak to you otherwise? Moreover, there are ways to bring such desires to fruition. Think on it, Jack—a veritable harem!"

"You mean this?" I asked, though my breath was quite taken away by her words, for the reader will recall that at the end of my last volume it was I who had used that very word—albeit that my harem had been intended to begin by gathering together Alice, Marion, and their maids, together with the beauteous young widow, Connie Blunt.

"I have never dealt with fewer than two, Jack," Helen declared now solemnly, her tone becoming now so businesslike that more than ever she completely gripped my attention. "I have played governess, companion, Mistress—call it what you will—and in the best of houses. Never, may I say, have I taken a penny for such services. I have no need to. The reward is always in the final acts of submission. Let us take, for instance, two young ladies of Society whom I will call Wilma and Elizabeth. Wilma was twenty-five, proud and haughty. She deserted her husband in an hour of need when he was bound with his regiment for Rangoon. Thereupon she landed herself upon her sister-in-law and brother with whom, I might say, Elizabeth was also living. The latter was eighteen and bothersomely shy. Shall I go on?"

"Please do," I begged, "and let us meanwhile partake of some better refreshment. Do you like liqueurs?"

"Of course," she nodded and arranged her skirts so that I might feast my eyes upon the exquisite lines of her calves and rounded knees, sheathed in the sheerest black silk stockings. Her tapered fingers touched mine as I handed her a glass of Cointreau. Her eyes danced. "Later—before I leave," she murmured in response to the look in my eyes. Trailing her glance down to the rigid state of my prick, which seemed fit to burst through my trousers, she waved me maddeningly back to my chair.

"Let me tell you first, Jack, though there are many details to be omitted. You may have those later if you are good," she laughed huskily whilst I stretched my legs before her and blatantly displayed my lewd state. "Wilma quickly proved tiresome to her brother and sister-in-law, though they had no wish to throw her out. I, being in my own discreet way known to them, was called in. Accustomed as I am in such matters, I befriended her, as also Elizabeth, whom I quickly perceived to be also ripe for awakening. Wilma being the more challenging, I engaged her in riding in the paddock whilst having a few alterations made in the stable. You will know the manner of these, Jack, from your own practises. They took not long to effect—a mere matter of bars and straps.

"Being accustomed enough to the stable, Wilma made no demur when I led her in there at an appropriate moment. She was almost of my height, with patrician features, high, firm breasts and the most adorable tight bottom—though not so tight after I had finished with her. It was a simple matter to sack her head quickly and thereupon to have her strapped over one of the lower sets of bars."

"To have her strapped?" I interrupted.

Helen's eyes sparkled. "My methods were known. The thought of them being practised upon Wilma amused my hosts no end. They were not loath to assist, though with a sack over her head—a slightly crude method, I admit—Wilma knew not their identity. Her screams were of outrage, of course, particularly when I removed her long riding skirt and lowered her drawers—displaying a perfect pair of nether cheeks thereby.

Then, whilst she howled and struggled in vain, I picked up a schooling whip."

The glow that showed in my eyes amused Helen. She laughed. "We are not finally cruel, Jack, you or I. The very tip of the whip suffices generally, does it not, and a schooling whip is excellent for that. Ah, how she screeched at the first burning sweep of it! I caught both cheeks first and then the deep groove between. Her squirmings were delicious to watch. Then, stepping forward, I removed the sack from her head whilst mine hosts watched from the background. The interior of the stable was gloomy, of course, but in any event she could not turn her head to see.

"Ungagged as she was, Wilma spat at me. I cannot permit that, of course, and thereupon the whip came to my hand again. Truly, Jack, I scoured her cheeks for long minutes until the full globe was a deep pink. By then her screams of outrage had turned to sobs of pleading. Ignoring them completely, I had her stock-inged legs widely parted and held so by virtue of what I call a holding block—that is to say, a three-foot length of timber with small straps at each end which are se-cured to the ankles."

"Good heavens!" I remarked, not so much out of astonishment as the most profound admiration, which caused a distinct look of pleasure to enter Helen's eyes. She distinctly liked the compliment.

"I wish indeed I could paint you a picture of it, Jack. Her legs were quite lovely—full thighed and slim at the calves. With her hot bottom thrust back, she could do naught but display herself. Her slit, I might say, pouted quite pleasantly after my attentions with the whip, but it was her other orifice that I meant to have attended first—after I had feathered her, of course."

I could contain myself no longer. Throwing myself to my knees before her, I clasped her slim waist and pressed my mouth to her mounding breasts through her dress.

"Helen, my love, you will drive me mad!" I exclaimed, whereat she stroked my hair and drew me up to her. Our mouths met in the most delicious of kisses, and no hand sought to fend off mine as I slowly raised her dress and rucked it up above her thighs.

"Do you not wish to know more?" she whispered, even as I imbibed her sweet saliva and insinuated my hand between the silky warmth of her thighs above her banding stocking tops. Smiling between kisses, she held her thighs tight. "How naughty you are—even as I was," she murmured.

"With Wilma?" I asked.

"Yes," she sighed and relaxed her legs so suddenly that my forefinger found the moist gap of cunny immediately, for she wore no drawers. The curls were thick about it. A slight hissing of her breath through her nostrils announced that I had found the pink bud of her clitoris.

"Dear Jack, what a pair we shall make when we have our harem," she breathed. Raising her farther leg, which lay against the back of the sofa, she allowed me to toy at will with the pulpy fruit of her cunny, sighing and working her bottom as my finger twirled.

"You lovely devil—I would whip you first," I croaked.

"Of course, for otherwise you will not know my mettle, pet—and then you shall give me what Wilma had immediately I had finished whipping and feathering her."

I rose, lifting her with me whilst her arms clung tightly to my neck. In that most blissful of moments, she was no longer a cool, commanding woman but one whose bottom desired to be burned and taunted.

"Which was?" I asked, carrying her into The Snuggery.

"Do you need to ask?" Her velvet lips brushed across my cheek, her bared legs hanging limp. "The prick in her bottom, my love. It was her first there, I truly believe. Ah, how she reared at first until it quelled her!"

Chapter 2

"DO NOT undress me," she murmured as I let her down. "I prefer it with my clothes on. Do you not like me all in black?"

So speaking, she stepped back from me and, holding her dress to her hips, straddled her legs, displaying to me the fuzzed dark of her trim bush, her white belly, the ivory columns of her thighs. Her garters, broad and dark gray, were speckled with glitterdust. So framed as all was by the jet black of her dress and her stockings and boots, she looked entrancing beyond belief. A gentle, teasing movement of her belly caused me to uncover my hugely standing prick in a trice.

"Oh, what a monster! But you have not answered my question, Jack. No—do not come too near. Is it not nice to wait?"

"Delicious," I declared, "and as to the black, my pet, no curves were ever more seductively delineated."

Helen laughed throatily. "We shall have our girls dressed like this, do you not think?"

"What girls?" I begged. "Tell me!"

One single step and she was against me. Ah, the warmth and splendour of that womanly form! I clasped

14

the cold cheeks of her naked bottom, feeling their firmness, their resilience, their proud weight. Unable to resist, I sidled my forefinger into the deep groove between the luscious cheeks and found her rosette, thereby causing her to wriggle coyly.

"Jack, I have been so naughty—you must whip me," she whispered.

At that I seized her hair at the back, forcing her head up whilst the tip of my finger oozed within her, causing her eyelashes to flutter and a slight flush to intrude into her flawless face. So held, she looked exquisitely submissive, and though I knew her not to truly be, yet the challenge was ever there. Hooding her large dark eyes, she gazed at me with parted mouth.

"Oh! you are going to!" she gasped and made as if to tear away from me. "No, truly you must not—oh, spare me—do not do anything so hateful, Jack—*Oh!*"

I had her as I wanted then, one arm twisted up behind her, her dress still fully folded up to her waist and her glorious bottom a gleaming orb of desire as I bent her over the waiting chair.

"Jack, no! Oh, my poor bottom—it will hurt so!" she sobbed.

Such a perfect actress could she be in such moments that I all but believed her, were it not that she made but a token struggle to rise. With my free hand, I reached for the silver-handled whip and, without delay, brought a whistling, stinging stroke full across that firm-fleshed orb.

"*Aaaah!*" she shrieked. "You dare! Ah, you dare! I shall tell Mama!"

Her brazen words were intended only to lure me on then, though her knuckles whitened upon their gripping of the farther arm of the chair as the hissing whip again scoured a path of heat across her bottom. Her hips jerked—a single long whimpering cry burst up from her throat. "You beast! Oh, you horrid beast!" she moaned.

What a bottom she had! It surpassed in its globular beauty even those of Alice and Marion. The deep undercurve of the cheeks stood proud and jutting even when standing naked. Bent over now as she was, its spherelike appeal, posed perfectly above her magnificent thighs, was no less. Where the cheeks inrolled was a faint gingery hue, all the more inviting for the pouting lips of her quim, which showed clearly with the slight parting of her legs.

"You were naughty, too, with Elizabeth, were you not?" I growled, fully entered now into the spirit of the game.

Another long-licking hiss of the whip across her bottom made her gasp and jerk anew.

"Yes, Jack, yes—ah, the sweet thing, how I birched her for some imagined wickedness. *Oooooh!* that was too h . . . h . . . hard!"

"Go on," I growled, "for you did not end at birching, I swear."

"N . . . n . . . no, I fear not. . . . Aaaaah! You are whipping both my poor cheeks! How they burn! I will . . . I will . . . I will tell you . . . her tears ran down his cock even as I brought her at last to suck it . . . 'twas but her in . . . in . . . initiation, Jack. . . . Oooooh! It st . . . stings me! P . . . p . . . please! No more! Put your cock there! Oh, darling, yes!"

I had brought the whip across her bottom but a dozen times, yet I could wait no more—no more than she. Casting the whip aside, I seized her hips in as powerful a grip as I knew she desired. Even then—so sweetly perverse was she in her playacting at such times—her hands beat upon the chair, her hips endeavouring to swivel as if to escape me even as my swollen prick nosed its crest between the deliciously velvety channel of her throbbing cheeks.

"You dare not!" she howled. "Oh, Mama, stop him!"

"Quiet, girl!" I hissed.

For a long moment, the apparently maddened rotating of her ardent bottom prevented me from nosing my knob against the crinkled orifice that awaited its coming. Then, seizing the nape of her neck whilst she howled most realistically, I thrust her head farther down and succeeded at last in centering upon the target. Feeling the elastic squeezing of her cheeks upon my shaft, I nosed it but an inch within whilst a further shriek came from her.

"T . . . t . . . take it out! Oh, my bottom! Ah!"

One powerful surging movement of my loins and my pego, thick as it is, was lodged halfway within the warm tight tube whose passage was faintly oiled with her secretions. Squeezing secretively upon it, she then relaxed, sobbing most realistically as the throbbing shaft urged farther up until, with a sensation of perfect glory, her superb bottom bulged fully into my belly and she was fully corked.

Hiding her face in her hands, Helen began to whimper, whilst at the same time slyly parting her legs wider in order to take a firmer footing for the assault. Assured then that she would struggle no further, I clasped the fronts of her thighs, caressing all that I could reach, even to the hairy slit of her snatch where I sought anew the budding of her clitty.

"Ah, you devil!" she moaned, whilst pressing her hot silky orb deeper into my muscled stomach.

"Do you not like it now?" I asked in the way of our pretence.

"N . . . n . . . no . . . it is horrid and you shall not wh . . . wh . . whip me again if you are going to put your naughty thing there. Ooooh! No! Do not move it in and out! *Ah!*"

I had withdrawn my flaming charger almost to the

tip and then rammed the piston of throbbing manhood
slowly within again. The suction I experienced in doing
so was such as made my head spin with the voluptuousness of the act.

"Oh-oh-oh-oh!" moaned Helen now as I continued
the action, sheathing my cock back and forth whilst her
divine orb ground against my belly with every indriving
stroke. Plump as her pubic mound was, I held it cupped
upon my left hand while continuing to twiddle her love
button. Tremulous quivers coursed through her, and
with her stockinged legs braced, she commenced rotating her hips so sensuously that I all but came. With a
certain instinct, however, I could sense her approaching
her own climax and so steeled myself not to loose my
sperm until the crisis was upon her.

In that moment we were truly lost for words. None
indeed could have added but a mite to the pure ecstasy
of so possessing her. The spongy route whereby I was
sheathed gripped me as sweetly as a baby's mouth
might take one's thumb, and the burr of the thick curls
around her quim, so warmly couched in my hand, was
but an added sauce to the feast. That her bottom tin-
gled deeply still from the whip I doubted not. Perhaps it
yielded to her even greater sensations than my own, for
the bouncing pressure of her peachlike globes against
my belly were ever more imperious.

"G . . . g . . . give it to me!" she mewed. I felt
her knees buckle momentarily, the thin spurting of her
love-pleasure oiled my palm. Turning her neck and face
toward me, she extended her tongue so that, bending
farther over her, I absorbed it in my mouth, sucking
upon it avariciously while the sperm churned in my
balls and then—to the deep, panting groans I issued
forth against her lips—jetted forth in long, thick strings
which spattered far within her, causing her to lap her
long tongue in the most sensuous manner around my
own.

I quivered, thrust, expelled—again and again—until it seemed to me that I had never before attained such a momentous orgasm. Indeed, as I finally withdrew my steaming prick, the rivulets of come ran immediately from her bottomhole and trickled down her thighs, leaving small pearls of the manly effusion about the rims of her stocking tops.

Weakly we tottered together and sank down upon a couch, where our lips met anew in a kiss as soulful as it was tender.

"How you made me come!" she sighed. The tip of her tongue licked my own.

"Tell me now," I begged.

"What?" She hid her face almost shyly.

"Who told you?"

"Marion. Oh, do not be shocked. We have long been friends, though until now she has known nothing of my propensities nor I—oddly enough—of hers. She was delighted to have been broken in, my pet, and swore me to secrecy, but with such plans as I have, I could not resist."

I was not so dumbfounded as I might have been. The change in Marion after I mastered both her and her maid, Kay, had been ever more notable than in her sister. There were many she could have told had she been minded to seek revenge. Instead she had turned to Helen, evincing almost a certain pride, it seemed—and, as I gathered from Helen—that among all else I had chosen her to be my "victim." The strangeness of woman thus caused me to muse aloud to Helen whilst we lay comfortably nursing and teasing each other's well-soaked genitals.

"Not at all, Jack—or at least I find no strangeness in it, but then being a woman, of course I am partisan. All females, at heart, desire to be conquered, and if thereby they must suffer some humilitiation, then—perversely, as you no doubt might think—they take it even as a compliment. That the person who breaks them in must be strong of character and at least liked or loved by them is of equal importance."

"Breaking in," I echoed. "That is a term you have twice used, Helen, and I like it."

"Of course," she murmured smoothly—a phrase she was much fond of if one flattered her sentiments. "We have yet to break in quite a few damsels, my pet, as I am now about to tell you. I make only one proviso, Jack; if I set the rules, they must be followed."

"Tell me who the girls are, and, if I agree, I shall set some also," I smiled.

"Set some you well may, but I may alter them. You, Jack, have already broken in Marion and have ravaged her, but we needs must have a more delicate touch with some, as I shall explain. Listen now and do not distract me by playing with my pussy, or I shall not be able to explain to you properly. You may have entrance to it later, if you are a good boy. For the moment, let us get up, retire to your sitting room, drink some more of your lovely Cointreau, and get down to business."

Chapter 3

ENSCONCED once more in the more comfortable adjoining room, Helen agreed to sit with me provided only that I "behaved" myself. Sensing that she had a serious purpose, I agreed, though my cock was already twitching for more play.

"Don't worry, I shall empty your balls again ere I leave," she said with a bewitching smile and arrayed herself against me, I sitting and she with her legs splayed full along the sofa.

"My plan is very simple," she went on. "I have told you only a little of my adventures, and you may take them as gospel. Both Wilma and Elizabeth were put several times to the cock, and in every possible way before I departed, leaving the one infinitely more obedient and the other much more lively, I can tell you. I have dealt with daughters, sisters, cousins, nieces, wards—oh, such a variety, and none have proved failures. There is no need for them to," she said giving me a mischievous peck before she continued.

"I propose now to concentrate my efforts, Jack—and yours, too. You will have to accept, I fear, that mine will be the outwardly leading role, but your pleasures will be none the less for that. To begin with, I am advertising in the most respectable newspapers . . ."

Before she could finish, I had blurted out with almost comical astonishment, "Advertising?" which caused her to laugh merrily. Indeed, so much so that she seemed not to have noticed that my errant hand had once more found her bared thighs and was luxuriously caressing the milky skin her position offered me.

"Really—you must wait until I finish," she chided softly. "I am advertising—most discreetly in the Personal columns—my services as a disciplinarian for young ladies of quality. Naturally, we want only the best, the prettiest, and the most shapely. Whether proud, haughty, nervous, or shy does not matter. They can all be moulded. My announced fees are high, for there is much more discretion among the wealthy than in the middle classes. My advertisement was very simple and yet invitingly worded."

"And do you really hope to receive replies?" I asked, rather too lightly for Helen's taste. Without a further word she rose, fetched her reticule, and fumbled therein whilst, to my profound disappointment, covering her lovely legs and taking the chair facing me. Symbolically, perhaps, our positions were thus reversed from the moment we had previously inhabited the room.

Drawing forth an envelope, Helen unfolded carefully a letter of several pages, the first of which—as I was able to glimpse—carried some sort of baronial crest.

"This is one of five I have received to date, Jack, and I will read it—or at least part of it. It begins by congratulating me on setting up an establishment—for that is what I mean to do—whereby recalcitrant young ladies may be trained. Observe, please, that that last word is the writer's own. I was naturally very discreet in my own first letter to him, but he obviously read well enough between the lines. He finds my proposed fee per term of two hundred and fifty pounds not unreasonable in the light of the service I propose to offer."

"Did you actually say what it was?" I asked in some bemusement, for with Helen now almost anything seemed possible.

She sniffed and regarded me levelly for a long moment. "Really, Jack, I am sure you have enjoyed my talents so far, and you would equally applaud them were you to know with what subtlety I can put such matters to paper. It sufficed for me to say that the whip, the birch, the strap, and what I carefully styled as 'other useful persuaders' would not be kept in the background, but rather applied to all the appropriate places. The gentleman writes that he has no doubt at all from what I say that I know well how to tickle them up. Perhaps he has heard of feathering also, do you think? Anyway, he goes on to refer to Samantha, who, he tells me, is twenty, given to overproudness—by which I feel sure he means that she will not lower her drawers for the birch—and is wayward in her habits. Her particular pleasure, it seems, is riding."

"Though not of the type he would prefer," I proferred, whereupon Helen laughed and nodded.

"He goes on to say", she continued, "that Samantha would prove a prime pupil for my course of instruction and that he wishes to enroll her forthwith."

I nearly fell off the sofa. "I say, have you accepted her?" I asked.

"Naturally," Helen replied smoothly, "as well as his cheque. He was generous enough to send the fee for two terms—as were several others. Listen, I will read you part of another. It concerns a girl named Victoria."

More envelopes and letters rustled and then Helen read aloud slowly: " 'Victoria is a difficult girl. She proves troublesome under the strap and most certainly requires to have postural instructions, such as your reply, Madam, but briefly outlined. I feel sure that you are of the same mind as myself in that the legs should

not be held together tightly at all times and that the
posterior should be held out fully and without undue
coyness to the width of the leather. Moreover, since
dresses are tiresomely heavy and given to sliding down
from the hips at the most inappropriate moments, the
attire should be of the lightest—preferably but a chemise and stockings with well-heeled boots or shoes to
display the lines of the legs.' "

"You adorable minx, you are surely making all this
up," I declared, as much to tease her as to gain a reply.
And reply I indeed received—not however in the form
of a quick riposte but by the quick tossing of two sepia
photographs upon my lap. One was clearly of Samantha, since she had been photographed in a field or paddock, leaning her head against the neck of her horse
and with a brooding and rather sullen look on her face.
She appeared to be a brunette with quite a fetching face
and most certainly a fetching figure.

"Observe," said Helen quite sweetly, leaning forward. "Three buttons of her bodice are unfastened—a
most unseemly way for a young lady to be photographed normally—and that there is a schooling whip
lying at her feet."

"By heavens, yes!" I declared, peering closer. The
photograph was not of the largest, and I could but
dimly make out the orbs of the girl's breasts revealed in
small but teasing part by her unfastened bodice. As to
the whip, I was no less quick in my thoughts than Hel-
en. It had clearly been tossed down there as a challenge by whoever had taken the portrait.

As to the other, it pictured much more boldly a girl
of some eighteen years, deliciously plump of bottom,
which was partly revealed by her lying face down on a
double bed with her legs over the side, her hips bared,
and her hand clutching down at her lacy white drawers,
which had been drawn down just sufficiently to show
the alluring split between her cheeks.

"Victoria, no less," declared Helen promptly, though I scarce needed to be told that.

"Have you had your likeness taken?" I enquired of Helen, who nodded.

"I, too, and by heavens I had to sit perfectly still for a full minute," I declared.

"So did Victoria, it seems—or rather she was bidden to lie still, no doubt under threat of a birching on her half-bared bottom. Is it not a lovely firm and round one? She will be deliciously tight for you, Jack."

"By heavens, you mean it!" I all but shouted rather senselessly. "But how on earth will you arrange . . ."

"Tut, tut," she chided me. "Have I not thought of all that? Each fee is a perfect fortune, my sweet. I already have my eye on a place that will be perfect for tuitions of the nature we intend. Yes, we, Jack, for I want you in this as guide, mentor, and companion. No, don't interrupt. We have little enough time to lose. The place I have in mind is an old vicarage, well secluded, for the nearest village is six miles away and the church itself demolished. There are ample rooms—certainly one for another Snuggery. In fact, I have already placed a deposit on the property," Helen concluded triumphantly.

I must confess that I gazed upon her somewhat in awe as well as an ever-deeper desire. At a tentative movement from me, she read my thoughts and rose.

"On the floor?" she asked, and with a laugh threw herself down upon the rug, drawing up her dress and lying full wantonly with her legs apart. The lips of her quim glistened, moistened by the excitements which had clearly been passing through her mind as much as my own. I would have thrown myself upon her there and then, but with a light upward movement of her arm, she stayed me.

"No, Jack, undress first. Yes, completely. I adore being mounted thus with most of my clothes on whilst

the man is naked—his cock and balls properly presented. Come—be my stallion."

"Dear God, what a fantastic woman you are," I
breathed in wonder, tearing at my clothes in the same
instant. "Truly, my love, our minds merge and comple-
ment each other in all things."

"Almost all," she whispered as at last I presented my
naked manly form to her view. Regarding me briefly,
she nodded apparent approval of my upstraining cock
and heavy pendant balls.

"You will be good for the girls," she smiled in the
most seductive fashion as I went down beside her. Half-
closing her eyes, she sighed as I very gently parted the
petal lips of her slit and exposed the pale pinkness
within. Her legs straightened, toes straining down, as if
to exhibit to me the long lovely lines of her limbs,
sheened in tight black silk which reached just over halfway up her sumptuous thighs. Her back arched as I
rubbed her and she began to purr. "You are delicate as
well as rough, Jack. I like that."

A quiver of lust ran through me as her elegant fingers reached at last to toy with the iron-hard shaft of
my prick. Very slowly they formed a loose ring about it
which moved slowly up and down. Turning her face
away from me, in a manner I was to learn she often
had, she smiled at the wall with such a mixture of sensuousness and yet girlishness that I could not help but
take her chin and seize her mouth. How passionately
we drank from each other's lips.

"Why did you say 'almost all'?" I asked, both delighted and annoyed that she could so enchant me and
make me ask things of her.

Her tongue intruded slowly into my mouth and then
withdrew. "The difference resides only in that I am a
woman, dear. Soon enough you will have me in bed
with you naked, but never entirely at your whim, even
though you may posses my bottom, my pussy, and my

mouth. I shall suck you off quite perfectly, Jack, when I want to. No, do not speak yet . . . oh, that is lovely, yes, move your finger around my clitty. I want to come before you fuck me—then I will come all the more when you do. I have decided upon a dozen girls, Jack. They will give us sufficient variety without amounting to a number we cannot initially control. There will be one young assistant whom I shall choose. It needs a woman's knowing. As to your role, and it will be a leading one, you will enjoy all of their bottoms in the first term as well as much else that we shall devise, but not necessarily their pussies, dear. *Ooooh!* I am coming! Faster, Jack, with your finger! Ah!"

Her slender back arched clear off the floor, her arms clinging to my neck as a child's might. Her eyes rolled until virtually only the whites could be seen. Her thighs were wide open, her belly trembling. Uttering tiny animal moans, she held her tongue extended but motionless in my mouth whilst such a spattering of creamy essence trilled from her slit that she might well have been pissing a little, save for the oiliness that exuded over my fingers and sheened the inner smoothness of her thighs. Then, with an exquisite quiver of her entire body, she fell limp, her head to one side, her eyelashes fluttering.

I passed my lips tenderly over her cheek. Her fingers felt for and touched my own. I, who had mastered half a dozen women in this very place—had put them ruthlessly to the whip, the feather, and the cock—was now acting the romantic lover! Yet such was this power that Helen exerted over me that I lay still with her until, recovered, she smiled and kissed me softly.

"Jack, that was perfect. In a moment, with your lovely prick in me, I shall come again."

"Not to fuck them?" I asked, for her remark had bemused me. Even as I spoke, I was easing upon her, pushing the front of her dress higher, until the exquisite conjunction of our bellies exchanged their warmth.

Looping her arms anew about my neck, but now more loosely, Helen drew up both knees so that my pendant balls nestled against her seeping slit.

"Put your cock in me," she murmured.

As ever, the feeling of a lovely woman's stockinged legs beneath my own added immeasurably to my sensations as the soft maw of her cunny parted to receive the first urging of my distended knob. Her mouth moved gently, dreamily, as she felt it insert inch by inch. Half-smiling, she moved the tip of her tongue across her lips and gave a little jerk of her bottom which lodged me another three inches within her. Ah, the sleekness, the incredible girlish tightness of her! The sealskin walls of her cunt seemed to part but reluctantly, and yet with some incredible skill of interior muscle power, as the piston drove relentlessly within.

Soft murmurs of pleasure came from her throat. Her head turned again to the wall. The Mona Lisa smile—yet a smile more tender than that—reappeared. Passing my hands around her hips, I cupped the bold cheeks of her bottom, drawing them slightly apart, savouring the fullness, the plumpness, the sheer feminine weight of her globe, which already I had injected.

With a little moue of her lips and still the distant look in her turned-away eyes, Helen whispered, "Do not kiss me, Jack. Ah! right in—yes! Now hold it there—let me feel it throb! Am I tight for you? Is it not lovely?"

I had forgotten my question for the moment. Her dark hair wreathed itself about her swanlike neck in large kiss-curls—and yet I was forbidden to kiss her adorable mouth. Even so, I sensed in part her needs, as surely as she knew my own. We were to fuck slowly and majestically, her bottom rolling and moving as it now began to on my palms, her full breasts moving beneath her dress.

Thus, in a tremulous silence, I began to fuck Helen

for the first time, her cunt squeezing upon my prick in a delicious nutcracker manner each time it slewed within her to the full. Much as she obviously tried to control her breathing, it came more heavily now with each in-pushing thrust. Slowly her legs rose, the heels of her boots sharp against the backs of my thighs where she knotted her calves tightly around my loins.

"Oh, God, you wicked man—you are fucking me!" she gasped.

The silence that until then I thought would hold was broken. Never had I known such a torrent of eroticism as now swept from our lips as our hot loins worked in unison. Scarce an obscene thought that I had entertained did not escape my mouth, nor yet her own. Yet withal her voice was soft and luring, contrasting with the ever-tighter clamping of her legs which rocked back and forth against the surging movements of my buttocks.

"How many have fucked you?" I ground as if possessed of a sudden jealousy that I believe she well sensed.

"A few—many—none," she taunted softly, "but only you have been so perfect in my bottom, sweet—ah, those long, slow, powerful strokes and—oh, yes—now, Jack, now. Make me come! Ram your prick in me! Shoot your sperm! Sperm me! *Ah!*"

Her entire body quivered anew in my arms. Her bottom ground and rolled violently, her cunt hairs rasping against me in a veritable ecstasy as her spilling treasures oiled my pounding cock and flooded my balls.

"Ah, you bitch!" I ground my mouth down upon her own, tasting the leaping of her tongue, her saliva. I determined now to give her no quarter, nor to loose my own essence until I was ready, grasping her shoulders, I rode her violently whilst her widened eyes stared into mine. Her legs slumped to the floor, heels digging into the rug as she arched her back, working her cunt back and forth against the ramming of my tool.

"Do-o-on't! Don't come in me—oh, it's naughty!" she moaned.

Had I not known her previous playacting, her words were uttered with such realism as I might otherwise have believed them. They caused me, of course, to fuck her even more vigourously and to hold her wriggling form tighter in a very rapture of possession.

"No! Oh-oh! you naughty man! Oh, you will fill me with it!"

"Come, girl, come, you must be spermed," I growled, delighting as much as she in the fantasy and to such extent that I truly believe we both all but meant it in that moment, so agitated were her struggles.

"Ah!" she screeched. Her hands tore at my hair, clawed my back, dug even into my buttocks while the ever-tight maw of her slit seemed literally to twirl around my cock. "Oh! you are going to come, you are going to come in me, I know it!" she moaned.

"Now, my little pet, now—take it—suck it out with your darling slit—every drop," I said huskily. The moment was nigh upon me, and I could no longer withhold the tribute she so sweetly deserved. Sheathing my pego so fully within her that my balls nestled against her bum cheeks, I expelled my jets. No less vigourous than my first injection, I shuddered on and on, swimming, as it seemed, among the very stars as the powerful spurts of creamy gruel exploded within, on and on, until the last faint dribblings when I sank full down, my weight pinning her tightly to the floor with the last weak pulsings.

And thus we lay, she unmoving, bearing all, until with cramped limbs we separated gently, floating upon the clouds that bear one in the aftermath of an amourous storm. Our shoulders touched. We kissed languourously.

"Because some, if not all, will be virgins, my love," she whispered in answer to the question I had long forgotten. Dandling the thick, limp worm of my shrunken cock, she smiled and leaned over me, playfully kissing my nose. "Their bottoms have no virginity that can be put to test, Jack—as well you know, but their pussies have. I doubt not, to put it delicately, that the first trials of some will be on their own beds at the end of first term. Thus we must return them a trifle intact. Naturally, when they return, they can be put to your own wicked cock at will."

"If they return," I grunted.

"True—but that has also been anticipated. We shall have more than enough enrolments for the first term, Jack—enough to spill over into the second. And, talking of spilling over, did I not promise you that I would empty your balls? Do you not want to pleasure me again before I leave?"

I groaned, but the sound was one of pure pleasure. Very slowly her lips began to trail down my neck, my chest, my belly. Holding my breath, I waited for the wondrous moment when my lolling, spermy knob would be drawn between her lips. I quivered in my waiting and felt the first lifting touch of her fingers beneath my balls. The tip of her tongue wafted out beneath my vision and climbed gently up my waiting conqueror.

"It will not be long before I have you ready again, Jack. I shall make sure of it. Lie still now and be a good boy, and Mama will bring it up."

Then my knob was drawn between her lips, and I quivered in an ague of desire.

Chapter 4

ENERVATED by our third bout, which was made all the more delicious by being prolonged, no delay attended the arrangements to which I had already fallen captive.

Helen, as it transpired, was staying at the Regency Hotel close by to Oxford Circus, and there I repaired the next day, she wishing to moderate our transports in order that I might be kept in "the best of condition," as she put it, and so refusing me the first complete night of her favours.

Of her history I learned that she was the third daughter of a wealthy cleric and that her bottom had frequently tasted the birch in her girlhood. That it had been wielded with skill rather than spite was the first cause of her conversion. Having learned to tolerate it, she then found herself taking a taste for the burning sweep of the softened twigs and so was brought amidst some pretended shame to remove not only her dress, chemise, and underskirt, but her drawers as well. Learning thus as she did to dissimulate a variety of emotions and reactions brought her soon to realise the delights of amourous flagellation.

I exclaimed, quite unguardedly, that if she had shown herself willing, it would surely have spoiled the sport.

"Do you not know me better?" Helen asked with a certain mild scorn as we sat together in the small drawing room of her suite. "I struggled sufficiently, my dear, to ensure that my bottom was well felt during the removal of my drawers. There was a spice in so doing, as I was not slow to discover. Had you but heard my sobs and cries as the birch swished at last across my proffered cheeks, you would have thought them as real as did Papa. Indeed, so much did I endeavour one afternoon to defend my nudity that he was forced to tie my hands with a kerchief. What a sensation I obtained therefrom—to be bound and so wantonly presented! Moreover, I was so left for an hour afterward to teach me, as he said, a further lesson. 'Twas but a small one, perhaps, but it made its mark upon me.

"Upon being released at last, I was in a condition of some desire, for a good birching gives one a longing to toy with oneself and I could not reach to do so with my hands bounds. Totally misunderstanding my state, however, Papa thought me to be truly distraught and sought to apologize for my prolonged ordeal, awarding me kisses and caressing my bottom, which he declared he had chastised too much."

"Your hands were still bound?" I asked.

Helen's eyes danced. A look of intense mischief entered them. "Oh, yes," she declared simply. "I lay perfectly still, however, and pretended to be both forlorn and bemused by such attentions, which did little enough to appease what I really wanted."

"And did you get it?" I laughed, for I was ready to believe almost anything now of this lovely, daring creature whose understanding of all matters which I myself had long cherished seemed infinite.

"Not on that occasion, Jack," she sparkled. "I was

not put to the birch thereafter for many weeks, which caused me great frustration, for like many girls I both desired and feared it. Is that not the best admixture? On occasions I even tried to bind my own wrists together—such was the excited state of discovery in which I found myself at seventeen. But then occurred an incident which was to change much. My Mama, being absent at the time with my two sisters, I had the run of the house and took to ordering about the maid-servants, which, though they resented, they had to follow. One was named Mary—a pretty little thing of no more than my own age.

"A great mood took me about Mary. I would frequently study her and would wonder how she would look naked—or, better, with her skirt piled up and her bottom displayed. Curious dreams overtook me in which I alternately birched and caressed her. I truly wanted to hear her squeal, Jack, although I felt quite an affection for her. Well, it so happened that one day I caught her out in quite a bit of untidiness—or so I pretended—for she had neither plumped my pillows nor smoothed down my bedspread. I thereupon told Papa that she was being particularly wilful and should be birched.

"Our temporary seclusion no doubt aided my plans as well as his own aspirations, for he advised me with a certain look of interest in his eyes that he would do so. Some astonishment followed when I told him somewhat boldly that I intended to see it well and properly done, to which he replied that it would be an exceedingly unusual thing to do. I, playing my part primly enough, said that one day I would have to learn to wield the birch and that I must see best how it was done."

"What perfect hypocrisy!" I chortled.

Therewith Helen shrugged and drew upon a Turkish cigarette, which filled the air with a most pleasant aroma.

"Are not all people so, Jack? The air was quite tremulous with desire, I can tell you, though we veiled it well. But, to cut a long story short, the miscreant was duly taken to Papa's room at nine that night. The hour was well chosen, you see, when cook and others would be abed. Ah, what a to-do and a fuss when Mary learned that not only was she to be birched but in my presence also! Her sobs rent the air. Papa would have sent me out if he could but I was implacable—yes, even at that age, Jack. She was quickly enough denuded from the waist down—such girls never wear drawers, after all. Laid over the edge of the bed, which was a high one, and so allowed only her toes to touch the ground, I held her whilst Papa prepared himself, removing his jacket and rolling up his sleeves.

"Looking back over her shoulder, Mary spied the birch and began to sob. I told her it was a nonsense, that her punishment was well earned, and that I would give her many a stroke myself if she did not desist. This brought a further howl from her, whereupon to the great surprise of Papa, I gave her bouncy bottom a resounding slap with my palm. Ah, what a sensation that was—the springy cheeks, the delicious orb! My excitement rose tenfold and clearly showed in my flushed expression. Kicking her stockinged legs as she was and while my palm fell again on her chubby cheeks for good measure, I told Papa that her wrists must be bound or I might never be able to hold her.

"Discerning therefrom, I am sure, the pleasure I was obtaining, he produced his kerchief in a flash, and just as quickly Mary's wrists were bound tightly behind her. She could only move then of course by virtue of rolling off the bed, and that I scotched by holding the nape of her neck.

"Papa then began to wield the green twigs with some gusto—each one causing such a turmoil of leaping hips, bottom, and kicking legs that her entire treasures were rendered to our view. Need I convey to you, Jack, how she sobbed, pleaded, and cried as her bouncing bottom reddened slowly under the steady swishing of the birch? 'Twas such an excitement that I would fain have removed my own clothes and taken place beside her for the very thrill of receiving what she was.

" 'More gently, Papa.' " I exclaimed somewhat to his astonishment when her writhing cheeks had been burnished to a fine glow. More sensitive than he to the sounds that Mary was emitting, I knew him to be on the point of bringing her on, for her face was as flushed as her bottom and there were certain betraying signs around her mouth and in her eyes that only another woman could truly read. My wicked thoughts then perhaps conveyed themselves to Papa for the first time. He could not conceal his state in any event, for his penis was as a veritable barber's pole beneath his breeches. Being slyly careful to let him observe that I had seen it, I thrust Mary's face deeper into the quilt. Her legs by then had ceased to kick and hung over the bed rather more wantonly parted than they had been while her glowing orb twitched and jerked most appealingly to the lighter coursing of the twigs it was then receiving.

"In that moment, Papa's haggard eyes met mine. He could no longer contain himself, nor could I. My eyes glowed with the same desire that had riven itself into his features. Kneeling upon the bed, as I then was, and holding Mary down by the shoulders, I nodded. His glance appeared glazed. The birch dropped. His febrile fingers sought and opened the flap of his breeches. Ah, what a stallion's tool appeared—rubicund, stiff, and flaming! With a groan, he was upon her. A shriek from Mary announced that the pestle had sunk at least part within. Crouched over her as he then was, I could but barely see the thick shaft entering her slit. She bucked, was held, and then it sank full in."

"Go on!" I begged when it seemed now she would hesitate.

"Would you believe that I then departed, Jack? Believe it so, for had I but stayed, I might have sought that which she was receiving. Silently, as I clambered off the bed and fled, I could hear her petulant moans flowing beneath the coarser grunts of his desire. My last backward glance was to see her as fully impaled as I had secretly wished her to be—and by such sweet force as between us we had applied. Indeed, I closed the door as if upon some voluptuous sacrament. But a few minutes later, Papa reappeared. His eyes haunted my own, where I stood in my doorway, and then he immured himself in his study.

"I repaired immediately to the bedroom, of course. There Mary lay, her eyes closed, her lips parted so appealingly that, without further thought I joined her upon the bed, rolled her face to face against me and partook of the nectar of her lips while foraging my fingers in and around her sperm-spattered slit. She murmured, gasped, and then accepted the luring of my tongue in her mouth. I sought her bottom which burned still from the birch. My finger found the puckered orifice which so intrigues me in untried young women. With wrists still bound, she bucked and moaned as I gently opened a path therein and found my forefinger tightly gripped. I caressed her hair, her heated face. Our tongues swirled in a sweet agony of pleasuring. With my finger fully ensconced in her bottom, I twiddled her clitty and brought her to such a delicious conclusion that her thighs were all bemseared with her cream. Then, untying her bonds, we lay cuddling in a wonderment—I having achieved my first essay in which I sought."

"Which is to conquer," I said, drawing upon her rich mouth and caressing her breasts which even then I had not seen.

"To master, to break in, to conquer, and to teach, Jack," she replied solemnly. "There will be times when

I shall use greater gentleness than I believe you applied with Marion. In her case it was but a partial breaking-in, though the virginity of her bottom remained to be taken by you, or so she would have it. As to the girls, I shall nurture them carefully. To rush matters might bring a certain chaos—and besides it would spoil the fun! Do you not agree?"

My features must have displayed a certain disappointment—if such it can be called in the circumstances—for she laughed.

"You will have all you want soon enough, Jack—and so shall I. Now, as to an assistant"—Helen went on, for I had earlier declared much interest in the matter—"I believe I have such a young woman as will suit us well. Her name is Angela and she is physically quite bewitching. Her age is twenty-seven, though her mind is infinitely older than that, as many knowing women's are. She has been put well through her paces, as I can tell you, and has emerged with a desire to expand her experiences and her philosophy. That they are as ours, I need not tell you. However, I will permit you to put her to it, for she knows she must have her trials. There—has that not pleased you?"

"Little enough at the moment will please me, my dearest, until I have you naked and bound as no doubt your Papa did."

"Did he?" she mocked and, as so often, escaped my grasp by jumping up from the sofa and going to the window. "I may tell you of that one day, as also of my other adventures, Jack—but are they not truly all of a piece? Is not practise better than reminiscence? You are about to have a little of the former, as a matter of fact, for there is the question of a maid. We shall need one, at least, to attend to the rooms and so forth—not to say a cook. She, however, must be a woman of middle years and total discretion."

"Or total stupidity," I ventured, for I had also turned

my mind to such practical measures. Rising in turn, I
went to Helen, placed my hands on her shoulders, and
felt her lean back against me in such wise that the glorious swell of her bottom rested against my prick. "A
dullard, perhaps—one who need never be aware of
what is going on," I suggested.

"Yes, that is possible—a woman from the village,
perhaps," Helen agreed without turning, though the
closeness of our bodies brought a sigh from her. "But as
to the maid, Jack, I believe I have a fine one here. She
attends my room of mornings, brings my tea, and generally looks after me. I judge her about twenty. Her
name is Lucy. I have arranged for her to come up this
evening when her duties are finished. Would you like to
be here?" she laughed and, turning, awarded me quite a
head-spinning kiss while her belly rubbed suggestively
against my own.

"I may just have time for it, Helen," I answered with
pretended formality. "Would you like me to bring anything?"

"Dear Jack, what could you possibly bring that
would be of use to a girl?" she mocked sweetly. "No,
my pet, I have all that we need here—see!" And, going
to a wardrobe, she produced there from several straps,
some lengths of rope, and a whip quite different to my
own. The handle, thickly plaited, was but some fifteen
inches long and held comfortably in the hand. What attracted my curiosity most, however, were the thongs,
for there were at least a dozen of them cut to some
twenty inches in length and so contrived that it needed
but a shake of the wrist to make them fan and splay
out.

The thongs and the handle were of black leather.
Passing them through my fingers, I felt a small protrusion in the ends, for the leather of each—tanned to the
fullest possible extent and made thereby no thicker than
silk—was doubled over, and sewn into the end of each

was what Helen explained to me was a tiny dried pea.

"The effect is startling, Jack—but you will see soon enough. A little practise is required to use it, but you will get the hang of it rapidly. It is my hotspur—no less—as I call it," she laughed.

"Your own invention?" I asked, not a little peeved in truth that I had not thought of making such a device myself, for I could perceive that the splaying-out of the tips of the thongs would serve to cover most female bottoms and so would assail them in multiple places at once.

"I would like to think so, but I fear I cannot claim it. In my early twenties I served as governess to two young daughters of an Austrian family who were resident in London for a period. It being a favourite tool of the household, so to speak, I was awarded it for my efforts—and you may be sure, Jack, that they were quite rewarding."

"Could I ever have doubted it?" I laughed, "But now, my love, will you never divest yourself of your dress and chemise and display your glorious body to me? Come, the bed is so close."

"No, Jack," she declared firmly, tapping her fingers chidingly though lovingly against the rod of my tool which was fully tenting my trousers forward. "It has some work to do this evening, and I want it in the finest fettle. Have you no business to attend to, you lazy rogue? Of course you have. Off with you, now, and I shall expect you this evening. At six-thirty, shall we say? I shall have her a little prepared by then."

And so, adamantly, I was hurried out into the unknowing bustle of the West End where, musing upon all and with feverish longing for the coming hours, I set my mind to a little inventiveness for the forthcoming harem. That it would be no less than such set my pulses ever racing. That very morn Helen had received six further letters in response to her advertisement and would spend part of her day in replying to them with the very subtlety of which she had earlier spoken. The innuendos were all, as I well understood, in her delicacy of phrasing, for to each parent, guardian, uncle, or "friend," she responded in individual ways, judging the tenor of her responses in part by what their letters contained.

Arising in my mind, as there now did, visions of the weeping, sobbing, but finally submissive damsels who would come into our thrall, a most excellent idea came into my mind. Changing my course and hailing a cab, I instructed the driver to take me to the very gentleman who had manufactured my excellent chair. He was a discreet enough fellow, not given to asking too many questions, though he had little doubt, I believe, as to the future of his products. His amazement, however, was considerable when I explained my idea.

"A board, sir, with a hole in it, and to stand upright?" he asked.

"Exactly that. The hole must be no more than twenty-six inches in diameter and cut perfectly out of the two halves, so that together and by virtue of a hinge at one end of the boards, they form a circle. The whole needs to be firmly mounted so that it will stand upon the floor and neither rock backward nor forward," I explained whilst his eyes grew ever wider.

I could see his mind indeed endeavouring to fathom what on earth such a standing contraption was for, but I had no intention of enlightening him. More, I had not finished and went on to explain the rest of my invention which I deemed quite as ingenious as my chair which ensnared and rendered helpless all who sat in it. This device, needing no concealing upholstery, would be rather quicker to make, I told him, whereat he agreed and finally settled down to noting all the dimensions to my instructions.

I must say I admired the fellow for restraining himself from asking what it *was* for. No doubt he would spend many a long week puzzling about it. A week and it would be ready, he told me at last. This was good news, for Helen and I intended to occupy the old vicarage without delay. I instructed him to have it sent by carrier and railway, for after my receipt of the chair, I had no doubt that his workmanship would be anything but perfect.

Rather pleased with myself that I had at least capped Helen's little whip in terms of ingenuity, I decided to tell her nothing about the device until it was installed. Such hours as followed seemed long indeed, for I could scarcely wait to make my introduction to Lucy. Consequently I was at the door of Helen's hotel suite promptly on the half hour. A quick double knock, as we had arranged, and the door opened.

"Go straight into the bedroom Jack, but do nothing, until I tell you," she begged.

I was minded not so much to obey her as to see what would transpire. Through the drawing room, I went toward a door that lay half-open. Helen followed me quickly.

There, arrayed on the bed, was a truly voluptuous young creature, her arms bound to her sides by two heavy luggage straps. A pink silk chemise enfolded her waist, being wreathed there prettily, the shoulder straps having been loosed and drawn down and the lacy hem well turned up above her naked buttocks. Save for black silk stockings, she was otherwise naked. Full length she lay on the bed, her thighs together, her feet toward me. So quietly had I entered that she did not turn her head until she heard Helen's voice bidding me sit down on a small love couch placed at a viewing angle to the foot of the bed.

Lucy's face was already flushed, as well it might have been. At the first glimpse of me, her eyes opened wide and she drew her knees up in that curious protective motion that girls have, and yet which they little seem to know exposes the bulge of their bottoms all the better.

"Oh, lord, no, ma'am!" she begged.

Helen closed the door and smiled down at her

"Lucy, do be quiet, please," she murmured and picked up the little black whip that lay in waiting at the girl's feet.

Chapter 5

W HAT I was about to witness was not so much a demonstration as a showing-off by my adored Helen who had arrayed herself maddeningly in the very tightest of black silk gowns beneath which I was prepared to swear that she wore naught but her stockings and boots. The bulb of her bottom being so closely and lovingly sheathed by the clinging material rolled sensuously and majestically as she took her stance at the end of the bed and—to a wail from Lucy—seized her ankles and drew her back until her feet hung over the edge of the bed.

"*Up* with your bottom, Miss!" Helen declared while the most appealing sobs came from the girl.

"Miss, no, please—oh, don't, it shames me. Send him away, Miss—please, Miss, do!"

"*Up,* girl, I say!" Helen spat. Her arm rose, wrist twisting, then fell. A horrified shriek issued from the maidservant as the thongs bit their separate paths across the tops of her thighs.

"No-oh-oh, Miss, please! It stings—oh!"

"What nonsense have we here, Lucy?" Helen asked crisply. "Have I not arrayed you prettily in my own chemise and stockings? Have you not contracted to

44

come into my service? You must be trained, Lucy. I will have your bottom well lifted up now or you shall receive a hundred strokes of the whip before I am through with you."

"B . . . b . . . but, Miss, I didn't want to . . . *Aaaah!*"

The thongs snicked and sprayed across that lustrous orb even as Helen spoke. I saw then their full effect, for in spraying out, each burning tip sought its separate target—some biting into the cheeks and others searing a path even into the tight groove where the hemispheres inrolled.

The effect upon Lucy was electric. Her hips bumped and jerked, and as if by some invisible leverage her bottom rose, squirmed, and poised itself precisely as both Helen's intent and my own burning eyes required. The fig of her slit, shrouded in a fine bosquet of curls, offered itself with such appeal that I immediately rose, doffed my jacket, and removed my boots. Nor did Helen give Lucy any respite. No longer had the girl's shrill cry died away than a further shower of hot sparks—as I thought of the thong tips—assailed her globe and brought to it the first sheen of pink.

"Oooh-ooooh-*Ooooh!*" How can you?" howled Lucy, thereby causing Helen such annoyance that she turned to me on the instant and demanded whether I had a kerchief.

I produced a large white one, which seemed immediately to satisfy her, for, turning back to Lucy, who had once more slumped down and lay squirming on one hip, she promptly brought a broad triangle of the linen between the girl's lips and, tying it at the back of her hair, so gagged her.

"Leave her to me, Jack," Helen ordained, as if I were on the point of taking possession of the girl, though that was an event that could be more pleasingly delayed. Striding to an armoire, Helen then produced a long fine feather, at the sight of which Lucy's eyes opened wide.

"Now, my pet, we shall begin," Helen declared, and, awarding the maid a sharp smack on her bottom with the palm of her hand, rolled her over easily enough onto her tummy, whereat the girl jerked and would have endeavoured to conceal her peppered globe had she not received an even more resounding slap that made her hips rebound.

"Jack, you will kneel upon the bed in front of her and hold her shoulders," Helen said.

Disguising the impatience that my stemming but still-covered cock already betrayed, I obeyed her with a mingling of amusement and desire while Lucy's eyes rolled beseechingly. The girl had a fair, soft skin which felt like silk to my hands as I bore upon her with no more strength than was needed to keep her from twisting over. Thereupon, Helen forced Lucy's legs apart and stood between them, running her palms sensuously up the backs of her thighs, where the taut black silk of the stockings gave way to delicious areas of flesh. Briefly she fondled the plump cheeks whose sheen of pink where the thongs had assailed her gave it an appearance of such inviting warmth. Then, to an anguished jerk from Lucy, she prised the cheeks just sufficiently apart with fingers and thumb to expose the crinkled rosebud of her bottomhole.

The upward urging of Lucy's shoulders as she strove to twist from our combined grasps was surprising, though I held her with ease as the tip of the feather, extruding from Helen's other hand, delicately approached its goal. Even through the gag then there emerged a muffled hissing cry as the tip of the feather—thinned back as I saw for its task—moved softly first around the puckered orifice and then, with a subtle twisting of Helen's tapered fingers, sank first one and then some two inches within.

Lucy's hips bucked and retracted, but in that instant Helen applied the full weight of her left hand to the small of the girl's back, and so securing her in her helplessly offered posture, commenced twirling and dipping the feather back and forth. Her eyes met mine in that instant, smoky with desire and more sensuous than I had ever seen a woman's eyes look.

The muffled gurgles that issued from Lucy's gagged lips and her attempts to buck away from the excruciating sensation merely added to the delights of the moment. With each rolling and twirling the feather inserted itself deeper until insensate quivers coursed down Lucy's spine and her head twisted from side to side in an ague of sensations.

"Remove her gag now, Jack. She shall not scream or she will have much the worse of it. She knows that now. Do you not, Lucy?" Helen asked coaxingly while I commenced loosing the knot which lay amid the girl's soft hair.

Her lips freed and twisting together, Lucy moaned.

"Do-oh-on't, Miss, don't!" she whimpered. "Oh, it tickles, it burns, it . . ."

"Quiet, girl!" Helen snapped. "I shall give you no further warning. Jack, you may give her your cock to lick whilst I continue warming her!"

"Wow-ooooh!" Lucy sobbed and buried her face in the quilt, for whilst the insinuating feather was ever deeper buried now, my fervent lance was displayed in a flash and her cheeks burned as hotly as her bottom doubtless did. I saw the feather move and twirl then faster until it became but a blur.

"Lick your master's prick now, Lucy," Helen said evenly. "Raise your head and attend to it—*now!*" And therewith, lifting her hand momentarily from the small of Lucy's back, she awarded the girl a sharp, uplifting smack beneath the bulge of her bottom, which brought a mingled squeal and moan.

"Miss—don't make me, please. . . . I never . . . oh, it's dirty; *Ah!* Oh, I can't bear the feather no longer, Miss—take it out!"

"Lift her face, Jack," Helen said calmly. "A little more of the feather, I think, and . . ."

"Whoooooo!" Lucy howled. Her neck strained, shoulders quivering as I eased her face up in such manner that the tip of her nose brushed first my balls and then the underside of my straining stem. With her arms bound, the globes of her snowy mounds bulging up from the top of her chemise, and the orb of her bottom frentically jerking under the ministrations of Helen, she looked as desirable a creature as ever I had seen. Slewing softly and with maddening tickling back and forth, the feather was now embedded in her at its fullest reach—a good eight inches.

Teeth chattering and with pearls of tears coursing down her pretty face, Lucy issued but the tip of her soft, warm tongue which touched my quivering rod for a second and then retreated as Helen, standing a little sideways, observed. Even so, her voice came as calmly as ever to me.

"Untie her arms, Jack, but keep them held. I will take the cords," she instructed and took them up the moment I had loosed the girl. "Hold still, Jack," Helen murmured. With that she retied one end to Lucy's right wrist and brought her arm around my back. This I then held while she attended similarly to the other and then, to my amused astonishment, tied the girl's wrists tightly together so that she was now locked to me with her flushed face hovering above my lewd erection.

Lucy had ceased to protest vocally. The strength of Helen's character and the firmness of her intent appeared to have conveyed themselves to her even more firmly than my own might have done. Such is the power, then, of woman upon woman, for though I had inveigled and indeed even enchanted Marion and her sister into wickedly enforced modes of *amour à trois,* here—so to speak—was a different flavour.

"I do-on't *want* to!" Lucy howled of a sudden, as if the realisation of the waiting presence of my swollen crest just beneath her lips had come upon her more unexpectedly than it had. Slump she dare not now, for then her mouth would have fallen full upon it, and thus her hips and bottom were of necessity held up in turn in the posture that Helen had desired. The shaft of the feather protruding from her rosehold during the adjustments did nothing to diminish my own erotic excitement. In any other circumstance, I would have mashed Lucy's lips down over my standing weapon, yet it intrigued me in this moment—and gave added spice to the occasion—to wait upon the whims of Helen.

With some speed, she now brought from beneath the foot of the bed two further lengths of cord which in a trice were secured around both of the girl's ankles and then extended tightly outwards to the legs of the bed, so that Lucy's black-sheened limbs were held wide apart.

"Oh! OOh, Miss, if you make me, I'll tell . . . Ow!"

The last exclamation was brought forth by the speedy application of the whip that Helen had retrieved and coiled around Lucy's brazen bottom in a flash.

"Yeeeech!" Lucy gritted, for by the snapping motion of Helen's wrist I could see even from my kneeling stance on the bed that it was a far fiercer stinger than she had received until now. Instantly Helen's eyes literally blazed into mine. The message, otherwise uncommunicated, was received and acted upon. Placing one hand firmly on the nape of Lucy's neck, I brought her sobbing mouth down full upon my urgent prick at last and felt with exquisite quiverings of pleasure the warm O of her lips enfold the first two inches, her salivia bubbling upon my buried shaft.

"*Suck* it, Lucy, suck it, girl—but do not draw forth the juice or by heavens I shall make your bottom as hot as a brazier!" came Helen's voice.

An inexpressible sound issued from the girl's throat as my cock, embedding itself another two inches in her mouth, made contact therein with her lolling tongue. The stem of the feather protruding from her bottom had scarce moved, even though now the surging thongs snicked and bit around her weaving globe again and again, causing Lucy's tears to trickle down to my balls.

In the ineluctable delight of that moment, with Lucy's arms enfolded about my waist by virtue of her bonds, my nostrils flared. I would have spouted gladly then for the sheer pleasure of loosing my jets upon her tongue and down her throat, but with inner knowing I sensed that the drama was not yet complete. Spongy as was the grip of those lips around my throbbing cock, I began to move my loins with impelling thrusts back and forth while, before my bleary gaze, Helen ceased her applications of the whip and delicately withdrew the feather from its lodging place.

"Another inch at least, Lucy—you can absorb more, girl," Helen murmured gently to the madly hip-weaving girl whilst in the same instant she slid the feather down under the fig of the maid's slit and commenced subtly teasing her there.

"B . . . b . . . b . . . !" Lucy bubbled madly on my cock, the sound emerging from her engorged mouth as a sobbing, trilling sound whilst my proud stander now was almost at her throat.

Helen's hitherto-suppressed excitement seemed then to emerge. I doubted not that it was her fingertips now that were flirting with Lucy's clitoris as she leaned full over the heaving girl's back and brought her own mouth for a maddening instant under my own.

"You shall have her now, Jack," she declared, where-with Lucy endeavoured to lift her head, but by clamp-

ing my hand upon her neck, I held my cock warmly
and wetly buried as Helen came to our side and released
Lucy's bonds.

"In the corner with her," Helen declared in unexpected fashion whilst Lucy wriggled veritably like a
fish, half-seduced as she was, yet still game for such a
struggle as revealed all of her treasures to me. She was
some five feet five tall, her nose rétroussée in a very
appealing fashion, her lips well formed and her bubbies
as perfectly round as melons.

"No-*Oh!* Sir! Miss!" came her frantic, hip-twisting
wail as between us we bundled her off the bed, her
smooth belly, hips, thighs and bobbing tits feeling all of
heaven against me until the darkest corner of the bedroom was reached.

"I wo-o-on't! He mustn't! Oh! Not that big thing!"
Lucy yelped, though I could not help but notice that
her voice was now never raised so loudly as to reach
any occupants of adjoining rooms. Bumped briefly into
the corner while I held in lewd expectation at her hips,
her head was forced down until her hands sought to
support herself by pressing against the walls. With Hel-
en's hand at her neck, however, she could not rise and
would have buried herself protectively into the corner
had I not drawn her hips well out.

Globing her well-strung bottom into my loins and
with my trousers thrust down, I had my cock now tight
between her cheeks and stemming upward, throbbing
between my belly and her flesh. That I did not take her
in the instant was again remarkable, for I would dearly
have pronged her in the moment that Helen bent her
over. Yet in these first hours of complicity between us,
I sensed a certain curious thrill in for once surrendering
my will to hers. There was indeed almost a perversity of
frustration that I had not known nor entertained before,
and most certainly not in all my hours of pleasure in
The Snuggery.

"Have her bottom, Jack. Her pussy has been rodded already—of that I am in no doubt. And as for you, Lucy," Helen went on, giving the squawking girl a sharp slap in the small of her back, "you will remember this, my pet, as one of the first postures of submission—well bent over in a corner with your palms flat to the wall, arms straight out, bottom projecting. Do you hear me?"

"Na-na-na-nah-*Nah!*" came Lucy's shrill, sobbing response, for in that instant I had split the warm globe of her peach and urged my insensate knob against the very aperture that the feather had so madly teased. Lucy's back rippled, her hips squirmed, but strongly as she was held, and with the warning hand of Helen still upon her neck nothing could now delay the insurgent power of my piston as it forced the tight, warm aperture and drove within.

"Wa-ah-*Ah!*" Lucy shrieked, this time well deserving the warning palm that Helen immediately clamped over her mouth. Cupping both bulging cheeks of her bottom firmly, I impelled the fleshy peg another two, three, four inches within the glorious grip of her until, to another muffled squeal from Lucy, she was as fully corked as ever a girl might be.

My hands now more at leisure gently caressed her stocking-banded thighs whilst at the same time holding her firmly into me. Seemingly daring no longer to wriggle, Lucy whimpered softly, the silken cheeks of her orb blaring their heat into my belly while my prick throbbed out its message of desire deep up her.

Releasing her hand slowly from Lucy's mouth, Helen leaned against the wall, regarding me smilingly while keeping still her fingers pressed lightly now on the girl's neck.

"How tight she must be, darling," she murmured. "Plug her well and deeply now, for she will soon get a taste for it—go on."

Needed I such a bidding? My head was swimming in the perfect delight of the moment, for few things are more to be treasured than the tight bottom of a girl whose shame and confusion melt slowly away in the uprising of the flood of desire. Withdrawing my cock almost to the tip whilst Lucy moaned and kept her head well hung, I slewed it half within, held it a-throbbing there—withdrew—and then, with a majestic action as of the mighty rod of an engine began to pump her, cupping the creamy gourds of her titties whilst the blissful moon of her bottom made its first tentative movements of assent.

Lucy's sobs became softer then and gave way little by little to a tiny mewing sound as the act of our unconventional copulation proceeded, her bottom bumping and grinding more eagerly now to my assault. Within she clenched me so tightly at times that I could scarce withdraw. At others some instinctive muscular action relaxed her so that my cock shunted back and forth as easily as it might have done in her slit.

Helen meanwhile scarcely moved, except for a slight sensuous movement of her hips. Lips parted, her eyes held mine and in that moment I truly adored looking at her. Then, with infinite stealth, her hands began to draw up the skirt of her dress. Inch by inch she uncovered her calves, rounded knees, upswelling thighs, her spangled black garters until at last, amid all the impassioned heaving of my body to Lucy's, the thickly tufted dark triangle of Helen's pubis appeared and her legs parted, long, straight and exquisitely curved.

"Come in her, darling," she whispered huskily, her words all but swallowed up by the cries and moans of Lucy, who, with her hot bum cheeks pressing their globular beauty firmly into me, received the long, thick jets of my libation.

Chapter 6

"**S**HE BEHAVED quite well, do you not think—our first pupil?" Helen whispered to me sometime in the night when at last I held her glorious body naked to my own.

Lucy had departed hours before—but twenty minutes after my juice had erupted within her and she had sunk down half-senseless when the long, thick cork was finally withdrawn. But then Helen had briefly feted her, coddling and caressing her and treating her to a glass of champagne. Blushing deeply and still unable to face me, Lucy had at last been persuaded that her true future lay with her Mistress, as Helen was pleased to call herself. I was not slow in remarking after her departure that the girl would be well paid for her domestic services.

"Not only her domestic ones," Helen had wheedled. "She will make a fair mount for you, Jack, during the holidays. You will see how she flourishes under my continued training. Unlike our cook, she will know of much that passes, and hence we must keep her both in thrall and in pleasure."

"Shall you treat all the girls so?" I asked Helen later in bed after we had enjoyed the most glorious fuck together.

Her finger teased my nose. "No, my pet. I was a trifle crude with Lucy, time being of the essence. Had she not had the lips of her pussy split already, it might have been even harder. As to the girls, I believe all will be virgins—otherwise there is no point in having them sent to me for training. I shall read their characters, fear not. Some will needs be whipped to it—others I may treat more subtly. Oh, do not look dismayed, Jack, at the thought of the latter category. All will come to your cock in the end. Meanwhile, I shall rely much on your inventiveness—you know that," she coaxed. "I am sure you have some splendid ideas already."

"I will think about it," I replied lazily, though I doubt that I ever disguised my thoughts and intentions from her. The "cornering" of Lucy had inspired me with another idea which I intended to put to work. It would be simple enough to produce, or rather more so than the one I had left in the capable hands of the furniture maker. My previous impetuousity was being diluted slightly by the wiles of Helen, but I resented this not since she had in its place found means of supplying me with a harem.

"The girls will be graded, Jack," she told me in all seriousness as we made a leisurely journey the next morning by train to our rural haven, as it was to be. "By that I mean that I shall bring some of them first to view your splendid cock in erection ere their lips even touch it. That I shall regard among the more shy as their attainment of first grade, though therewith their bottoms, too, must be graded by virtue of an increasing number of strokes of the strap or birch or whip. Not that I shall hurt them terribly, Jack, nor you—but a firm and guiding hand is definitely required.

"Some may attain their first grade only by removing their drawers," I said half-jokingly, though I had Victoria a little in mind, and others of her coyness.

Helen's delight at my "sensitivity," as she called it, was apparent.

"Dear Jack, how right you are! They must be taught to display first—by which I mean to unveil their bottoms to full view. Yes, I like that idea very much. We will call *that* Grade One. After all," she added slyly, "that is how most of us begin—though rather later than sooner in some cases. Did I not tell you about Maude?"

I raised my eyebrows enquiringly and then reached within my valise for a silver flask which carried my favourite brand of whiskey.

"Shall we toast Maude?" I asked with a smile, fully aware that I was about to be regaled with a tale that would further pass the time nicely whilst the train rattled on.

"Toasted, my dear, she certainly was," Helen responded with a sparkle. Taking the flask from me, she quaffed a fair mouthful of the delicious brew, gave a small ladylike choke, and handed it back to me for my own delectation.

"Jack, I do not wish to bore you," she teased, and, seated as she was close beside me in a happily otherwise empty carriage, passed her fingers over a certain protrusion in my trousers.

"You will probably bore me to distraction, Miss Hotspur," I remarked in a languid, affected tone that made her laugh. "Nevertheless, you may proceed, though first of all I have a fellow here who would listen as well."

"And no doubt be fondled the while," she laughed as I displayed my upstanding prick, "but be careful, Jack, that your inquisitive friend does not spill over with excitement, as he is well likely to do." Thereupon, clasping my tool and rubbing her thumb about its glossy, glowing head in the most exciting manner, Helen stretched her legs and leaned her head upon my shoulder.

"Do not exclaim with astonishment, Jack, when I tell you that Maude Hopkins, the honourable daughter of Sir Charles of that ilk, was all of twenty-seven at this occurrence. She was the last of the unwed daughters and indeed had been despaired of marrying until a foppish and exceedingly dull aristocrat turned up. Minded to win not merely her heart but her dowry, he set about courting her with one eye firmly upon the opportunities for business and social advancements that such a marriage would bring.

"Suffice to say that he succeeded in obtaining a date for the happy day. The least-liked of all the suitors of the four daughters of the family, he won neither respect nor affection from her relations. As to Maude herself, she was scarcely a family favourite, being haughty, proud and overweening—and given much to playing what we call 'the Madame.' She would have had her drawers down for many a birching ere this had it not been for an over-protective Mama, who, at the time of the wedding, had retired temporarily to a nursing home, there possibly to imbibe even more champagne than she did at home.

"I confess to having been called in too late, Jack, to effect my intended purpose with Maude, for by then she was under the eagle eye of Gerald, her intended. However, being of determined disposition, as you now know me to be, I weighed the chances carefully of the general unpopularity of the pair and found them not wanting. Thus, a few days prior to the wedding, I dropped certain hints as to how a dual effect might be obtained. These being accepted with a certain amount of glee—I saw to it, despite Maude's attempted interferences, that the guest list was both selective and discreet. I need not tell you, Jack, that among the *nouveaux riches* and the aristocracy are many who fill their empty hours with all sorts of lewd games and tricks. An invitation to do so on such a bibulous occasion was not to be missed."

Interrupting Helen for a moment, I cast my arm about her shoulders and kissed her moist lips whilst my cock thrummed in her gently moving palm.

"Your loquacity, my sweet Helen, is never less than charming, but do please get on with the story," I chided her.

Her large eyes met mine closely and with all apparent innocence. "Oh, but Jack, I *do* like to set the background. However, I will hasten matters slightly by informing you that Maude, while facially of a slightly imperious look, was extremely well-endowed by nature in respect of her bottom, legs, and breasts. By then, of course, all was well-matured and ready for the fray—a fray, indeed, that she had not yet encountered, for I doubt that she had even taken sight of a good upstanding cock. As to Gerald, he was three years older, slender of build—not overstrong—and a perfect target for the ladies. Yes, Jack, for both were to be dealt with.

"Naturally I ensured that the wines flowed freely and that in the general hustle and excitement of the event— which took place in the drawing room of Maude's home which, being of a large size, was well isolated from any other residence. By four-thirty of that afternoon, I had plotted so well, that Gerald—being induced to accompany a lady upstairs on the pretence that she felt faint—was seized by several of her companions, gagged, carried into a bedroom and there first bagged.

"The plot, in his respect, was first to accord him a sound birching for his impudence in marrying into the family. The ladies would then take turns in his undressed state to exhaust him so thoroughly that he would prefer to spend the next fortnight in bed rather than on honeymoon.

"Maude, meanwhile, had imbibed quite as much

wine as I intended her to and became prey to the lusts
of the assembled guests. Flushed of face by the wine
and preening herself not a little that she was merely
being admired in her wedding finery, judge of her astonishment when one held her hands as if about to
compliment her whilst another, moving behind her,
raised her skirts to her waist and, with some well-
developed aptitude for the task, loosed the ties of her
drawers and brought them fluttering to her ankles.

"I tell you truly, Jack, that for a moment Maude was
quite speechless. Her mouth opened to scream, but no
sound emerged as all was displayed of her long-hidden
charms. Her thighs were plump—even lusty, I would
say, and most prettily gartered at the tops of her white
silk stockings. Her polished tummy was well-furred at
the base, where her thighs strove desperately to conceal
the rolled lips which for too long had failed to part to
the invading cock. As for her bottom, which was truly
as much on display as all else, it was a work of gran-
deur—fully fleshed, of delightful roundness, and by no
means small.

"When her frozen shriek finally emerged, Jack, it
was of course far too late, but would have gone un-
heeded in any event. Whilst her ankles were firmly held
by the very gentleman who had denuded her lower half,
two ladies who had been deputised to assist in the ceremonial came forward and, with the greatest of ease, removed all Maude's garments except her wedding shoes
of silver, her fine white stockings, and her garters."

My brow wrinkled. "With the greatest of ease?" I
asked, knowing what frills, furbelows, underskirts, and
heaven knows what else women array themselves in on
such occasions.

"Oh, yes, Jack, for I had provided scissors for this—
sharp, clean dressmaking shears. After all, she was
most unlikely ever to wed again, and so the clothes
would have soon been cast out in any event," Helen

explained by way of what I thought was a quaint excuse for the delightful outrage.

"To a table first the struggling, shrieking Maude was taken. I had tossed a cushion upon the edge of it already, and there upon it her belly was laid as she was bent over. The two ladies, I might say, stood on the opposite side of the table, holding Maude's arms extended. She could kick with one leg, had she tried, but this possible exercise on her part was soon put at fault by the immediate application by myself of a nice green-twigged birch.

"Ah, dearest, what rising cries of shame, embarrassment and horror rose from the haughty Maude, who knew too well the possessors of all the pairs of eyes which were by then lecherously scanning her magnificent posterior, her full, creamy breasts, and that well-thatched treasure which lay already half-visible by virture of her posture. You can well imagine her oft-repeated cries, Jack: 'Oh! Do not shame me! For pity, let me go! Cover me! Oh, you monsters!'—and so on. How foolish such females are that they do not realise how much the appetites of males are increased by such appeals even as the birch was swishing steadily across her bottom and bringing it rapidly to a fine glow.

"I accorded her a fair dozen, Jack, before I desisted in that respect. By then her proud features had crumbled, her hips squirmed madly, and her tears coursed freely over the arm on which her face was laid. Oh, my pet, who could be more enticing than a denuded bride with a bared and glowing bottom and freely wriggling hips? Her earlier shrieks were as nothing to those which resounded when—held still over the table as she was and in a prime position of presenting herself—I duly presented the knob of the first cock to her. That it belonged to him who should have birched her long ere this I need hardly say. Gross in size as it was by virtue of the general display Maude had given, the longing crest

forced itself between the pouting lips of her quim and
urged itself slowly up the while that, overcome with excitement, he growled her name into her ear.

"Ah, how the table shook as Maude realised who her
first stallion was! Her shrieks of protest would have
raised the roof had it not been firmly raftered. Her
torso twisted, breasts bobbing heavily on the table until,
flexing his knees and cupping those wobbling gourds, he
sheathed himself with many a groan to the root.

"Maude's anguished cry of *'No!'* appeared for a moment to be her final effort, for, feeling as she did the
great throbbing of his prick within her, she fell to sobbing. Indeed, I would have thought her crying her heart
out were it not, after a few seconds, for the febrile
movements of her bottom as he commenced to ream
her. Again and again the oak table trembled and quivered as belly and bottom met again and again in a loud
slapping.

"Thereat a curious silence fell otherwise on the
room. At a signal from myself the two ladies released
Maude's arms. In response her hands beat in apparent
anguish on the polished table while the emergence and
renewed indriving of his thick cock in her channel
made the most succulent sounds.

"I made myself then quite a circus and gained several new clients thereby, for would you believe that in
the midst of this frenziedly erotic scene I accorded any
gentleman who attempted in turn to broach and breech
the other two ladies a fair crack of my birch? I intended
the divinely wriggling Maude to receive all the favours,
and this she did perforce. As was evident to all who
observed the lubricious scene, her submission was by
this time only partly enforced, and such resistance as
she had offered was slowly dying away as her polished
rump—now being most fervently caressed—responded
in agitated fashion to the excited surging of the cock
back and forth in her cunny.

"The moment of utmost delight could not, however, be long delayed, and with many a desiring groan, he loosed at last his spermatic bliss within the altar of desire whilst Maude's fingers clawed at the tabletop and her mouth opened in a soundless cry.

"Thus freshly injected, she was half-carried, half-dragged to the rolled arm of a sofa where it was deemed an even better posture and greater comfort for the combatants would be obtained. The round padded arm, being somewhat high, pushed her bottom up exceedingly well whilst the upper half of her body slumped down into the well of the seat where one of the ladies held her head.

"Some instinct of the perhaps even greater outrage that was then to occur must have entered Maude's mind, for she made frenetic efforts to rise—but alas (or rather, all to the good) too late. In a flash the next of the gentleman was at her rear, his tool well presented for the fray and his hands taking good purchase on her curving hips. Whether 'twas sweeter to take her by her narrower portal I know not, but ah! the horrified shrieks and cries that arose from her as the crest of his lance urged itself against her rosehole! Indeed, I regret to say that the second of my female assistants was required to apply momentary weight upon Maude's shoulders while the thick syringe was inserted inch by inch in her lovely fundament until at last she was well and truly pegged or—what is your favourite term, corked?"

I nodded, not trusting myself to speak, for my pego was throbbing fit to burst as I imagined the scene that she was so graphically describing. Perceiving my state, Helen loosed her fingers somewhat and let my prick throb like a captive bird against her palm.

"Well, then," Helen continued, "as fully corked as Maude then was, I motioned to the ladies to let go their hold upon her, for I ever insist, Jack, that once the manly shaft is properly inserted, all future fortunes must be left to the combatants. Truly Maude once more attempted to rise, but her posture—with the back of her thighs pressed tight to those of her rider—made this nigh impossible. Slumping down once more while he kept it deep embedded, she moaned, sobbed, and flailed weakly with her arms while the same perfect hush as before settled upon the observers. With her legs forced to remain straight by virtue of the fact that they were squashed between his own and the side of the sofa, her bubbies extruding their hardened nipples, and the arrogant globe of her bottom thrust tight into his belly, she looked as perfect a fallen Venus as any I have seen.

"Hiding her face in the brocaded cushions, she moaned unceasingly as the sturdy cock then began to plough her tighter furrow. The sofa creaked—all withheld breaths seemed to expel, and thereupon sweet, proud Maude was as truly buggered as any female might be until with the final emergence of the foaming lance the sperm trickled from her rosehole and ran in little rivulets down the insides of her thighs. As I expected, then, Maude made no further attempt to rise or to wriggle off the arm of the sofa but waited—whether in expectation or despair—for a third assault. That this was but a moment in coming, I need hardly say. Meanwhile, curious as to events upstairs, I repaired there and found Gerald in such a ruined state that he could do naught but lie as limp as the ladies there assembled had left him. Well-birched as his rump had been, it showed still the red streaks, whilst his cock had shrunk to the size of a sparrow's leg after the juice had twice been drawn from it.

"The ladies, it seemed, were quite in contempt of his lack of virility, for two of the four remained to a great extent unsatisfied. Tying him about therefore with his own shirt—an operation he had no strength left to resist—he was left upon the bed whilst we descended. Some ten minutes having passed by then, Maude it seemed had become converted. Not entirely to my surprise she lay now upon her back on a rug, her stockinged legs well spread, while the fourth gentleman—a relative quite well known to her, I might say—was entertaining his piston in her pussy, she seconding his efforts in the most langourous manner. As to my two erstwhile assistants, they, too, had by then quite naturally been put to the cock—the drawing room fairly resounding with their cries."

"Oh, my love, I can bear no more—kneel up upon the seat, I beg," I pleaded hoarsely.

Submitting without a murmur, Helen so placed herself upon the padded seat with her glorious, uncovered bottom well-protruding. The gentle rocking of the train added not a little to the exquisite sensation of parting the petals of her quim and inserting my swollen prick.

"Oh, Jack, how I wanted it!"

"So you concluded that wicked occasion with a general orgy," I groaned quite beside myself with her lustful inventiveness which so well matched my own. By some curiosity of human nature, I experienced quite a pang of jealousy in so saying and so imagining.

"I, Jack? Heavens, no!" Helen panted. Her neck, twisted about, offered her long, pointed tongue to my mouth. "One d . . . d . . . does not, as a Mistress of Disciplines, my pet, offer oneself up publicly, or all submissions to one's will come to an end. No, darling, I most tactfully left them to it, being well aware that the orgy would continue unabated and that Maude had no more to learn from me. It was too easy a victory, I fear, though I saw to it by further visits that she did not deviate from the path. Oh! faster, Jack, for I want to feel your flood!"

In a trice—such was our mutual state of arousal—her bubbling slit had received my effusions and responded with her own. With a merry laugh from Helen, we slid backwards together onto the floor of the carriage and there lay for a moment in a tumbled heap, my dripping cock still gripped between the lips of her maw.

"How I love you!" I declared hoarsely and of a sudden, though the words spilled so quickly from my mouth that they all but surprised me.

Turning her lovely face about once more to mine, her rump full upon me and our tangled limbs rocking to the movement of the train, her eyes met mine in a perfect glow of pleasure.

"Of course, Jack," she whispered softly. "What else? Be sure that I shall see to it that neither Maude nor any of the others entrap you now."

Chapter 7

"MAUDE?" I had echoed several times in astonishment, but Helen had simply smiled, shaken her head, and refused to answer me. This I took to be a mere mischief on her part, for the name is by no means uncommon. Hence I desisted from asking further and absorbed great pleasure from the rolling countryside, the lanes and the hedges whereby we wended our way in a carriage from the rural halt on our arrival. For such it was rather than a station proper, being only a tiny platform with a small ticket office on the other side which was reached by way of a footbridge.

It was a summer's day such as befitted our first visit together. Passing through the single street of a village, Helen waved briefly to a stout middle-aged woman who responded with some attempt at a curtsy and a vacuous smile.

"I have already chosen her to be our cook, though she knows it not," Helen explained. "She is a simple soul, prepared to be totally obedient, and will have no inkling of the world that goes on about her at the Academy. Indeed, were she to hear of it, she would neither understand nor believe it. As to Lucy, she will follow in a few days. Meanwhile we may make ourselves comfortable, Jack, and examine the letters which will surely have arrived here. My newest advertisement gives the address, you see."

A further fifteen minutes' drive, and our coachman led his horses at last between the stone pillars of the entrance to the house. It lay well back, shielded by elegant, tall firs and a veritable bustling of rhododendron bushes in full flower, and other shrubs. The ivy-covered facade looked exceedingly pleasing and gave, as Helen remarked, a pleasant air of calm and propriety to the place.

Within, I was astonished to find all already furnished. The wide reception hall was carpeted, and glass and brass ornaments gleamed upon small tables on either side. So it was, too, in all the rooms to which Helen led me turn by turn whilst our luggage was unloaded. Upstairs, on the second floor, the bedrooms had been divided up into what Helen termed dormitories and tuition rooms. The former each contained three single beds with cabinets, chairs, and whatnot spread between.

"Two girls together might get into collusion, Jack, but with three the variance in characters is such that that is unlikely. The tuition rooms have one double bed each, as you can see, and I scarce need to explain their purpose. The doors to these have a double lock. Selected girls will have a key to but one—I shall have the key to the other and a master key for the first. The purpose thereof, as you will come to know, is when they attain their graduation honours. I love to have my little inventions in this respect, as I am sure you, Jack, will have your own. However, I shall not ask you, for I know you may want to surprise me," Helen twinkled.

"You have anticipated all," I remarked with fond amusement, for I had expected to find naught but bare floorboards and empty rooms. Instead, all was fully prepared down to the kitchen, scullery, larders, laundry room, an exquisitely furnished drawing room and two dining rooms—the larger being for the girls.

"Naturally, Jack, for I have learned human nature well enough. But twelve young ladies per term will see me paid off for my expenses in a year. Thereafter we shall continue to profit in every way. But now as to your own intended accoutrements, I have a room laid off for you from my study. I have furnished it but with a carpet, couch, and lamps, for I know you will want to do the rest. It is large enough, as you will see."

Being led there—as I was truly being led—I agreed that it was. Helen's study was a perfect picture of formality, its large bow window giving out on to one of the prettiest views of the grounds. Bookcases were arranged on one side and a very comfortable leather divan, well piled with cushions, on the other. Betwixt these two principal pieces and with its back to the window stood her large desk. To the left of that was an armoire, of which I did not need to ask the contents. It held what Helen was pleased to call "correction pieces."

In the wall facing the window and to the left of her own entrance door was another, discreetly plain and with a spring lock, as she showed me. Larger by far than my Snuggery, it measured some sixteen by twenty feet, but the perfect surprise was to find that in addition to carpet, rugs cushions and couch, the walls were mirrored all around.

"All shall be seen, from all angles, and nothing shall be hid, Jack. Think of the all-round views you will obtain," Helen laughed, seeing my pleasure. "But come, the luggage is unloaded, the coachman awaits his tip, and then we shall have some refreshments."

"Very well, I will see to those," I said gallantly, for as a bachelor I had even been a dab hand at preparing repasts and had seen how well the larders were supplied with comestibles. Having seen the fellow off, I betook myself inside again and saw Helen lounging at her ease on a huge sofa in the drawing room.

"Come, sit with me. Wine will be brought in a moment," she declared.

So used was I to her surprises that I was careful to envince none myself. Lighting two cigarettes from an onyx casket, I handed her one and laid a crystal glass ashtray between us.

"Let us hope then that it will be nicely chilled," I said.

" 'Tis the only thing that ever will be here, my pet," Helen laughed, and then came to my ears the tinkling of glasses upon a tray. Modifying my expression as best I could—being determined not to be put out by Helen's little japes—I turned my head toward the door and there saw the very one whom I knew of instinct to have been described to me on the train.

Not a word was said as she laid down the silver tray on an occasional table beside us. Dressed in a clinging russet gown, girded by a thick oatmeal cord at her waist, the young woman presented the most placid but comely of appearances. The swell of her buttocks showed clearly as she bent momentarily to place the tray, as did the globular fall of her breasts through the thin material. Her brown hair fell in a long sweep between her shoulders, being secured and drawn together at the base by a blue bow that looked pleasingly girlish. Her face was round to oval, the lips full and slightly sensuous. Her eyes, smaller than Helen's pools of wonder, spoke I thought of both slyness and shyness.

Turning toward us and affording me no more than a flickering glance, she stood gazing with a mixture of wonder, adoration and—I thought—a wisp of apprehension at Helen.

Helen leaned back and issued a cloud of blue smoke from between her lips.

"Present yourself, Maude," she murmured.

Only the slightest hesitation showed and the merest
hint of a flush appeared upon the young woman's
cheeks as, standing but a few feet in front of us, she
turned about, bent over and raised the hem of her
dress, affording it a final flick in its uprising so that it
settled neatly in a long loop about her hips.

Thus did I make first acquaintance with Maude's
bottom. What a deeply split orb of glory she presented!
The bulging cheeks, of ivory-tinted pallor, were flawless, supported upon thighs of perfect roundness that
midway up their columns were banded by black stocking tops. Moreover, from my seated position, the fig of
her slit showed clearly, the rolled lips crowned by a
bosquet of thick, dark curls.

Helen's hand crept into mine.

"You see now what I mean, Jack?" she asked whilst
Maude remained unmoving. "What a waste such treasures would have been upon the foppish Gerald—
fortunately long discarded, of course. Her second name
is Angela, but it would have spoiled my little treat had I
told you all earlier. Come to me now, Maude, come!"

I expected then the accolyte to rise and turn, but instead, to my amazement she remained fully bent over
and shuffled carefully backward until the pale glossy
orb of her bottom loomed against Helen's face.

"What a pet she is," Helen said huskily and, whilst
Maude uttered a small, choked, "Ooooh!" Helen
parted the sumptuous cheeks, thereby exposing the
crinkled orifice into which the tip of her long tongue
immediately darted. Therewith also the passed her left
hand up between Maude's straddled legs and gently
fondled her plump pussy, bringing a soft murmur of
contentment from her.

Eyes glazing, I watched the brief proceeding of the
incredibly sensuous operation as the curling tip of Hel-
en's tongue inserted and withdrew itself, snakelike,
again and again whilst the quivering thighs and soft-

breathing moans of Maude spoke well enough of her pleasure. Then of a sudden, Helen ceased her ministrations and gave Maude's lustrous globe a loving smack.

"Go—back to your duties," she commanded, and thereupon as if nothing had happened the young woman delicately smoothed down her dress and literally wafted from the room as quietly as she had come.

Helen's eyes gleamed as I solemnly then poured wine, with my cock at such full stance that it bid fair to split my trousers.

"A naughty operation, was it not, Jack, but she adores it. Besides, she is perfectly clean there, for she washes upon the hour every hour. You have seen her now in servile pose, but, my dear, she can now be as strict as I when called upon to be. A case of the bitten learning to bite, but she is best kept now on tenterhooks, for it sharpens her wonderfully. Her dosage from a weapon as valiant as yours shall be not more than once a fortnight. The girls will benefit therefrom, I can tell you, for the strands of frustration in her will keep her at them."

"How often was she put to it during her post-nuptial training?" I asked, "and what happened to Gerald?"

"Gerald was dispensed with, as I said, by mere virtue of Maude's father despatching him off to a plantation he owns in the West Indies, thus to clear the ground, so to speak. Maude regretted not his going and has no idea now why she intended to marry him. Her haughtiness and general demeanour had been in part a disguise for the frustrations she had imposed upon herself. I refused to let her slacken, however, after the orgy in which she had been brought to indulge and knew well that she might again retreat into her shell if matters were not in the first place properly orchestrated.

"Giving her twenty-four hours' rest after the wedding reception—during which time she was in a thorough daze—I had her birched on her bare bottom in her

room. On this occasion I merely acted at first as specta-
tor and controller of affairs, so to speak—quelling such
protests as she uttered about the 'horrors' she had en-
dured. The cock was well up during her birching, as
you can imagine, but to the despair of its eager posses-
sor, I dismissed him and took to tonguing and caressing
her myself, which delights I might say brought her almost immediately into my domain.

"The next day, partly by cajollery and partly by
threats of whip or birch, I had her move about the
house clad only in a short and flimsy chemise, stockings, and shoes. At the first signs of revolt I smacked
her bottom sharply, then kissed and fondled her and all
but brought her to real tears. By then, Gerald had already been despatched to town in anticipation of his departure. Within two days—for my methods are not always so crudely immediate as with Lucy—I had taught
her to 'offer' by raising the hem of her chemise on command. No fondlings or touchings were permitted. On
the fourth evening, whilst I had thus ordered her to
stand, the cock was presented to her view. I sat with
one hand holding my whip. Ah, the blushes that came
and the visible quivering of her stockinged legs as the
monster that had first injected her slit was revealed. She
made to run from the drawing room, but a warning
lash of my whip around her calves stilled her. I ordained her then to play the young mare to her stallion,
which, finally, with many supposedly horrified cries,
she did by virtue of kneeling in readiness on a rug, her
chemise looped up about her waist.

"The struggle that followed was quite delicious to
watch. For once I did not interfere. Finally, with
Maude overpowered, his prick found lodgement between the cheeks of her bottom. Her cries rent the air.
For a moment, with the long, thick pestle of flesh
sheathed but half within her, she bucked like a filly. A
groan and a grunt and it was lodged to the full. A long,

quivering cry escaped her, and then her shoulders sank. Cupping her blazing face in her hands, her struggles ceased, she pretending no more than a sob or two whilst the big shaft moved slowly in and out between her cheeks. In but two minutes, during which their moans mingled, she was inundated with his flood. He sank down upon her, ever buried still, their bodies quivering in the sweet aftermath of desire.

"Thereafter I have had no problems with her," Helen finished simply. Aroused as I was, I drew her hand to my cock, but she moved it away. "No, Jack, you must not be spoiled. Have you not work to do whilst I go through my letters? There is a full score of them in waiting."

It was indeed true, for we had come across them at our entrance, though it had not occurred to me then who had neatly placed them on a table in the hall. Besides, I had my first new contrivance to prepare. There was wood and tools enough in an outbuilding to the stable. This had been prepared also for "visitors," the floor being swept and cleaned and all put away save for several interesting trestles, some wall rings and chains, and a few bales of straw.

I contented myself therefore with my frustration—if such a condition may be so called—by attending to "first things first," as Helen put it. Besides, I had a perfect will to work, for but minutes after she had refused even a gentle handling of my prick, she advised me in a soft and enchanting whisper that Maude's two weeks of waiting was already up and that I could "attend to her if I were a good boy" that evening.

Thus heartened, and whilst Helen settled to her letters, I began my carpentry, stopping only for a brief midday meal which the ever-quiet Maude both prepared and served. By six that evening I had my "cornering" device installed. It consisted first of a hinged piece of timber some six inches wide by three and a half feet long which could be lifted up and outward from the corner to whatever height was desired. This I affixed to the further right-hand corner of my new Snuggery and therewith attached to the free end of the timber a curved piece in the shape of an outward-reaching half-moon.

The next step was to provide footholds, and these were no less easy to devise. Each comprised two pieces, which, when placed close together, formed the mould of a female foot. The toepieces were secured to the floor some three feet out from the corner. To the rear of these, but sliding in grooves, I fixed the heelpieces, which were thus perfectly adjustable to small- or medium-size feet. The final touches were to add a stout piece of strap on either side of the hinged piece—one of the lengths being buckled—and then wall rings with attendant wrist manacles to the walls themselves.

Seating ourselves at dinner that evening, Helen remarked on my industry but was tactful enough not to enquire as to the exact nature of it. This enchanted me since it was obvious that she considered the room adjoining her study to be my own domain and one that even she might enter only by favour.

Once the liqueurs and coffee were finished, I therefore invited her in the most gallant fashion to view my contrivance.

"Shall I be safe?" she asked me archly.

"Perhaps not, but how dull it would be to be so," I rejoined, making her laugh. "Maude shall come, too," I added, whereat she agreed and summoned her. Maude had eaten alone, but in future would share our table occasionally when the pupils began to arrive, Helen said.

Leading both up—for I thought it not proper on such an occasion to display any deference—I lit the oil lamps that I prefer to gas for my "entertainments." Oil casts a lambent glow and does not hiss in the sometimes irritating manner of gas.

"Oh, Jack, whatever is it?" Helen asked in a manner quite deliberately intended to convey to Maude that I was total master of this particular domain.

"Let Maude be its first victim," I declared, and whilst the young woman hung back instinctively, I seized her wrist, dragged her forward to the corner and placed the soles and heels of her lace-up boots in the prepared footholds, easing the heelpieces forward until her feet were so tightly secured that only by standing perfectly upright could she prevent herself from falling forward.

Were she to do so, of course, her hands would have to reach out and forward to support herself against the walls. This being my intention, I gave her a gentle prod in the back which made her cry out in alarm, her hands grabbing immediately for the two iron rings which were just below shoulder height.

In so doing, Maude was already in a nigh-perfect posture of submission—arms held all but straight before her and slightly downward, her back extended, legs braced and held, and her bottom well up.

Quite bewildered, since she had never been put to any such contrivance before, Maude cried out in alarm, "What are you doing? Oh, I'm quite helpless like this!" And indeed she was, for with the upper part of her body stretched forward, no amount of strength would allow her to lever up her otherwise unsupported body again. Were she to let go of the rings, she would simply slump further and remain doubled-up. This, however, I did not wish her to do, and so secured her wrists in the manacles, these being fixed to the rings in such position that the fingers could still grasp them.

Then, to a cry of alarm from Maude—which I am perfectly sure was in part real—I swept her gown up to her waist and found to my delight that it was the only garment she wore. By the light from the oil lamps, the pale roseate glow of her moonlike bottom and supporting thighs was truly superb—the cleft and the well—furred slit beneath showing in full offering, as Helen was always to term it.

"No! Oh, let me up, please!" Maude panted, endeavouring to shift her feet, which the securing blocks, however, held as well as I intended them to. Besides, I had yet to demonstrate my *pièce de résistance,* which I did by bending half beneath her and lifting the hinged piece up so that its padded cresent nestled firmly into her tummy while the two halves of the stout strap affixed to it were passed around her waist and there buckled.

"Oh, Jack, it's splendid! What a marvellous idea!" Helen purred. "And now a taste of the leather will warm up our assistant nicely."

"No!" Maude howled, making the wall rings clink as her arms attempted in vain to move. Her hips endeavoured to retract instinctively, but were unable to do so by virtue of my "supporter," the hinged piece. Her bottom could still squirm indelicately, however, for nothing prevented a slight bending movement of her stockinged knees as I had anticipated. The movement merely added to the brazen allure of that naked orb, whose plump cheeks endeavoured to clench defensively as she peered beneath her arm—eyes wild with wonder—and saw me select a tawse from several straps that hung nearby.

For the totally uninitiated, I should say that a tawse is a Scottish implement of thick, supple leather some five inches wide and a good quarter of an inch thick. It possesses a split end—sometimes split two ways and sometimes three—these splits producing "fingers," which add to the suppleness and effectiveness of the leather as it sleeks across a naked bottom.

"A full dozen, Jack," Helen murmured even as Maude's wailing protest was cut off at its height as the first sharp, cracking slap of the tawse impacted itself across that glorious orb.

"*Ya-ah-aaaah!*" Maude shrieked, her hips endeavouring in vain to press inward. "Oh, God no, it burns!", she cried, and indeed, such was the weight of the leather that a full pink band had appeared already across her luscious hemispheres.

"No more than your Papa's birch, my sweet," rejoined Helen, whose face was bright with pleasure, for she was truly enchanted by the posture which my device enforced.

"*No-ooooh!*" Maude shrieked, though whether in protest at this revelation or the fact that the tawse was once more searing a path across her, I knew not. Rolling her head from side to side so violently that her hairpins dislodged and allowed her hair to fall and cloud her face, she most ill-advisedly bent her knees under the impact, which merely served to bulge her nether cheeks out more. Taking immediate advantage of this, I brought the heavy strap in an upward snaking curl full under the plump wonder of her hemispheres, which caused her wailing cry to run around the very walls.

"A moment's respite now, Jack," Helen whispered, and, stepping between us, laid her open hand upon the heated globe in such fashion that her delicately extended forefinger slid beneath the palpitating cheeks and caressed with maddening brevity the rolled lips of Maude's quim. "Deliciously warm—a trifle moist already—but she needs more—I know her, don't I, Maude?" she mocked affectionately.

"P . . . p . . . please, no-oh!" Maude sobbed, while, moving again to my side, Helen gently stroked my fiercely upstanding prick and murmured, "Go on— she's always like this—be neither too hard nor too soft, dear."

I needed no such instruction, but showed no resentment at it. The art is to lather the bottom well, to induce its hidden heat to the surface and to put a fine gloss on all, preparatory to inserting the peg. Thus now I assailed first one cheek and then the other, giving no respite despite Maude's sobs and cries while adding my favourite "intermediary" stroke, which is to snap the leather up sharply beneath the bottom and so stiffen the lines of the legs to their most attractive extent. The tawse, moreover, is perfectly designed for such an exercise, since the fingers at the end curl up beneath the pussy and so titillate and excite it in a fashion that the victim can do nothing to prevent.

That Maude was only partly assenting gave added spice to the occasion, and while I betrayed nothing that I knew of her seductions, the very images of them added a fiery warmth to the occasion.

The very weight of the tawse is as if designed to lure nubile maidens to perdition. It needs no great swinging of the arm to effect the very loud CRACK! that is heard upon impact with the wriggling cheeks. Nor does it leave the bottom unduly marked, as oftimes does the birch. Its usage is betrayed, rather, by a deep glow which invades the hemispheres—a roseate sheen which fades slowly and leaves the female bottom simmering for such added attentions thereafter as it deserves.

At the tenth stroke, Helen loosened my attire and drew out my champion in readiness. Naught was heard now save the wails and sobs of the shapely accolyte, whose bottom was by now almost burnished to the full and whose black-stockinged legs alternately flexed and straightened under the loud-smacking slap of every impact.

"Oh, no, oh-*oh!*" came the rising shriek then from Maude as upon the final searing caress of the tawse she heard it fall. Her cheeks tightened upon instinct, her long hair so now cascading down on either side of her flushed face that I could glimpse only the tip of her nose.

"Be quiet, Maude! What have I always told you?" Helen scolded while without further ado she grasped my throbbing cock and brought the flaming crest to rub up and down between the mucous lips of Maude's slit, causing my head to spin with the delicious contact. Bending my knees slightly, and so forcing her own inward, I unbuckled the waist strap whereupon—the hinged piece falling down—more freedom was left to her to wriggle. Taking her well-curved hips then and so quelling her would-be evasive movements, I urged my shaft slowly upward into the clinging maw of her slit.

Ah, what warmth, what delicious moisture, what spongy clinging! Her attempted writhings served but to give the act greater appetite. With a groan of perfect pleasure, I waited no longer but rammed if full within her and so held her glorious hot bottom tightly into my belly while a cascade of bubbling cries came from Maude. Thereupon Helen decided to inject even more pleasure into the occasion. Casting herself down beneath the bottom-wriggling young woman, she slid her feet between both Maude's and my own and, clasping Maude's thighs at the back, brought her lips and tongue up to caress and delight the close conjuction of our parts.

A soft mewing issued from Maude at the wicked flickering of Helen's tongue, which swept both the lips of her cunny, the root of my embedded shaft, and my heavily dangling balls. Strongly pumping, I began to pleasure the young woman, whose heat glossed bottom was a veritable orb of delight in its incessant squirmings. Doubting not from Maude's panting that Helen had the tip of her tongue working around her clitoris, I began to ream her with such energy as I felt she required. The artless nutcracker action of her cunny was almost as skilful as Helen's, and in but a trice I felt the sperm churning in my testicles.

The licking and lapping sounds that came from beneath but added to the lewd joy of the bout, causing me even in the midst of such raptures to make a mental note that the footholds must be even farther apart in future. But all was then lost in the bumping, heaving, gasping rise to the very peaks of bliss as my embedded weapon commenced spilling its load in such veritable streams and powerful jets as flooded down my prick again, oozing from within Maude's luscious nest to trickle upon Helen's luring tongue.

A few frenetic quiverings more, and then the delicious tableau stilled whilst I rapturously clasped Maude's bottom tightly into me, fondling her hips and thighs whilst Helen—bright-eyed and wet of mouth—brought herself up from beneath us once more. Then was Maude gently released. The inner surfaces of her thighs gleaming and sheened with our combined spendings, she threw herself with apparent confusion into the arms of Helen, who smiled over her shoulder at me and stroked her hair.

"She is always thus, but with the girls she will be a true martinet—will you not, Maude?"

The young woman's whispered "Yes" came from between Helen's breasts, where she had buried her face.

"Come, Jack, you may have the best of us both tonight, for we shall call this a celelbration," Helen announced. With the most mischievous of smiles, she drew her gown up so that it coiled about her waist in the same fashion as Maude's. Then, putting her arm about Maude's waist, she led her before me toward the open, waiting door of her bedroom. Their hips moved together, their naked bottoms rolling in blatant invitation. Then the milky gloom enfolded us and the long night unrolled its veils of passion.

Chapter 8

THE DAYS that passed were ones of bustling activity. Freed from her kitchen chores by the arrival of the cook, Maude assisted Helen in preparing the curriculum and in replying to the letters that continued to arrive.

"Fifty-one, no less—did I not tell you, Jack?, Helen crowed. "Of those, twenty-eight have accepted my terms and sent their fees. You will have a fair browsing through their letters and photographs, my lad. Such a culling we have here of some of the most attractive damsels in southern England, I am sure, aged from eighteen even up to twenty-two. And not a one who may not be fully tamed. Are your own preparations now complete, my pet?"

"Thoroughly, and the stable, too," I was able to assure her, for evidently Helen was looking forward to surprising herself and had deliberately avoided seeing or overlooking the installation of my other devices. That which I had ordered in London was already in place and delightfully elaborate it was, though requiring—as shall be seen—two shapely girls together. I suspected I might see no more of its operation than Helen herself, once she had viewed it in action.

As to my own official role, it was decided after much discussion that I should be the Riding Master, though my presence would not otherwise be announced to the outside world unless by some quirk of misfortune it should be called for, in which event Helen would know well how to put a bold face on it. Together we selected the first term's entrants. They included the selfsame Samantha and Victoria, of whom something has already been said together with a very evidently slender and nubile girl named Monique, whose father was a high-placed official of the French Government now posted in London. Monique had been presented both by portrait and in full figure by means of two photographs sent. They indicated, unless the sepia tone of the prints was misleading, a deliciously smooth and faintly olive skin, two melon-round breasts that strained distinctly through the corsage of her dress, a mouth that spoke of mischief, and eyes that uttered strains of sensuousness. Being corseted, as she evidently was in the full-length portrait, her figure—turned sideways to the camera—displayed a wasplike waist and a wickedly appealing apple of a bottom.

That Helen had as much a taste for her as I was in no doubt and hence she was among the first to be interviewed. This little ceremony took place upon the arrival of each girl and was conducted in Helen's study. To apprise myself of all that took place I had made a peephole between the wall that separated it from my improved Snuggery. Placing a chair there where I could lounge at ease, I furnished myself with a small side table bearing cigars and a flask of my favourite whiskey. Thus was I fully prepared to enjoy the first interview when Samantha was ushered in.

Her carriage having been the first to arrive, her bags had been unloaded and she had been given a pleasant collation accompanied by two of our best table wines. Such, I may say, was ever a matter of surprise to the incoming girls, who expected in all matters a harsh regime and were amazed to find the comforts of the table no less than they enjoyed at home. But on this point Helen was rightly insistent that there were a few areas in which they might be coddled, as with her provision of perfumed soaps, warm towels, and even Turkish cigarettes for the daily smoking hour that was allowed to follow dinner in the evenings.

But I shall delay no longer the entrance of Samantha who was as proud and lovely as one might ever see in a girl of her years. Five feet seven in height, she was possessed of long and perfectly curved legs, surmounted at their height by a bottom as tight and round as a drum. Her breasts formed two perfect orbs, her face oval with large, well-curved lips. Blue eyes complemented the corn-gold of her long hair, which, when unpinned, reached halfway down her back. Her walk, long-striding, was an appealing admixture of the imperious and the nervous, as if at any moment she expected the flicking of a crop across her tight buttocks.

Helen arrayed herself formally for such introductory occasions, wearing a black, form-fitting gown, a black choker in which gleamed a small solitary diamond, and with her hair drawn up in a bun. Beside her chair—almost as if waiting to swing a chalice—stood Maude who was similarly attired save for the choker, which gave Helen greater authority. From Maude's waist, however, hung an item that quickened and intrigued me. It was a black, silver-handle crop, secured to the waistband of her gown by a steel clip. At each movement it swung against her thigh.

No chair being placed before Helen's desk, Samantha thus stood, though her eyes sought briefly for one.

"Samantha, we are very pleased to have you here," Helen said gently. Of a purpose, she had, laid before her, the girl's photograph and the letter that had accompanied it. Samantha's lips parted slightly and then closed with what I felt to be an affectation of primness as she noted them. "A charming photograph—I particularly liked the casual way that your corsage was unbuttoned at the top. Perhaps you would like to loose the one you are wearing?" Helen asked with a great affectation of casualness that even so caused Samantha's colour to rise.

A moment's silence ensued whilst Helen remained apparently engrossed once more in the contents of the letter whose pages she turned idly. "I am waiting, Samantha—unbutton to the waist," she said with a trifle more asperity in her voice, "or was it perhaps unbuttoned for you to add greater charm to the picture? Maude, you had best assist her."

"Oh, no, I . . . ," Samantha began. Her arms wavered and rose, her fingers distinctly trembling whilst she loosed the tight buttons of her gown. Helen now looked up again,—a frown crossing her lovely features.

"A bodice beneath? Oh, come, Samantha, you wore no such guardian of your bust when this was taken. You intend surely not to displease me already? Remove your dress and all else beneath except for your drawers. Quickly now—we cannot have the day held up."

"Oh, really, I never thought—" Samantha began, only to be cut off by the quick rising from her chair of Helen, from whom I expected a more biting outburst. Instead, however, she moved lithely round her desk and placed her hand upon the girl's arm.

"Really, my dear, we are all three females here, are we not? What have you to conceal save the bounteous gifts of nature, and with which I am led to believe—and in part already perceive—that you are well endowed. Bend forward on the desk and let me assist you."

"Madame—please—I would prefer—oh, really, the

impropriety!" gasped Samantha. "Why am I to be examined like this? I have never permitted—"

"Yourself to be examined?" asked Helen with a laugh. "Then more's the pity, my dear. However, it is not absolutely true, I believe? Let us take an occasion last spring. Ah, yes, here it is, on page three of your introductory letter. Shall I read from it to you? 'Exceedingly well-figured as Samantha is, she garters not tightly and should be taught to do so, for her thighs are quite splendid. Her drawers—on the solitary occasion when it proved possible to raise her skirts—' "

"Oh, no!" Samantha shrieked, covering her ears. "It cannot possibly be!"

"Really, Samantha," Helen said calmly, returning (somewhat to my suprise) to her desk, "were it not so, I would scarcely be privileged to know that you have a pretty dimple on the left cheek of your bottom. You wish me not to read this out in Assembly tomorrow morning? Then off with your things, Miss, and *now!*"

For a long moment, Samantha gazed wildly back and forth from Helen to Maude. Then a sob broke from her.

"Madame, you would not shame me so? It is but a wicked invention, I assure you. Oh! I cannot believe my ears that such things could be written. How hateful, how hateful, how hateful!" Samantha cried and actually stamped her feet, such was her petulance.

"Untrue? Then we shall see for ourselves," Helen declared. "Maude—up with her dress and apply the crop."

"*No!*" Samantha shrieked and ran to the door, rattling the handle so violently that I thought it might come off.

Quite undismayed, though emitting a small sigh, Helen motioned to Maude whose stillness was broken as she advanced upon Samantha.

"The door is self-locking, Samantha, and cannot be opened until the Principal ordains. Come to the couch—you will be more comfortable there," Maude uttered in a voice I had never heard her use and which was as steel sheathed in velvet. With a grip which I sensed was as strong as Helen's—and thus betrayed to me once more the strange duality of woman—she took the girl's elbow and guided her, sobbing and apparently bereft, to the couch. Samantha's legs tottered. A wailing cry escaped her as, with an agile twist of Maude's arm, she was spun face down upon the leather and Maude's left hand clamped firmly upon the nape of her neck.

Helen tutted gently and rose.

"What a foolish girl you are, to be sure, Samantha. Are you then to be undressed like a child, or will you at least sustain the dignity of disrobing yourself? Come— for at least I give you the option, do I not?"

Samantha's form stirred. She moved nervously for a moment, as if expecting to be under assault from Maude, but then, as the woman stepped away she rose. "I will undress myself, Madame, though I see no purpose in it," she said quietly. A single tear pearled down each silk-smooth cheek as she spoke, though it clearly had no effect on Helen, who waited and regarded her commandingly as Samantha's hands reached down and commenced drawing up the hem of her dress.

What limbs, what legs, what loveliness! Were I a poet, I would have penned a sonnet about every curve and dip of her ankles, calves, rounded knees, and ivory thighs. The flouncing of a lacy underskirt showed, then white cotton drawers whose pink silk ribbons so prettily adorned her waist. The drawers were loose—too loose—and had no doubt been the subject of complaint in the letter. Tighter ones would have better delineated the sweet mound of her pubis and the impudent out-curving of her bottom. In a moment she stood, with eyes downcast on the carpet, attired in but her brown silk stockings, her drawers, a chemise, and button-over shoes.

Turning away, Helen regained her seat. "Bring her to the desk," she told Maude curtly. Before Samantha could move, the broad flow of her blonde hair was gathered swiftly together in the fingers of Maude, who, jerking upon it, caused Samantha to squeal, her eyes opening wide and a deeper flush suffusing her features. With her head drawn helplessly back and another impelling hand in the small of her back, she was led forward there and thus held whilst Helen lectured her rapidly and quietly.

"I have given you leeway, Samantha, such as I shall afford to few of our young ladies. As from now, I will brook no further rebellions. No, girl, you will *not* speak, but you will listen."

A further sharp squeal from Samantha announced that the grip on her long hair was proving no less imperative in holding her head back. Her lips pursed as if she were about to cry, yet by some particular effort, as I felt, she restrained any further tears from flooding into her blue eyes. Meanwhile, as Helen continued addressing her, Maude's hand, that for a long moment had fisted into the small of her back, relaxed and descended inch by inch until, with a hip-jerking start, Samantha felt the hem of her chemise taken up and the silk ties of her drawers being slowly loosed.

"Obedience at all times, Samantha . . . complete compliance with my wishes . . . you will emerge from this establishment all the better for it—yes, let her drawers fall now, Maude."

"No! Ow!" The two exclamations came fast upon one another from the girl's lips as, with an additional warning jerk of her hair-gripping fingers, Maude crowned the pleasure of the moment by letting Samantha's white drawers crumple and descend slowly to her ankles. Mindful, as I liked to believe, that I was watch-

ing, she then held up the hem of the girl's sole remaining garment so that I might feast my eyes upon the utterly delectable bottom that was now revealed. Were one to cut an apple precisely in half, coat it with alabaster and carve with infinite delicacy an inrolling groove as secretive as that which faced me, one might then have some semblance of Samantha's bottom.

"A little better," Helen smiled. Reaching down into a small compartment in one pedestal of her desk, she brought out her multi-thonged whip and laid it carefully on the desk so that its thongs fanned out toward Samantha, who, with her face still jerked up toward the conjunction of wall and ceiling above the window, must have glimpsed it just within the lower line of her vision, for her nostrils flared and her breath hissed out softly.

"Forward, Samantha, round the desk, to the chair," Maude then intoned, and just as any proud female captive might have been led in a Roman slave market of long ago, so Samantha now was urged step by step forward to Helen, whose chair swivelled round toward her so that the arm of her chair came within inches of the sweet conjunction of those superb long legs which, compressed tightly together as they were, offered at their meeting a floss of golden curls in neat triangular shape. Her legs quivered distinctly, her eyes obtaining a blank, tear-sheened stare.

"Look at me, Samantha," Helen murmured, whilst in that moment Maude slackened her hold on the girl's hair so that her face lowered slowly. Watching as breathlessly as I was, I saw the whip glide into Helen's hand, the handle inverting itself so that it rubbed suavely up the side of Samantha's left thigh, causing her to start. "I do not intend to break your pride, Samantha, dear. A proud girl offers her bottom nobly to such attentions as it may receive."

"*Ah!* Madame! *No!*"

The exclamation ripped from Samantha's throat as

the polished bulbous end of the whip handle moved
sleekly between her thighs and with consummate ease,
as it seemed, wormed its passage between them, moving
sleekly upward until it nestled against the sweet lips
that pouted all but invisibly to myself in the golden fuzz
of curls. Therewith a screech came from the girl, for as
her head was jerked back from behind once more, so
Maude's questing hand descended and a seeking digit
found the forbidden path between those tight cheeks.

Even as Samantha's shriek died, a long, bubbling
whimper emitted itself from her throat and her eyes all
but bulged. I needed then no words to convey to me
that Maude's forefinger had found its rosetted target
and had wormed gently up into Samantha's bottom.

"Hold her so, Maude," Helen murmured and bent
down. For a moment all but invisible to me, I wondered
at her purpose until, straightening up, she cast upon the
carpet the two halves of Samantha's drawers, which she
had severed neatly with a pair of scissors.

"Whooooo!" Samantha moaned and wriggled madly
as the working motion of Maude's finger became evident to me. Naught but the clasping hand about her
hair restrained her now, and yet it was enough. A puffi-
ness appeared about her features, her eyes rolling up,
lips compressing and then parting again whilst a thin,
shrill sound came up from her throat. Then, as suddenly as the invasion of her hitherto-unbreached pri-
vacy had begun, so it ended with a sudden succulent
withdrawal of Maude's finger.

Samantha sagged and might have fallen, had she not
leaned with one hand upon the desk, her legs trembling.

"Loose her hair, Maude. Leave her. She will struggle
no more. Come, Samantha, a step forward—quickly!"

I saw then Helen's subtle purpose, for now she held
forward the handle of the whip again, but at such
height and at such an angle that in making a full, quivering step toward her, Samantha could not help but part

her thighs to the knob and so come upon it in such a position that the lips of her slit again sleeked over it. With a sharp inhissing of breath, she thus stood as one transfixed, blushing so hotly that the delicate skin of her features looked as pink satin.

"That is better—a little better," intoned Helen suavely. "One move, one further hesitation, and Maude will crop your bare bottom as surely as it should have been cropped that spring morning in—where was it?— the summerhouse? *Answer!*"

"Y . . . y . . . yes, M . . . Madame."

"You received how many strokes, Samantha?"

"Th . . . th . . . three."

"Yes—with your drawers on, of course—but then they were drawn down and you shrieked out, causing— as I understand—much embarrassment, confusion, and interruption. A young lady must learn discretion, must she not, Samantha? Was it not infinitely wicked of you to cry out in such an alarming fashion and thus disturb the nap of your poor Mama? *Well?*"

"M . . . M . . . M . . . M . . ." stuttered Samantha, whose blazing cheeks and incoherence betokened not only her apparent dire shame at all events in the study, but the fact that Helen was gently soothing the knob of the whip handle back and forth beneath her pussy.

"Do I take it that you agree with me, Samantha?"

"Y . . . y . . . yesssss, but I . . . *Ow!*"

I marvelled at Maude. Was this the selfsame young woman who had been led like a lamb to the altar of lust—the same one who but a few nights before had herself howled and wriggled while I had tawsed her? For, like veritable lightning, it seemed, the crop had unhooked itself from her waistband and sleeked with a sharp cracking sound full across Samantha's proud buttocks. A yelp, a straining of legs and back, and a veritable cascade of tears flooded down Samantha's cheeks, for the up-prodding of the whip between her thighs all but forbade her to move forward or back.

"There was no 'buts,' you see, Samantha," Helen said softly. "You will be a good girl now, will you not? Put your dress on. Our pupils are permitted to wear no more than a single covering over their charms. And see to your garters. I will *not* have slovenliness. They are to be tighter in future. I desire to see not a single wrinkle in your stockings."

Samantha seemed unable to speak. The sting of the crop had clearly caught her so deeply and unexpectedly that she could scarce get her breath still. Maude moved away, and she was permitted to step back—a vision of perfection in her young womanhood and with the single pink stripe of her initiation showing across her pert bottom, where the crop had whistled its path. Moving with a proud elegance that was never fully to leave her, she bent to pick up her fallen gown, thus displaying perfectly to my eyes the succulent fig of her pussy and the glinting of golden curls around it.

"There will be riding lessons, Samantha," Helen observed, having put her whip out of sight. "You like those, I believe?"

Samantha's face was at that moment hidden and submerged in the cascading of her dress over her shoulders. To my infinite regret, it descended with many a lithe wriggle of her torso until her thighs, knees, and slender calves all were hid once more. For a second I thought she might not reply and wondered, with a further inner thrill, at the consequences, but Helen seemed not over-disturbed at her hesitation.

Finally a quiet, "Yes, Madame" came from her lips and she stood waiting. The interplay of wills in that moment was truly fascinating, for I knew her in no sense to have succumbed completely and watched the slight creasing of her lovely face as she strove to keep her bottom stilled against the continued inner stinging of the crop.

"You may leave, Samantha. You have been shown your dormitory. Think not of dressing again beneath your gown. I may examine you later, and this time the whip will make much closer acquaintance with your bottom than the crop did. One question, my dear, and you will answer it directly. What is the proper behaviour of young ladies when their posteriors are being duly heated?"

For a moment Samantha's eyes locked with Helen's and then dropped.

"To . . . to strive not to cry out, Madame."

"And if their drawers are being removed, Samantha?"

This time a greater battle appeared to be taking place in the mind of the young beauty, for the interval of silence extended for longer. Then at last, as if by a great effort, she found the words.

"To . . . to permit them to be, Madame."

An ironic smile crossed Helen's features for she sensed even more acutely than I that had Samantha been able to, she would have fled on the instant and quickly cast aside both of her admissions. Maude went then to the door and unlocked it by means of a spring device that few others would have known even to search for. With Samantha's going, I sprang out, the condition of my trousers such that both women burst into laughter.

I made to seize Helen first, but she escaped me.

"No—you will have neither of us, you wicked man. This indeed may be the final arbiter, but it is not the interim solution," she laughed while my cock prodded aggressively through the cloth. "Heavens, Jack, if you are to fuck one of us every time you see a girl being interviewed, we shall never get through the day. Restrain yourself, you monster, for I now have to see Victoria. Maude, go and see whether she has arrived and if Lucy has seen to her welfare."

Then, turning to me, she pressed her glorious form tightly to my body, her hand squashed between us, squeezing upon my erection.

"Wait just a little, dear, for Victoria may prove an earlier prize than Samantha, who needs a little more prolonged schooling. Think on it, though, that in a few days you may give her her first riding lesson."

"You devil!" I squeezed the resilient cheeks of her superb bottom through the material of her dress whilst her perfumed breath mingled with my own. Had we had but fifteen minutes, she would have surrendered to me on the couch, but no sooner had the tips of our tongues met than a gentle knock sounded upon the door. Helen jerked away from me.

"Go to your peephole again, darling, for you are about to view a luscious little Venus!"

Chapter 9

VICTORIA, it may be recalled, was the girl whose photograph had depicted her lying face down upon a bed with her drawers well lowered. As I had remarked to Helen, at the time, such was the patience required in posing for a photographic plate that she must have lain there for a deuce of a long minute, else her posture would have been blurred. Even so, it was her "postures" it seemed that were at fault and which Helen was implored to correct.

I had secured my seat in hiding just a second or two before the girl was brought in. Her appearance did nothing to alleviate my near-bursting state, for much as I had fallen for the elegance of Samantha I now did the same as my eyes scanned the trim and smaller figure who entered in the company of Maude. Rounder of face than her predecessor and giving way to her in height by at least two inches, Victoria had a small but poutingly appealing mouth, lustrous eyes that seemed ever full of wonder, and gently waved nut-brown hair which fell in a broad fan across her shoulders.

Her footsteps were dainty—neither hesitant nor ea-

ger, which betokened a watchful spirit in her. Slim ankles peeped from beneath the hem of her blue dress
which was prettily frilled with white. Her shoes of the
strap-over type with low heels were a gleaming brown
and her stockings white. Hugging her slim waist tightly
as it did, her dress flowed out around hips that showed
a pleasing fullness whilst—as for the exquisite "ron-
deur" of her bottom—I had viewed it in part already in
her photograph but now awaited with some palpitations
its complete denuding.

Unlike Samantha, this new entrant was motioned to a
chair which Maude drew up facing Helen's desk. There
then ensued a conversation of such casualness and propriety that for long moments I feared Helen would
never come to the point. For this impatience on my
part, which I but jokingly expressed to her afterward,
she chided me, saying that all girls needed handling dif-
ferently, but that she could expect no such subtleties
from a man who was over-led by his cock. This being
said in good humour, I might say, I then presented it to
her with some success. But that is another story.

Certainly my ears pricked up when Helen observed
now that she had received "a very pretty photograph" of
Victoria—to which the young lady replied with a silent
biting of her lip as if she knew not whether to giggle or
cry.

"Was it your first such posing, Victoria?" Helen
asked gently whilst even Maude accorded the girl an
encouraging smile.

"Oh, yes, Madame—well, no, once before . . ."

Victoria's voice trailed off uneasily whilst Helen nodded, as if in sympathy with her. "Quite, Victoria—there
were greater difficulties on that occasion? I do understand." It was then that Helen produced the sepia print
and laid it face up, causing Victoria's cheeks to become
infused with a delicate blush. She stared across the desk
at it, looked away, stole another peep, and then ap-

peared to take a fixed interest in the corner of the ceiling.

"She really looks quite adorable in this—do you not think so, Maude?"

Maude nodded. "Indeed she does. I feel, though, that her knees might have been drawn up more. She has such an attractive bottom that it well deserves to be displayed more. I believe she will take well to postural lessons—will you not, Victoria?"

Victoria's gaze returned reluctantly to eye level. Her breath seemed to catch in her throat. Her blush deepened. "M . . . M . . . Ma'am?" she stuttered.

"The couch would be best. Would you like to go and kneel on it?" Helen asked. Smiling sweetly, she added, "Maude will show you how."

Victoria's small lips parted in the most appealing of gestures. A cloud of breath that one felt should have been accompanied by words that had failed to catch up with it issued therefrom, for Maude—stepping forward—had lifted her persuasively by the elbow and was guiding her across to the couch with such firmness and despatch that not until her knees met the side of it did Victoria throw a look of appeal over her shoulder to Helen.

Quite of a purpose, as I judged it, Helen made no attempt to move, but remained seated in an attitude of obvious authority.

"The basic posture is one I would like you to practise first, Victoria," she said, to a small, surprised squeal from Victoria who found herself gently bent over by the attendant Maude so that her hands were forced to support herself by virtue of lying her palms flat on the seat.

"Oh, please, Ma'am, may I get up now? pleaded Victoria with such naïveté that Maude laughed for the first time since the interviews had begun.

"What a silly goose you are! We have scarce begun, Victoria. Remain exactly as you are whilst I lift your skirt," Maude said. "Do you not have it lifted for you at present and your drawers taken down? Yes, I'm sure you do. No silliness, now Victoria—*No!*"

This last exclamation was drawn forth as Victoria wildly thrust one arm behind her in a blind, evasive fashion to endeavour to prevent Maude from carrying out the very operation I most desired to see. For her pains, however, she received a sharp slap on the wrist which brought a blubbering cry from her. At that Helen came round from her desk and, seating herself beside the girl, fondled her hair gently.

"Now, Victoria, I have very good reports of you and I expect the very best of behaviour from you, young lady, for I am sure you can turn out to be one of our most apt pupils. Yes, remove her drawers, Maude, dear. I want them off completely." Whereat, to a wail and a cry from Victoria, whose back was so bent that her head touched the couch, the white linen garment was slowly withdrawn and the treasures of this eighteen-year-old Miss laid bare.

To few are vouchsafed the extreme pleasure of the comparison I was now able to make between the charms of the leggy Samantha and those of Victoria. The white silk stockings suited the younger girl perfectly, giving her the appearance of one who had just come from boarding school. Her calves were well-turned, and from her rounded knees there swelled upward two utterly delicious thighs, neither plump nor thin, but of such proportions as most please the wandering male eye. Her bottom itself had a certain chubbiness, presenting to the view two warm and unsullied hemispheres which inrolled into a groove whose very slight gingery hue made enticing contrast with the creamy pallor of her skin. Her quim was little to be seen, though Maude saw that I was not disappointed in that respect for, carefully tucking up Victoria's dress and underskirt, she slid her hand twixt the girl's thighs

and gave her some pinch or squeeze as made her yelp
and part her ankles.

"Good girl," observed Helen quietly, as if the act had
been purely voluntary. "The feet must be kept a regula-
tion two feet apart, my dear, unless otherwise ordained.
And the toes turned inward a trifle. Come, Victoria. I
am watching you."

"I w . . . w . . . want to get up!" Victoria now
truly howled, her posture being such now that her naked bottom jutted well out and the perfect fig of her
cunny was enticingly displayed. Plump as her mound
was, its lips showed clearly together with their delicate
inner creases and a perfect froth of small brown curls.

"But you must not—not yet—must you, Victoria?"
Helen intoned, keeping the girl's head well down whilst,
by warning taps of her shoes against Victoria's heels,
Maude ensured that her feet did not slide together
again. "I am going to put you on honour, dear, to remain exactly as you have been placed whilst I get up. I
can trust you, can't I? For if I can't, Victoria, then I
fear this beautiful little bottom of yours is going to feel
my wrath. Still now, please."

"Wh . . . wh . . . what are you going to do,
Ma'am?"

"Why we are going to play a little game, Victoria.
First, I propose to blindfold you—so—and then we are
going to have a guessing game"—saying which, Helen
strode to her desk, took up a folded piece of black velvet, and bound it quickly around the girl's eyes despite
the fretful turning of her head from side to side whilst
this intriguing operation was done. A sharp "Ouch!"
came from Victoria amid this, for the watchful Maude
had observed that her feet had begun to edge together
and with remarkable speed and deftness she awarded
those chubby, upstretched cheeks a resounding smack
which, for a brief instant, left the imprint of her palm
on the bulbous hemispheres.

"Tut, tut, what silliness! Are you not frequently spanked, Victoria, and do you not sometimes get a round dozen? Of course you do, but your postures are awkward and silly, as I was given to understand—and I doubt it not now that we have been given this exhibition. You are here to prove your worth, Victoria. Thrust your bottom up and out and let me see it!"

"Oh, please Ma'am, I hate to do this!" Victoria whined, receiving a further smack which made her jolt and squeal.

"All the more reason why you should be brought to enjoy it," Helen replied crisply, and striding to her desk, brought out the black whip which I was to learn she was pleased to call a teasewhip. With due caution, then, Maude secured a gentle hold on the nape of Victoria's downbent neck whilst passing her other hand under her bared tummy to ensure that she did not "wilt" from her position. By slightly pinching her skin there, she could well maintain her in a bottom-up posture as the thongs effected their first searing caress of those adorable cheeks.

"Ya-oooh!" Victoria screeched as at the same time a quick nipping of Maude's fingers made her bottom jerk out again to the hissing thongs.

"Knees straight—legs apart, Victoria," Helen commanded as the first spots of pink speckled the split peach of flesh and the girl's hips waggled madly whilst a perfect trilling of sobs and yelps came from her.

"Ma'am, oh, don't, please—oh, it stings, it burns! *Ah!* Oh! I haven't been naughty, I haven't!"

"Haven't been naughty?" echoed Helen with a laugh, bringing a deft undersweep that lifted Victoria clear onto her toes and brought a long quavering cry from her. "Of course you haven't, my pet, but you will be if you don't succumb to training. How prettily she wriggles it, does she not, Maude? I believe we have effected a littel improvement in her already."

"*Yooo-yooo-yoooo-yoooooh!*" bubbled Victoria, for with every word the thongs snicked and swirled about her upthrust bottom. Several, as I saw, teased their tips into her groove and beneath there flickered around her pussy in a way that agitated her squirmings even more and made her glowing orb rotate to such degree that I could not help but release my straining pego and fretfully rub it with my fingers. Little as I had thought or cared to count, I had no doubt that Victoria by now had received a full score of caresses from the burning tips, and her sobs were now bubbling out full one upon the other. But then, as meaningful smiles passed between Helen and Maude, Maude slid her hand full down from Victoria's tummy and cupped her pussy in such a manner that her forefinger deftly inserted itself between the petulant lips.

"M . . . M . . . M . . . !" Victoria stuttered, though what she intended to say one would never know. The restraining hand upon the nape of her neck was withdrawn, and for a moment her head tossed and turned as the insidious caress was accompanied now by a lighter swirling back and forth across her bottom by the thongs.

"Yes, Maude, she needs a little comforting now—what a brave girl she has been," Helen declared, and, twisting Victoria about so that she fell with a startled cry onto her back on the couch with her legs hanging over the edge, she cast herself down beside her and gathered the sobbing, wriggling girl into her arms. Maude, in turn, slipped to her knees on the carpet and held Victoria's stockinged legs apart, awarding her slit a little kiss which made the girl give a tremulous jerk whilst her hot bottom squirmed on the cool leather surface.

"There, dear, there," Helen coaxed, "this now is to teach you the second posture, Victoria. Do you not like a cuddle after your spankings? I'm sure you do."

"Oh, Ma'am, oh, Ma'am, Oh, Ma'am!" Victoria whimpered. Her silken belly rippled, her bottom lifting a full two inches off the couch as the flickering tongue of Maude swept a path up and down between the puckered lips of her cunny, artfully brushing her clitty as it did so.

"Nooo-nooo-noooo!" Victoria mewed. For a long moment, she strove to close her thighs against the outward pleasure of Maude's hands. Blindfolded still, and gasping, she squirmed madly in Helen's embrace until a shriller cry rose from her throat. Her back arched, her eyes rolled, her very panting seemed to fill the sudden silence in the study which was otherwise broken only by the steady lapping of Maude's long tongue. Victoria's teeth gritted, her hands opened and closed several times, and then with an out-rushing sigh, she fell back, released from Helen's embrace. Her legs quivered distinctly, stretching out wide and unheld now on either side of Maude's body. Her mouth opened, was lax, and then she lay still.

Maude rose, wiping her lips delicately. As she did so, Helen bent over the girl and laid a single soft kiss upon her mouth. Then, rising slowly, she uttered a sigh of satisfaction, gazing down upon the clearly moistened curls that fringed Victoria's quim. As if conscious of the glance, though still hidden in the darkness of her blindfold, the girl's arms stirred, whereat, bending down, Maude carefully slid her hands beneath her bottom and gently drew her dress down once more. A soft "Oh!" came from Victoria whilst Helen returned to her desk, her own face lightly flushed.

"Remove your blindfold now and come to me," she uttered. "Come now, Victoria—you have been such a good girl. Has she not, Maude?"

"Indeed, quite remarkable—she has attained her first grade already," Maude replied solemnly, though she made no attempt to assist Victoria, who fumbled the velvet band about her eyes and rose unsteadily, her eyes downcast, lips trembling as if about to cry.

"She would like a glass of wine now, I am sure," Helen said and beckoned the girl's faltering footsteps to the chair she had previously occupied.

"Oh, p . . . please, may I go now, Ma'am?" Victoria implored, twisting her fingers nervously whilst Maude placed a glass before her. Her request being met with silence, she gazed first at the desk, then all about her, and finally, with a quick, nervous gesture, raised her glass to her lips.

"We might perhaps make her a prefect, Maude," Helen observed, causing Victoria to gape at her and flush even deeper with surprise.

"I do think so indeed," Maude answered solemnly. "She has passed her initial test with flying colors. Shall I award her a garter?" she asked, whilst I sat thoroughly bemused at all the intricacies of their behaviour.

"A blue one, yes, Maude. Now, Victoria, we are about to bestow a most unusual honour on you. Your comportment, though it merited a little punishment, has been excellent in the main. I am quite content already to believe that not only will you more freely adopt the basic posture without demur in future—and with your drawers off, naturally—but may assist us even in monitoring the behaviour of others who quite simply do not have your *delicatesse*. Raise your skirt, now, and extend your right leg so that Maude may exchange your present garter for a blue one. It betokens, you see, a privileged rank."

I doubt that Victoria was any the less astonished than I at this patent comedy. Quite in a daze, she permitted the operation to take place and even gave an assenting wriggle as the bright blue garter was slid tightly up her thigh. So bereft of words was she that she continued to listen openmouthed and in total wonder-

ment to the little lecture that was put upon her. Now
and again, a nervous little smile tugged at the corners of
her pretty mouth whilst, with due solemnity, Maude refilled her glass, her charms being constantly extolled,
and her head made quite to spin with all that had occurred.

"But M . . . Ma'am, I don't think I could . . .,"
she began in a virtual whisper when Helen once more
brought up what she was pleased to call monitoring. I
had no doubt now that Victoria was beginning to feel a
confusion of pleasure and wonderment at what had
passed, as her mentor fully intended her to do, whilst
keeping her mainly in a state of naïve bewilderment.

"On your own, you will naturally not be expected to
correct the other girls, though in due course, if you
should take a mood for it, Victoria, then I might not
object. No, Victoria, I simply want you to let me know
of any untoward events in the dormitories that may
come to your ears, and for this your privileges will be
increased. Do you like riding, by the way?"

"I have tried, but only a little, Ma'am."

"Well then, we have a quite handsome Riding Master
here who will be able to teach you much that you will
want to know about that," Helen said smoothly. "I
would like you to be at the stable at three-thirty. Will
that suit you?"

"Oh, yes!" Victoria replied, quite astonished to be
asked. I verily believe that she no longer knew where
she was at all as Maude conducted her out and I literally burst from my hiding place and took Helen in my
arms.

"Well, Jack, what did you think of all that?" she
laughed.

"A perfection of hypocrisy, my love," I marvelled,
"but why behave so with her? Have you not coddled
her now overmuch?"

"Really, pet, I thought you would see clearly through

it all. She has a charming naïveté, has she not, and knows not now whether she is coming or going. Every word and every act on my part was quite deliberate, Jack, for I judge her to be more easily overcome than some of the others. That she may bring me occasional tittle-tattle is neither here nor there. She has had her first taste of things now—though not quite her first, for I believe her to have been fingered up a little after her spankings. Believing herself to be priviledged now, I am quite sure she is ready for stabling, as we might call it. Do you think you could attend to that little matter at three-thirty? You will not be disturbed, I assure you."

"Good heavens, you mean it!" I marvelled whilst Helen answered me with a loving smile and a kiss.

"Keep this naughty thing in prime condition, Jack, for you will need it then. A taste of your tawse first, I think, and then breach her slowly. You may have a deuce of it getting it right in at first. A gentle urging rather than a rude assault were best, I think—don't you agree?"

All this was said with such sensuousness that I all but came in my trousers—a condition that Helen endeavoured to prevent by easing herself from my arms.

"No, Jack, you must cool your ardour for the moment. We will have lunch now, for afterward I must attend to Monique, and that, I believe, may be an encounter almost as pleasing as your own!"

Chapter 10

THREE-TWENTY of that afternoon found me waiting in the stable, where I had duly made all my preparations. The steed that the delectable young Victoria was to mount stood ready within and comprised yet another of my inventions for such a contingency. Within, a pleasant gloom obtained, broken by thin bars of sunlight that filtered through the large doors and the cracks in the timbered walls.

Clearing my throat, I consulted my watch a dozen times, though having little doubt that the girl would be perfectly punctual. Indeed, she was. Precisely upon the half hour, I parted the doors and saw her approaching. Her eyes widened a little at the sight of me, attired as I was in a loose shirt, riding breeches, and boots. As she approached, I saw more clearly than I had been able to from my peep-hole the attractiveness of her features and the most promising thrust made by her breasts within her dress. Stepping forward onto the short grass which surrounded the old stable, I made my introduction gallantly, and, without ado, took her wrist and led her within, barring the doors quietly behind me.

"Oh! the horse!" Victoria delcared in her softly

modulated voice when she perceived what stood before her.

"It would not do for you to be thrown by a live one," I observed solemnly whilst she gazed with some wonder, though not unpleased, at the grey-dappled rocking horse which stood in waiting. Her eyes did not perceive the alterations I had made to the original, and I did not intend them to. It was the largest I had been able to secure and stood glossy in its new paint on its rockers, with a fine saddle and steel and leather stirrups.

Victoria gave a little start as I moved toward her and placed my hand gently in the small of her back.

"Here, of ourse, we do not ride sidesaddle, for it is considered quite rightly by Miss Hotspur to be unsafe. Young ladies are prone to slide off their mounts in that way, Victoria. If you care to raise your dress and place your left foot in the saddle, I will assist you over," I said smoothly.

Victoria's body pressed back immediately, though prevented from doing so overmuch by my hand. "B . . . but, sir, I will need raise my dress too high—oh, pray do not. Oh!" For, obtaining already such impatience as would surely have made Helen frown upon me, I had swiftly bent, gathered up the hem of her dress and swept it up to her hips, thereby revealing anew to my eyes the lovely lines of her legs which, more appropriately sheathed now in black silk, rendered all the more enticing the milky pallor of her thighs. Her round bottom was naked, a faint translucent glow upon it from the bath she had evidently just taken.

Quelling the urge to caress it, I placed my palm beneath the luscious bulge and lifted her manfully in one upward sweep. With a shriek, she landed full upon the saddle in such a turmoil that she was forced to bend forward and cling to the neck of the rocking horse, a deep blush flooding her features the while.

"Excellent, Victoria!" I said, as if a half-naked maiden were common enough already in the stable.

"Oh, sir, let me please—let me cover myself!" she babbled and would have reached behind her with one hand to draw down her piled-up skirt had I not slapped her wrist much as Maude had done in the study. Therewith also I leaned hard down upon the rump of the horse, causing it to rock back and forth to such extent that with a further high-pitched cry, Victoria was forced once more to fling her arms wildly about its thick, polished neck.

"Let me . . . let me . . . let me *down!*" she screeched, whilst her thighs, parted widely by the broad saddle, displayed to me perfectly the plump mound of her quim. Giving the horse a further push so that its rocking became for a moment even more violent, I then moved to its head and quickly clipped Victoria's wrist to a pair of manacles that were studded at their centre link to the forward part of the neck. This causing her to wail even louder, I then attended to the tucking up of her skirt well above her hips, whose curving was quite delightful for one of her age.

"Sir, sir, sir, I beg you!" Victoria howled, her voice rising up to a startled shriek as my palm cracked smartly against her bottom.

"*Quiet,* Victoria!" I commanded sternly, "or you will stay thus all afternoon, my girl. You have been lectured well enough about postures, have you not? Your posture astride a mount is just as important. Now let us see to it that it is improved even more."

So saying, I reached down to her feet, which were gripped uneasily in the stirrups, and drew down upon the toes of her shoes two adjustable metal bars, which in turn served to lock her feet into position so that she could not withdraw them from the stirrups. Realising this, she jerked her head up and began howling anew and sobbing in such a fashion that I was forced to give her bottom yet another smarting smack, making an "*Aaaah!*" of shocked surprise burst from her. Giving her no respite, however, I attended next to the most ingenious of my devices which appertained to the saddle. This finely fashioned piece of leather had at its front a broad and deep upcurving pommel. Here its form was exaggerated, and for good reason, for now by pressing a button which released a strong spring at the rear of the saddle, that part of it was caused to rise. With its movement, and forward toward the horse's head, Victoriaa's delightful bottom was lifted upward a good foot off the back of the horse while the pommel in front prevented her from being tipped forward.

"*No-oh-oh!*" Victoria screeched at this, for her bottom cheeks were now so lewdly raised and exposed that she could not but guess the purpose of her exposure.

Stepping back, I viewed her thus for a moment. My device had worked to perfection. Her head and shoulders were now slumped down at the very base of the horse's neck around which her arms were firmly secured. Her legs being forced down in straight lines by the clamping of her feet in the stirrups, gave her a posture of perfect loveliness and appeal, with the pale apple of her bottom poised high for my attentions.

"Oh-oh-oh! Let me *down!*" she shrieked. "I shall tell Madame—I shall tell Mama!"

I ignored her, of course. Walking to the rear, I surveyed the plump glory of her young bottom and the curl-fringed nest of her slit beneath. That I was not yet to enjoy it was a little of a torment. I prayed devoutly that Victoria would return at the end of the term having then been mounted fully, and ready for further injections in that adorable tight-lipped pussy.

"Please, please, please, I beg you!" Victoria continued to sob whilst I produced full out of sight of her my worthy tawse. Not unmindful of Helen's teachings, I afforded Victoria first but a warning swing of the thick leather full across her delightful rump. *"No-ow!"* she squealed. Her legs swayed as little as they could in the rigid stirrups, her hips writhing under the truly resounding smack of the tawse, which makes noise in equal measure to that whereby it induces heat. At my leisure, I watched the first contraction of her cheeks.

"Remember, Jack, that this is a training session and not a punishment," Helen had observed to me before I left the house. Her expression had been as solemn as her voice. How much she had tempered my previous impetuousness was a debt I first truly owed to her during this hour with Victoria.

"You are learning to display, Victoria," I said quietly. "At the moment, your posture is enforced. In due time it will become voluntary, will it not?"

"No, you can never make me, never—*Ow!*"

I scarce have need to say that this final exclamation was drawn from her as once more the leather seared its path across the very centre of her cheeks, making her hips rebound and a pink flare appear across the milk-white hemispheres.

"I must ask you to measure your replies more carefully, Victoria. On the next occasion you are spanked, will you not remove your drawers, your dress, and your chemise and adjust your bottom to the position required of it?"

"No! Oh, no! It is naughty. I won't, I won't— *Aaaah-ouch!* St . . . st . . . stop it! It hurts me, it burns, it stings. . . . *Yeee-ow!*"

Scra-aaaack went the tawse twice now, changing driection from left to right so that in the very midst of her squirmings, her cheeks moved in the direction I wished them to, right into the swirling path of the leather. Watching the ever-tighter contractions of her bottom, I saw that I had struck home deeply and that a deeper flare had spread over her glossy orb whilst mov-

ing briefly to her side I glimpsed the helpless pearling of
tears upon her cheeks.

Unable to resist any longer, and standing sideways
to the horse as I then was, I passed my upheld palm
beneath her splayed thighs so that the delicious padding
of curls around her quim nestled thereon. Moist and
succulent as it was, I longed to dip my forefinger up
within, but by a great effort of will desisted and simply
allowed her slit to pulse gently on my hand whilst her
eyes screwed up with seeming shame and emitted from
beneath their lids two further rolling tears.

I rubbed my palm gently under the pouting lips,
causing her to sob and turn her flushed face away from
me to the other side of the horse's neck.

"Have you not had it fondled before, Victoria?" I
asked quietly.

"No-oh-oh! What a wicked thing to say! T . . . t
. . . take your hand away, Oh!"

"Truthfulness is a first precept here, Victoria," I observed with a perfectly hypocritical tone in my voice,
for I had not forgotten Helen's remark that she believed
Victoria to have been a little tickled up already. "I
must ask you again, Victoria."

"No, no, no, no, I h . . . haven't, I haven't. I
wouldn't let . . . *Neee-ynnnng!*"

Scarce were her first words out of her mouth than I
had stepped smartly to the rear once more and with
considerable effect brought the tawse flashing with a
loud *cra-aaaaack!* across her already tingling bottom.

"*Ooooh-aaah! Ooooh-aaah!*" she howled at the end
of her first gritting screech whilst her hips waved more
wildly than ever. "*No-oh! Don't!*"

It was a long, long moment before her sobs subsided
in part, at least, her hips waggling as do the hindquarters
of dogs when they shake off water.

"*Not* had it fondled before, Victoria?" I asked again,
sleeking my fingers once more beneath her pulsing slit.

The lips felt now distinctly more mucuous, leaving a faintness of oily moisture upon my palm.

Her head hung once more away from me so that her features were concealed. I gave her a while to regain her relative composure, desiring as I did to fondle all within my reach but restraining myself. The hairs of her quim burred deliciously on my palm, which I eased back and forth as if comforting her.

"A l . . . l . . . little . . . ," she burst forth at last. "Wh . . . wh . . . when I was sp . . . spanked . . . after . . . after I was spanked."

I slid my longing hand from beneath and then glossed it gently around her glowing peach, which throbbed beneath the hot-sheened skin, so silky and velvet smooth it was to the touch. Thereat she sobbed louder, but more for effect than anything, as I was convinced, for her bottom seemed a trifle more eager to impress its bulge onto my palm than to retract, seeking there no doubt the comfort of pressure to oppose the burning within.

"So far, Victoria, you have been a good girl," I murmured, imitating—though not consciously—the manner of Helen. "I am now about to let you down. When I do so, however, you are not to attempt to lower your dress. Otherwise I fear that I must tell Miss Hotspur that your first riding lesson has been less than successful. Are we agreed?" An imperceptible movement of her head came to me then, but I was less than satisfied with it, if it were to signal assent. "*Are* we agreed, Victoria, or must I attend to your bottom further?"

"No—I mean yes—I mean, I won't," she quavered, whereat, assuring her solemnly that I accepted her word as a truthful young lady, I loosed first her feet in the stirrups and then caused the saddle to lower at the back. A trifle more cautiously, then, I attended to the manacles which secured her wrists at the front of the horse's neck. In that moment, however, Victoria

seemed all but resigned to her fate and remained otherwise still, save for the further slumping of her body
along her wooden steed. For a second or two, I considered my next move. I could lift her down and carry her
immediately to one of the bales of hay, or I could make
her dismount by herself. The second course seemed
best, for it came upon me then that every movement of
the girls in such training periods must be modulated
and brought about by their own actions, rather than by
force.

Stepping back, I told her quietly to dismount, which,
after a moment of uneasy and embarrassed stirring, she
did, revealing to me in the process the momentary parting of her cuntlips as she must well have known, for her
hand fluttered there briefly and then hastily withdrew
as she attempted to stand shakily in a sideways posture
to me. That she did so was perfectly admirable, for it
gave me in her standing position a seductive view of her
pert and reddened bottom on one side and, on the
other, the smooth tranquility of her tummy and the pro-
file of her neat crop of dark-brown curls at the junction
of her thighs.

Standing but a foot or two from her, I moved in
closer to the delectable warmth of her form and felt her
tremble expectantly. A vibrant quiver of her curves
came with the gliding once more of my palm beneath
her bottom, which I cupped most gently.

"You may kiss me now and thank me for your lesson, Victoria."

A soft "Oh!" scarcely audible, came from her lips,
as only by the most stringent effort did she quell the
previous wriggling of her derriere on my palm. I allowed her the hesitation that ensued and then tipped
her chin up and around toward me whilst her brown
eyes literally melted in tears. More softly, perhaps, than
I had ever kissed a woman before, I laid my lips upon
her own and moved them gently from side to side. Feel-

ing then my forefinger begin to sidle in between her throbbing cheeks, she made to start away, but by gliding my other hand behind her neck, I trapped her hair in my grasp and stilled her movement whilst her expression strained up to mine almost appealingly.

A softly choking gurgle escaped her as my seeking digit found the crinkled rosehole that the meeting of her cheeks concealed. Once more my lips passed lightly across her own.

"Be perfectly still now, Victoria. This is the correct upright posture to adopt, when required, after your bottom has been attended to. You may wriggle your hips a little, but no more than that." A moan then issued from her throat, her eyes literally bulging as fraction by fraction the end of my forefinger urged itself gently within her bottomhole. Her legs quivered, teetered, and her feet shifted, but the hold I had obtained on her hair held her otherwise captive to me

"No-oh-oh, please!" she bubbled. "Ooooh, your f . . . finger, you mustn't!"

The tips of our noses touched. I assailed once more her lips, which she managed still to keep pursed at the approach of mine, albeit this time they felt subtly softer.

"I am going to let go of your hair now, Victoria, but my finger will remain in your bottom. I am putting you again on trust, do you understand?"

Her eyes appeared to glaze and but the faintest movement of her lips made itself known as I slowly loosed my hold upon her hair, which fanned out again across her shoulders. In doing so, I urged my finger up a further inch within her bottom, causing her to jerk out an *"Aaaah!"* Her heels drummed on the floor, her lips parting so prettily that I seized upon them again and this time held her in the most luscious of kisses.

"The tip of your tongue now, Victoria," I whispered huskily, for I was all but beside myself with lust to possess her. "The tip of your tongue must ever emerge in the kisses that follow upon attendance to your bottom. Bend forward a trifle, protrude your bottom more, and give me your tongue."

"*Blub!* she choked, for even as she obeyed, I had sucked her tongue in upon my own and given her a further inch of finger in her deliciously tight tube. Her knees buckled, forcing her to fling one arm around my shoulders for support. My embedded finger then moved gently back and forth, causing her to moan and bubble in my mouth. "*Neee-ooooh!*" she whimpered of a sudden and would have tried to burst from me had I not held her. The hurried flowing of her breath into my mouth was itself a perfect delight. Her head hung back in a posture of helplessness now whilst I recommenced working her bottomhole, which now exuded a faint oily secretion in her arousal. I felt her tongue work a little about my own and then retract. Then, with a sudden sigh, she tore her mouth from my own and laid her head on my shoulder, moving her hips quite adorably whilst my digit insinuated back and forth.

The throbbing and burning in her bottom had eased now, I felt, and she was better able to accomodate herself to the pleasure she was secretively obtaining.

A momentary, rebellious quivering seized her as I then drew her hand down to my rigid cock. She gasped, made to retract her hand, but I held it there until her fingers could properly feel its strength and pulsing. Little by little the tension in her hips had relaxed, so that the orb of her bottom moved itself more engagingly to my finger. Then began, as I thought of it, the "Helen Method" of extracting from her such confessions as I could. No, she had not felt a cock before . . . well, yes, she had once . . . once it had been shown to her and it was big and horrid and she had managed to pull her drawers up again and she wouldn't, she wouldn't touch him.

"How naughty you were, were you not, Victoria?" I

chided her and of a sudden withdrew my finger from her luring hole and bending, picked her up half-kicking and laid her with little ceremony face down upon a waiting bale. Immediately she shrieked and made to rise, but a most effective *smack!* of my full palm across her derriere made her yelp and subside.

"Shall it be the strap again?" I asked sternly, standing over her as she lay bottom-up before me.

"Oh *no!*" The cry came with horror and she hid her face, making the straw rustle as she moved.

"Has not Miss Hotspur endeavoured to instill obedience into you? Am I to report that you are as rebellious as when you were being spanked?"

"No! No, please!"

"Very well, then, so be it. Legs apart, bottom well held up—the basic posture that you have already been taught, Victoria."

"*Yow-oooh!*" came her rising scream as on the instant I seized her hips and, manoeuvring myself close forward, buried the glowing crest of my pego between her inrolling cheeks and there held it quivering against her most secretive aperture. "*Nooo-ooooh-ooooh!*" she squealed, wriggling so vigorously that I could but just contain her, urging my prick remorselessly inward until, as with a silent "Pop!" her sphincter yielded and my engorged shaft sheathed itself a full three inches within.

"*No! Ah! Ooooh!*" she continued ejaculating, though with my cock now somewhat embedded, she ceased to wriggle and held herself as if in waiting tension. Knowing her a trifle better then in such matters as she perhaps knew herself, I made no further forward movement for a moment, but contained her thus, savouring the infinite bliss of so observing the heady spectacle and the myriad sensations afforded by her chubby half-corked bottom.

With a speed that she could not anticipate, I then loosed my grip upon her rounded hips and moved my hands down to clasp them strongly about the fronts of her thighs. There I was able to savour also the conjunction of her gartered stocking tops and silky flesh whilst holding the backs of her legs tightly to the fronts of my own.

"Tay-ay-ay-ake it *out!*" Victoria then all but screamed and, thrusting her left arm back twisted her face and shoulders about at the same time and in the same direction so that her face came perfectly into view. It was her undoing. The sight of those pouting lips, the tear-streaked face and the seemingly wide-open innocent eyes enervated me as much as did the warm clenching of her tube. With a veritable growl I fell then full upon her, mashing my lips passionately over her own and—with a single powerful lunge—burying my cock completely in her virginal bottom.

Ah, the sweet elasticity of her rectal muscles that could yield to receive so doughty a shaft! The bubbling, sobbing cries that flooded my mouth were ignored as the luscious bulb of her hot bottom ground into my belly. Her knees bent forward, pressing into the straw beneath the pressure of my own. She was truly corked and held, my cock throbbing its imploring desire within her.

"*Whooooo!*" she moaned into my mouth as now I withdrew half the length of my sturdy prick, thrust in again and then sucked out almost to the knob. Therewith I groped beneath her moistened quim, parting the lips to seek her budding clitoris. A moan that was softer and more yielding issued from her throat. I absorbed her tongue, sucking upon it while keeping her literally at fever point by maintaining the knob of my cock just within her orifice.

Drinking her very saliva, stroking her hair and her neck beneath, I began whispering in her ear such tender eroticisms as must have left her as dazed as my assault. Licking within the shell-like folds into which my words poured, I began to assure her of the divine pleasure she was now giving and that she must so learn to yield on all such occasions. With each phrase I moved my tightly sheathed cock but an inch or so back and forth, the better to titillate her and so draw her on.

"Your tongue, Victoria, now—flick it in and out of my mouth and work your bottom slowly back and forth. You must learn to come onto the cock, Victoria," I said huskily.

I found her lips again. The upper one rolled up more willingly now beneath my own, her breath coming in rushing gasps as I twiddled her clitty.

"Oh, but it's so b . . . b . . . big!" she stammered. They were her first coherent words since I had plugged her, and I knew them as the final signal of her surrender.

"It pleasures you—confess it. Is it not delicious to urge your bottom back onto a manly cock? Come, press it back a little whilst I hold still . . . your tongue, now . . . *ah,* Victoria!"

The minx had obeyed! Hissing her breath in through her nostrils, she wriggled, jerked, and thrust her bottom, embedding my cock a full five inches within and gripping it so possessively that I almost came. Warm and snakelike, her tongue protruded fully within my mouth and swirled.

"B . . . b . . . b . . . b . . . !" stuttered Victoria, helplessly. "Oh, it's so naughty! Oh, yes, do it, do it, ah, *ah!*" A rippling surge sounded from her then as I felt her first libation sprinkle its salty effusion over my fingers.

Her surrender being complete now, I came upright, drawing her legs straight in turn and rammed her in full earnest whilst her heaving shoulders and rotating hips evinced the sudden lustful pleasure that had overcome her. Smacking loudly again and again into my belly, her bottom churned, gripped, and sucked upon me in a perfect melee of rhythmic movements until, unable to conserve my forces any longer, I seized her thighs as I had previously done, rammed myself in to the root, and effected the powerful jets of my come in long, burning shoots which made her quiver ecstatically.

"Haaaar!" she sobbed, her rosehole so lubricated by my sperm that I continued pistoning her vigourously until the last leaping pellets were expelled whilst the warm, velvety cheeks pressed amourously into my belly. So we remained for a long moment whilst my prick continued to throb and tick within her, then— withdrawing the piston slowly—I sank down half upon her, caressing the backs of her thighs as the last dribbles of come oozed upon her now-responsive flesh.

Chapter 11

GIVING VICTORIA such respite as I felt she needed, I rolled her at last onto her back so that we lay together atop the bale. With a murmur that seemed to betoken both surprise and renewed shyness, she made to close her legs—a gesture I prevented by passing my hand between her thighs at the tips of her stockings and holding them apart. Closing her eyes, she clutched as if protectively at my shirtfront and then turned her head away. Pursing her lips tightly, she felt my fingers insinuate themselves up the silky inner surfaces until they brushed the damp curls of her mount. A distinct tremor rippled through the pale silky surface of her tummy, and she attempted once more to close her legs upon my hand.

"No, Victoria" I barked at her sternly. "Open wide, now—open them!"

"Oh!" she whimpered and would have refused me had I not given her nearest thigh a slap that made her jerk and squeal whilst her hand covered half her face so that her expression was hid from me. Rising, then, and with my cock lolling thickly from my opened breeches, I increased the pressure of my hands until her legs were skewered wide apart and the salmon-pink interior of her quim gleamed its luscious invitation. At that, she covered her face completely whilst I half-bent over her.

"Remain so, Victoria, or I shall deal with you again sternly," I uttered. "Have I your promise on it?"

No reply coming from her and her eyes and mouth being completely concealed beneath her cupping hands, I slowly lifted off, prepared to slap her again at the slightest move. The manner of my voice, however, and the swirling of sensations in which she must have found herself, took sufficient effect for her to continue to lie thus in the most wanton of postures. Her white belly with its whorled navel, the nut-brown thatch of curls around her pussy, the milky plumpness of her thighs and the black banding of her stocking tops all combined to present such a picture of voluptuousness that my prick immediately stirred again.

Before she could sense my intentions, I fell to my knees and—lifting her own wide-spread ones—quickly hooked them over my shoulders so that her bottom lifted entire from the bale and was immediately cupped on my hands. A low gasp escaped her, but she was now as truly captive as she had been when I held her corked. My tongue protruded, licking gently up between the lips of her slit whilst she bucked and moaned. Heady as the salty musk taste of her was in those shell-like folds, I savoured also the lingering cream of her libation which had oiled her cunny as much as my pego had done in her bottom.

"*HOO-HOOO-HOOO!*" came from Victoria then, for parting her lips at the upper folds, I had found the pink bud of her cunny which had erected itself like a tiny penis. Her heels drummed against my shoulders, her torso twisting, the silky cheeks of her bottom squirming on my palms whilst the very tip of my tongue flickered remorselessly back and forth over her bud, diverting now and then to the creamy aperture of her cunny itself.

She would not be long in coming again as I sensed from the increasing twisting from side to side of her shoulders whilst I gripped her bottom tightly. Of a sudden, her legs shot straight out from my shoulders, straining in ague. Her quim literally mashed itself to my mouth, loosing therein a fine salty sprinkling of her pleasure whilst I held the peach of her bottom drawn apart. One long, quivering sigh from her, and then she slumped again whilst I, rising, placed my lips upon her mouth so that she might taste herself, as I whispered to her, the very essence of her pleasure.

"You will be a good girl now, Victoria," I said to her, rubbing my now-stiff ramrod in agonising frustration against her bush.

"Yes," she whispered simply, then, to my utmost surprise, gave a little giggle and, groping down between us, took hold of my cock in her warm fingers. "Does it . . . does it always get big again so quickly?" she asked hesitantly and then hid her face in my shirtfront at so bold a question. "I cannot believe it all went into my bottom," she murmured with such plain disbelief in her voice that I laughed and kissed her, rolling her sweet upper lip about beneath my own.

How I desisted from plunging my piston within her pussy I know not, for the little urging movements of her soft belly under my knob were such that I felt she would take it, despite such cries as she might utter. Another second or two and I might have ruttingly betrayed Helen's principles, had not a sound come to me from beyond the doors, causing me to jump up and Victoria to follow suit.

"Oh! they will know!" she gasped naïvely whilst a gentle tapping sounded at the doors and she hastily covered herself.

Knowing the doors to be safely barred and that it would be none other than Maude, I gathered the flushed girl in my arms. "You have had a cock in your bottom, my pet, but who is to know? This is the delight of it all, Victoria, and a lesson you must never forget. Such secret pleasures are now your priviledge," I assured her, whereat—so simple are the minds of such young girls—her hand went to her mouth to suppress a giggle of relief. Restraining my prick in my breeches as best I could, I opened the doors and saw Maude standing patiently there. With but a quick, discreet glance at my condition, she swept past me and took Victoria's hand, asking politely whether she had had an enjoyable riding lesson. Blushing to her eyebrows, Victoria assured her in a single stumbling phrase that she had. A more sedate-looking pair never walked back across the sward to the house.

I, for the sake of appearances, lingered a moment or two and, seeing them enter, followed on. I had reached the stone steps to the entrance when a carriage appeared. I turned about and waited, little doubting that it was a new entrant. As it drew up beside me, the face of a young woman stared at me momentarily from the window and was then withdrawn. From the opposite side, a gentleman of good aspect and in his middle years descended and came around the rear of the coach toward me while the cabby lumbered down to remove the baggage that was piled atop.

For a moment the gentleman's eyes regarded me with some hesitation. Not doubting that I must take the initiative, I made him a slight bow and extended my hand, introducing myself as Helen and I had agreed. To do so was to put a somewhat bold face on, yet it might have been worse had I retreated hastily within a domain that was outwardly intended for female habitation.

"I, sir, am Lord Bidcock, and have brought my ward, Amelia, for a course of—er—that is to say . . ."

Given his difficulty in finishing the sentence, and whilst a profound silence reigned within the carriage, I ventured to ask politely if he did not mean correctional excerises, whereat his face quite lit up.

"By Jove, exactly that. Lovely girl, but tiresomely disobedient—needs a touch-up of the crop now and then, what? Over-abundance of clothes. Quite troublesome to get at, so to speak, what? Deuce of a time with my dear wife about the matter, too. No understanding, eh? Needs a chap's mind. Devilish difficult to discuss with Miss Hotspur."

"Nevertheless, you wrote to her about the problem, for I do recall her mentioning it, and she was entirely at one with you," I replied to his evident relief. Morever, I actually recalled the young woman now, since such she was at an announced age of twenty-one and fair ripe for it, by the look of the portrait sent.

"Ah, well, I say—jolly good," he puffed, evidently relieved that I was not immediately escorting him within to meet the Principal. With that he cast his eyes around the grounds and beyond to the meadow, appearing to espy, as if with some instinct, the stable I had just vacated. Such outbuildings would be common enough on his own estate, and yet his eyes lingered there as if he meant to ask a question he found not able to put into words.

"For postural corrections, sir," I observed, giving a nod in the direction of the stable, whereat he flushed a little and looked around a trifle furtively.

"Deuced interesting. No one else there? Ought to see it. Then must be off," he said as the tip of Amelia's nose appeared at the side of the carriage window.

The slight bow I had made him initially was repeated. "We are pleased at all times to demonstrate our methods, Lord Bidcock. Perhaps if you care to bring your ward?" Of deliberation I then walked straight back in the direction of the stable, knowing that he had no recourse but to follow. The opening of the carriage door sounded behind me. A flustered female protest was heard.

"Oh, no! I thought we were to go inside, though I do not wish even to do that, as you know. Why must we go there? Please do not take me! May I not wait within?"

Amelia's voice was deliciously mannered and held all the strains of anxiety that I suspected it might. Much as I longed to turn my head and view her, I maintained a leisurely pace, with the two following a few yards in my rear while her plaintive protests continued. At each one my cock twitched a little more. I knew her from her photograph to be well enough curved and full of figure for such a venture, though the thought of putting her upon the horse or over a bale in the presence of another man was strangely odd. That Lord Bidcock wished to indulge such a whim I could not doubt. The fellow must have had such a thing in mind all the way here, yet probably never thought to realise it. As to Helen, I wondered what her wrath or amusement might be to hear of such an escapade, if that it were to be. Wondering indeed if I were not letting my own imagination run riot, I was yet emboldened by the fact that Amelia—after several muttered words from her guardian—had fallen silent.

Reaching the doors, I open the righthand one but slightly and turned. What a picture of flushed confusion she was already! Of middle height and attired in a light-brown dress trimmed at the neckline and hem with white lace, she had a visage of total innocence that was much adorned by her thick curly brown locks. Her nose was aquiline, her lips thinnish but well formed, her eyes as appealing as a spaniel's. Scenting no horses within, as she was perhaps wont to do at home, she made to draw back, but a firm leverage on her elbow from Lord Bidcock urged her forward.

"I—er—suppose, dear fellow, if you perhaps show

her but a little of your—er—that is to say, Miss Hot-spur's methods . . ."

"You would wait here, sir, yes," I concluded for him and to his great satisfaction. There were cracks enough in the old timber walls through which he could peep within, and I had no doubt whatever that that was precisely what he intended to do. I, never having before provided such a peepshow, found myself being led by my cock rather than moral intentions as I firmly drew Amelia within and barred the doors. Immediately I did, she stared about her wildly, espied the waiting horse, and covered her face, crying, "Oh, sir! What are you at! I wish to see Miss Hotspur!"

"In due course, and indeed in a short time, you shall," I replied. To get this filly astride my rocking horse would present a fair struggle, I knew, and one that I did not intend to indulge in before the eyes of her master. I had scanned his letter but hastily amid many others and recalled not a jot of it, but suspected that he had attempted her already and that she had been too coy to succumb, or that Lady Bidcock had intruded at awkward moments. Speed therefore seemed to me of the essence, for I had naught to lose and Amelia—in truth—little enough either. At her age she would be bedded soon enough in any event.

The spirit of my first adventures with Alice was truly upon me as I took the girl in my arms. She screeched and endeavoured to wrench herself away from me. In that brief moment, however, the warm contact of her thighs, her belly, and her firm breasts was sufficient to bring my cock to straining point.

"How dare you embrace me! Stop it! Let me go!"

Kicking and struggling fiercely as she did, I lifted her by the waist and carried her immediately toward the bale, which of a purpose had been built up with flat-top and of sufficient height so that a girl of such build when placed over it found her toes just touching the ground.

To the sound of her horrified shrieks, I cast her face down upon it.

"My God, you horrible man, what are you at! Let me up, let me go! I will tell Lady Bidcock—*Ow!*".

In a flash, with my elbow pinning her down between her shoulder blades, I had scooped up her skirt, displaying thereby a most elegant pair of legs sheathed in silk stockings of the same shade as her dress. Above flourished a pair of white thighs whose skin was so flawless that the merest speck of dust would have shown like a stain upon them. Indipping briefly, they gave way then to a bottom well-concealed in batiste drawers of a straw shade—a bottom plumper than I had thought from the loose fall of her dress and one that looked exceedingly enticing.

"I shall die if you uncover me! Oh! Do not! What a monster you are!" Amelia howled whilst my free hand then sought for one of several thick straps that I had laid about the bale for such a purpose. That she had not shrieked for help to her guardian was sufficiently significant to assure me that she knew well enough of his own intentions, whilst he for his part was plainly not minded to stir from his peephole until all had been concluded to his satisfaction. Precisely what that was meant to be, I knew not, but since the fellow was lewd enough to lend himself to such a spectacle, there was a certain price he must pay.

In a trice, though not without some dint of effort, I had secured Amelia's arms to her sides by means of the strap passing round her body. My brief fondling of the proud pumpkins of her breasts during the process had raised such cries from her that I suspected it might be their first such caress—from a male, at least. Now, however, the fair prey lay relatively helpless, her bared legs tightly held together whilst she sobbed appealingly.

Neither from Alice nor her sister nor even Lady Betty of the past had I however heard such a shriek as burst from Amelia's throat as I loosed the waist ribbons of her drawers, drew them down to her ankles, and then whipped them off her feet.

"*Ah!* The shame of this! Oh my God, you will pay!"

Deliberately I then stepped to one side so that her guardian might share in the pleasure of viewing her naked rear for the first time. Plumper, as I say, than I suspected it might be, the cheeks were full and bold, jutting out proudly from the tops of her thighs between which even in their clenching I could see a tiny peep of hairs. One tiny brown mole, perfectly round, floated, as it were, upon the right cheek of her bottom, appearing not as a flaw but a minuscule decoration as if by some indiscreet mark of Nature that here indeed was Amelia's most treasured spot.

Her shoulders shook, enveloped as she was in sobs. Indeed, she would have endeavoured to slide backward and fall upon her luscious derriere had I not anticipated the move and given it as fair a *smack!* as ever I had awarded Victoria's. The answering yelp that came from Amelia was deliciously satisfying, for it had a broken ring to it which betokened her despair at trying the trick again.

"Be still, young lady," I warned her sternly. "You were brought here for one purpose, and well you know it."

"Please, I beg you, please, please—he is w . . . w . . . watching, I know it!" she blubbered.

"What a nonsense," I replied. "The walls are stout and cannot be seen through by any observer. Spread your legs now!"

"*No!* Oh God, no! You cannot make me—*Oooh! Ouch!* Oh, don't sm . . . sm . . . smack me again. I cannot bear it! I hate it!"

One clue at least had been given to me. The minx had been spanked before, though whether with her

drawers down or not was in question. I suspected not.
Unlike Victoria's, they had probably never come even
to half-mast, nor would she had sullied her image—as
mayhap she thought of it—by being photographed in as
wanton a posture as the young girl I had earlier
plugged.

"Your *legs,* Amelia!" I repeated, giving her then
such a loud smack across her glorious cheeks as made
her jerk and leap whilst a fair imprint of my palm and
fingers blurred its pink upon the white satiny hemispheres.

"Never, never, *no!*" came her protesting howl despite the deep stinging I must have afforded her and
which had made her cheeks tighten visibly. Brooking no
further delay or repetitions, I then levered her ankles
apart by force and—whilst her screams bid fair to bring
the rafters down—held them so with my own straddled.
I intended not to strap her then and there, but to give
her a more teasing taste of other treatment, and that
which I sought lay fortuitously to hand. For amid all
the straws were several that retained still their feathery
soft ends, and such a one I drew out, mindful that
Amelia's guardian now must have shifted farther along
the outside wall to better view what I was at.

"St . . . st . . . st . . . stop *it!* I shall tell Lady
Bidcock, I shall tell . . . *Yeeeee-oooooh!*"

Her commencing sentences of wild protest were broken off as I parted the rich cheeks of her bottom with
thumb and fingers and brought the fluffed end of the
straw to twirl about her tight rosette. The effect was
electric, causing her widespread legs to quiver, strain,
and lock, whilst she endeavoured madly to squirm her
hips and so remove her orifice from the tickling taunt-
er. In vain, however, did she writhe, being unable to
move backward or forward whilst I stood so close over
her and kept my feet strongly against the insides of her
own. Rotating the straw rapidly, I inserted it in her bot-

tomhole to a rising shriek that died away rapidly into bubbling sobs.

"Oh, my God! I cannot bear it! *Ah!* You beast! *Wooooooo!*"

Delicate as my fingers were at their task, the feathered end had slid full within her virginal orifice, causing her to buck crazily, though having now little enough space to do so, she could only suffer with quivering moans the devilish tickling and enforced excitement as I continued twirling and drawing it back and forth. It being secured within her a full five or six inches, I had no further need to keep her cheeks prised open, but rather—stepping to one side and so allowing her to clap her thighs together again—gripped the nape of her neck and continued urging it gently in and out.

Her face was muffled now in the bale, such muffled sounds coming from her as mingled sobs, moans, and pleas. Affording her no respite, I then swiftly fisted her thighs apart once more, withdrew the maddening "feather," and just as deftly sought her pussy with it.

"Yeee-eeee-eeeek!" she screeched, for rather by fumbling luck than judgement, on this occasion, I had evidently slid it up so far that it made immediate contact with her clitoris. Enchanted that I had reached her spot with such ease, I then rubbed my forefinger about her puckered rosette and inserted it slowly to knuckle. "No-ah-aaaah!" came from Amelia then, her head jerking back and up in a quick, wild motion and then slumping again whilst her bound arms strove helplessly to free herself.

"No, no, no, *no!* I can't, I can't, I can't, I can't!" she ripped out in sobbing cries—a phrase that was then a trifle incomprehensible to me, though I knew well enough what strange words and unbidden phrases came often enough from females in such excitement. I had not long to wait, however, before its meaning was revealed. The doors, unbarred, burst asunder, and from without came the figure of her guardian, his breeches already unbuttoned, his prick at full erection.

"By Jove, she can! She has already tasted my knob there, but no more! Let me have at her!"

"*No-oh-oh-oh!*" came then the shriek of Amelia, whose body bucked in a veritable frenzy as he reached her and, without ado, took hold of her bared hips, thrust her delectable thighs apart, and with a groan of bliss urged the swollen crest of his taut penis slowly up between the rolled lips of her quim.

"*Nooo-nooo-nooo-nooo!* Take it out! *Ah!* Oh, Mama!" came then from Amelia, whilst I, stepping back, watched, as if hypnotised, the steady urging of the thick pestle of his flesh into her divine cunny until at last his balls hung at her bottom and she was secured.

"Undo the strap, sir!" he panted, hooking his hands therewith over her shoulders so that her bottom remained rammed into him.

"Sto . . . o . . . o . . . op him!" Amelia wailed whilst I, obeying her master rather than herself, loosed her arms with some wonder and watched them flail all about, then fling themselves forward as if to grab at the farther side of the bale. Finding no secure purchase there, she wailed loudly, whilst with a massive jerk of his buttocks, he all but withdrew his cock and then rammed it slowly up again, holding her stockinged legs well apart by strength of his own.

"*Dooo-oooh-ooooh!*" came her moan as she felt the full insurgence of his weapon once more, the fleshy smack of her lustrous bottom to his belly sounding loud within.

"You shall have it, Amelia, as I have promised you," he ground, and she sobbing "No!" and he responding "Yes!" he commenced to pestle her in earnest, her rump quivering and bouncing at every stroke as the succulent lips of her slit gripped his cock. Little by little

then, as I fully expected from the ever-changing shade
of expression that crossed her apparently anguished,
lovely features, her bottom indicated by its febrile little
jerks the pleasure that she was slowly obtaining from
the bout. Hiding her face from my view, she began to
whimper softly, the distinct squelching sounds of their
transports coming faintly to my ears whilst her legs
stiffened slightly and her derriere began to respond more
boldly to his thrusts.

"*Ah! Oooh!*" came from her now in more encouraging tones as the slurping thrusts of his cock urged deep
within her, withdrew, and rammed again. Bending farther over her now, he commenced unfastening the front
of her dress, to which she made no defence. Burrowing
his hands deep within, he brought out the pale, full
pumpkins of her breasts, whose rosy nipples were stiff in
an instant to his palms.

"Ah! how tight she is, how exquisite," he croaked.
"Give, Amelia, give! Work your bottom! Ah, my
treasure, I am coming in you at last! Aaaargh!"

A low, singing moan from Amelia and a sensuous
twisting of her hips announced, in turn, that his juices
were pulsing forth within her maw, her breasts fervently
caressed the while. The white froth around the lips of her
cunny announced the power of his effusion. In a moment
the thick worm of his cock reappeared from within her
slit. He tottered, staggered, and fell back on a bed of
straw.

I was at her in the instant. One startled cry from
Amelia, and my own fervent prick had nosed its offering
against her tighter orifice.

"Not *there!*" she shrieked whilst I, taking advantage
of her bared titties, cupped them in my turn and
rammed my pestle a full four inches within the firm
balloon of her bottom. How she reared! Her back all
but met my chest before I thrust her down again. "Na-
ah-aaaah!" she yammered, all in vain. Tight, warm,

and spongy withal as she was, I had her fully corked in but a moment more. Her shoulders and back rippled and quivered. The magnificent orb of her bottom glowed to my skin as I thrust my breeches down and drew up my shirt.

"*Oh-no!* It's too b . . . b . . . big there! *Aaaah! No-oooh-ooooh!*"

So on and on went her moaning cries as I screwed my prick gently back and forth whilst her rump squirmed about deliciously.

"Plug her well, old chap, for she will take mine there, too, before the day is out," I heard from her master, who lay prone and watching where he had slumped. Therewith a shivering sob came from Amelia and a further long "*Oooooh!*" sounded from her lips to the slow urging of my pestle which her plump cheeks and rose-hole nipped so closely.

"Shall he not, Amelia?" I croaked in her ear.

"No! Yes! *Ah-ooooh!*"

Tight as she was with each withdrawal of my prick, yet her rectal muscles eased just sufficiently with each long forward stroke to absorb me to the full, my balls swinging and smacking under her cheeks as they surged back and forth to my thrusts. Where I had thrust her dress up higher, her spine showed faintly, the wondrous violin curve of her hips rolling beneath the power of my piston. Head slumped now on her arms, she uttered little mewing cries that told me well of her increasing pleasure. Passing my hand forward and beneath her plump mound, I felt in a moment the delirious sprinklings from her, falling in a fine spray on my palm.

"Your tongue!" I growled. Working my loins ever more frantically, I experienced with shivers of bliss the exquisite gripping of her hole whose once-puckered mouth was now sucking in a tight O around my shaft. Long and pointed, her tongue entered my mouth. I sucked it within, savouring her perfumed breath as her

urgently bucking bottom commenced drawing the long
jets of sperm from my prick. Her gasps flooded into my
mouth as the delicious tremors of release shook us, her
sagging knees impelled forward into the side of the bale
by my own.

Long did our lingering quivers last until with a faint
"Plop!" the seeping knob of my cock oozed from her
bottom and dripped its last down the backs of her
thighs. A deep sigh from Amelia, and her luscious
mouth slipped from mine. Her eyelashes trembled and
she would have slumped backward onto the floor had I
not held her.

Her hands covered her face then as if—recovering—
she could scarce believe all that had passed. "Oh, let
me go," she moaned so piteously that I was all but de-
ceived, though not so her master, who had indeed a
worm's eye view up between her stockinged legs. With
his cock at full reach once more, he clambered to his
feet and, before Amelia could move to draw down her
dress, the knob of his tool was presented to her well-
buttered bun, causing her to utter the most horrified
shriek.

"Not *him!* Not *there!* Oh, you wicked man! Stop
him! *Ah!* Oh, my God, no!"

Squealing and squirming as if I had not but moments
before breeched her there already, her hips sought
madly to evade the strong clamping of his hands whilst
his cock urged within the now-well-lubricated passage
that I had just vacated. His eyes glazed over with delight, the thick shaft of his manhood protruded half
from between the cheeks of her bottom.

"Ah, how tight she is!"

"Stop him, stop him! Oh! He is doing it! Ah, no
more, I can't bear it!"

One long despairing cry from Amelia, and he was
lodged persuasively full within. Once more her shoulders lifted, her throat working, mouth open. Then again

she slumped, deep sobs racking her that I yet knew to be of hidden passion that she dared not convey, for little enough resistance came from her as he lifted her hips up farther and commenced reaming her vigourously.

"Wha-ah! Wha-ah! Wha-ah!" came from her now in repeated jerks, the responsiveness of her supple hips becoming ever more visible to my eyes as the pestle of his cock surged back and forth in her ripe bottom. Sheened with perspiration, her face twisted and turned blindly toward mine where I stood beside the bale, her eyes rolling up into her head until only the whites showed. Thereupon such a deviltry seized me as they, too, seemed now possessed of. Drawing the upper half of her body closer to the side of the bale, I urged my risen cock against her mouth, and with but a small effort, slipped the swollen knob between her lips. With a gurgling choke and some pressure from my hand at the back of her head, she absorbed it, sniffling and snuffling through her nose whilst I manoeuvred it back and forth over her tongue.

Naught then was heard save our groans until Amelia, truly mastered, impelled with her mouth and bottom the long shoots of sperm that coursed with her at both ends.

Chapter 12

"I HAD thought that Lord Bidcock would bring his ward today," Helen remarked to me that evening after dinner.

Flushing a little and then recovering myself by pretence of having choked on the wine, I nodded agreement. "By Jove, yes, they are the only ones unaccounted for," I replied, for all the beds in the dormitories save one were full and Helen's register now held eleven names.

"Possibly she has changed her mind and yielded without a fight," Helen smiled, whereat I laughed and agreed with her, thanking all the gods that be that no one save myself had been aware of the arrival and departure of the pair. For departed they had, within half an hour of completing Amelia's conversion, which Lord Bidcock must have counted as the most profitable bargain he had ever come upon. Pretending great dismay, confusion, and shame, as she had continued to once order had been restored, I had been put to it to admonish her severely for her hitherto "wayward conduct." Wishing as she had done to run to the carriage, I had restrained her from so doing.

Amelia, believing that I intended her to enter the training couse still, had struggled pettishly. "What are you at? Oh, I shall not be able to live for the shame of this," she cried, quite oblivious to the way she had succumbed in the end to our dual assault.

"How far have you to go, sir?" I asked Lord Bidcock whilst holding Amelia's elbow, the three of us standing still within the stable.

"Thirty miles and a change of carriages en route. Why ask you?"

I believed him to have been in doubt about Amelia's future conduct or degree of compliance, for his glances upon her were more nervous than would have been my own in the circumstances. Much as she might deny it, the minx had seconded our efforts to the full when we had engaged in the final and delightful trio.

"I think you may now well consider whether Amelia requires the course of training she would otherwise have received from Miss Hotspur. Dare I suggest that you stop over the night at some convenient inn or hotel and there discuss the matter in a private bedroom?"

His eyes lit up at that. "By Jove, sir, what a splendid idea—eh what, my love?"

Amelia's brown-shod feet shifted nervously on the wooden floor, her eyes downcast and her cheeks more flushed than befitted a healthy young female who had just taken both our cocks together. For a moment we waited an answer that did not come, whereupon I, boldly asserting that all was thus arranged, guided her to the doors.

"Oh no!" she jerked and started back.

"Would you have me report your conduct to Miss Hotspur?" I asked, whereat she wilted, covered her face, and whispered in a shocked manner, "Oh, no!" Her eyes sought her guardian's quickly and then dropped again. "But—" she began.

"It is settled then. Lord Bidcock, may I suggest the

Crest Hotel? It lies but five miles from here, has splendid double rooms, each with an attendant private bathroom. You will have naught to disturb you whilst you make your—er—deliberations. Should Amelia decide otherwise, then doubtless you will return her here in the morning. Well, Amelia?" I asked abruptly.

Her face suffused, her breasts rose and fell beneath her bodice. For a moment I thought her to challenge me, but then, with a slight sniff and an attempt at regaining her poise, she assented softly, but with such reluctance that I turned back within, took up the strap that I had first secured her with and proffered it to Lord Bidcock, who received it with a rare smile. To this gesture, Amelia gave a little jump and uttered a sharp cry.

"Go to the carriage, Amelia," I said sharply and in such a tone that she bit her lip and with quickly mincing footsteps began walking across the grass toward it.

"I say, dashed strange occurrence, what?" Lord Bidcock exclaimed, flushed of visage as he was. "Not a word, eh? Total discretion. Gentleman's bond, what?"

"You have my word on it—neither shall I hint of this pass to Miss Hotspur, lest she be shocked. Keep her in fair trim tonight. A good strapping after dinner, I suggest. By morning, sir, she will have been well enough saddled to become docile. Must get back. Duties call, eh?"

Such had been my departure, quickly and tactfully taken. I had few doubts about Amelia, now, save that he—being more ruttish than knowing—might rapidly be wound around her little finger. But that was a problem that need not concern me. For every Amelia there was a Samantha, a Victoria or, as I learned now more closely from Helen, a Monique.

"That one is a cock-teaser, of the first order, Jack," she told me whilst I, raising my eyebrows, questioned what such a maiden had been sent here for. "Because

she is so good at it," Helen went on. "A wicked tease
and a flirt who is viewed by her doting Mama as quite
the tomboy of the family and as innocent as the day is
long. She little knows what a rare teasing-up she herself
is about to get before I put her to your cock. The salute
will be well overdue and will prime her best fot the reception she will get when she returns home at the end
of term, for I shall send as detailed a report of her as I
mean to. I have asked her to come down in half an
hour."

"Here?" I jerked in surprise, for it was not, as I understood, to be Helen's custom to receive girls in her
drawing room.

"She is used to luxury, Jack. They all are, of course.
The fact that they have all been so dreadfully spoilt is
but one reason why they must all be brought down a
peg—or put to it. Maude will bring her down. Besides,
I am sure you are dying to make her acquaintance. She
is deliciously sylphlike—breasts as firm as melons and
the very naughtiest apple of a bottom you ever saw.
Her eyes, I swear, are as large as my own, with long
dark lashes. Her mouth is as sensuous as you will ever
encounter. Shall we drink to the thought?"

"Have you tasted her yet, you delightful witch?" I
asked. The fact that I had got away with my escapade
with Amelia had put me in the highest of spirits.

Helen shook her head. "No, I received her quite de-
murely and in the most formal fashion. She believes, on
the word of her Papa, that she is here purely to extend
and perfect her English and to brush up on her knowledge of the English. She will get a fair surprise, at that,
when we polish up her bottom."

"A form of correction not yet attempted?" I asked.

"Oh, indeed yes, but there lies the nub. Brought to
the strap by her fond parent—for it is a more desired
instrument apparently than the birch among the

French—she has had the effrontery to lower her drawers herself, displaying her naked charms in the most alluring manner you can imagine. Thus thinking her fair
fit for it, he has several times begun to warm her up,
but ever on the third or fourth stroke she has leapt up
in pretended horror and confusion calling for her
Mama, who has ever rescued her."

"Until now," I said shrewdly.

"Precisely, Jack, and this, of course, is the real reason for her presence. I have her in the same little bedroom as Samantha and Victoria. The former will be too
proud to say anything to her of what she now knows
passes here. As to Victoria, you gave her such a lusty
pumping that she is still in quite a daze about it, though
not too unpleasant a one. Now, my boy, cast off your
jacket and tie in readiness for Monique—but I want her
bottom not yielding yet. I shall tell you precisely what
to do. Listen now . . . ."

My cock was in right fettle by the time Helen had
tutored me, and thus she intended it to look, though
concealed to full view by my trousers, which were fully
lumped foryard when at last Maude conducted Monique within.

All that Helen had said of her came clear to my eyes.
She was a bewitching young creature, not then having
attained her nineteenth birthday, but with eyes that appeared as old as the Sphinx. Having no doubt at all
where those selfsame eyes would fall when I was introduced, they indeed did so and fastened themselves for a
long, wondering moment on my obvious projection.
Then, raising her oval, clear-skinned face to mine, she
treated me to a look of such patent flirtatiousness that I
could well understand the havoc she could cause.

"Our practise, Monique, is to entertain the young ladies separately in the evenings," Helen declared to her
glibly with many a bubbling smile whilst she motioned

the girl to the divan on which I was seated at one end.
"You would like some wine, of course? All French girls
adore it, do they not?"

"Ah, oui, Madame," replied Monique in a delicious
accent, whilst preening herself in a self-congratulatory
manner on the royal manner in which she was being
received.

"By the way, are you wearing drawers, Monique?"
Helen asked suddenly when we were all seated.

"M . . . Madame?" Monique's lips quivered. I had
no doubt that she had never before been asked such a
question in company or otherwise, and, being used to
taking the initiative in such matters outside of her Mama's hearing, she was quite thrown back on her heels.

"It is not the custom to wear drawers here, Monique.
Did Maude not tell you? Oh, tut tut. Really, Maude,
you are quite forgetful. Have them off her, will you,
Maude?"

For a moment, Monique remained as if frozen, for
she had only just finished her glass and had placed it
down in evident anticipation of having it refilled and
acting the sophisticate. Her legs uncrossed immediately
and she made to rise, whereat, I playing my rehearsed
part, took her shoulders and spun her quickly about.
Maude, rising in the same instant, seized her ankles and
pulled upon them, thus bringing Monique to full reclin-
ing position on the divan with the back of her head
drawn down on my lap whilst my hands grasped her
shoulders.

"Oh, no Madame, Madame!" Monique cried as
Maude, sleeking her hands slowly up the girl's slender
legs, uncovered their shapely forms until first her
tightly banding stocking tops and then her gleaming
white thighs came into view. Forcing her arms beneath
my own, I then began to unbutton the front of her
dress. At that moment, Maude, amid unbelieving
shrieks from Monique, lifted her bottom firmly and

ripped down her drawers, ignoring the kicks of her feet
as she drew them off.

"Ah! you cannot do thees!" Monique howled, for
by then I had bared the creamy hillocks of her breasts
and was rolling her perky nipples between my fingers
and thumbs whilst below me, where her dress had been
thrown up to her navel, I had the delicious vista of her
mound, whose dark curls made a perfect triangle at the
base of her belly.

"Hold her legs apart and let me see her," Helen said,
facing me from the other end of the couch. "What a
pretty one we have here, haven't we—well-furred and
so tightly pursed, but you are used to presenting it, Monique, are you not—though not quite in this position?"

"Nevair, Madame! Oh, how can you treat me so
naughtee?"

"Naughty? Naughty is delicious, is it not, Monique?
Let us see you now the way you offer to the strap.
Turn her over!"

"Non! non! non! non!" howled the superbly curved
young girl as in a trice, Maude at her ankles and I at
her shoulders spun her over like a sack so that by pressing her face down a little, I brought her warm lips to
nestle at the base of my rearing cock which I had rapidly bared. Pushing Monique's knees forward, Maude
forced her to present the luscious little globe of her bottom to full view whilst her mouth struggled in vain to
break contact with my swollen organ.

In a prime position as I was, I watched Maude produce two feathers from the neckline of her dress, one of
which she passed to Helen. Thus armed, and whilst I
maintained a firm hold beneath Monique's armpits, the
one attended to the tickling of her rosehole while the
other glided the tip of her feather in the most maddening way all about the fleshy fig of the girl's quim.

"C'est terrible! c'est terrible! Ah! Non!"

Monique's bared hips writhed frenetically, but in no

way could she escape the excruciating torment of the two feathers, both of which I now guessed from the deeper movements of their wrists had invaded her and were causing her to mouthe and splutter.

"Over again!" Helen commanded whilst I, regretting the adorable pressure of the girl's moist warm lips on my cock, brought her about once more on her back and, leaning far over her struggling form, clasped her beneath the knees which I brought full back. Thus with her bottom half raised off the divan, she was on full display, her calves jerking in vain and her howls of protest—mostly couched in fluent French—resounding.

Her posture was not such, however, as befitted protest, her head being securely held between my thighs in such a way that every attempted movement of it caused her thick soft hair to caress and tickle my prick delightfully.

"A sweet furrow indeed to be ploughed," Helen sparkled, running her forefinger between the soft lips and so parting them to reveal the mucuous glistening within. "Hand me your feather, Maude. I think just the tip of it around her clitoris will almost bring her off, though I mean not to give her the entire pleasure of that."

"*M . . . M . . . Madame! Ah, que c'est horrible!*" came Monique's long wail as the skilful flirting of the tickling tip made itself felt all around her budding clitty. Her hips writhed torturously as each moment, in addition, Helen awarded her a sound smack on her half-lifted bottom. "Do not do eeeeet!" the girl shrieked, "Ah! for the shame, the shame!"

"Ha! Do you but hear her, Jack, this selfsame one who has so naughtily bared her bottom to the strap and teased her poor Papa to distraction? Still her mouth, my pet.

This now was the invitation I had most desired. Whilst Maude now took purchase on Monique's upheld legs, I got from under her, casuing her head to fall back on a cushion I quickly placed there. In a trice I had thrust my trousers down and knelt at the side of the divan. Taking the shoulders of the shrieking, quivering, writhing girl, I forced her chin toward me and— pinching her nose so that she was forced to gape— inserted the knob of my cock smoothly between her moist lips.

"Suck but do not bite, Monique, or I shall bring the whip to you!" warned Helen instantly, brushing the feather constantly all about the girl's quim. Her hands free, Monique even made to slap at me and force her mouth away, but smacking her wrists sharply, I caused her arms to drop again and her mouth most lusciously to tighten on my prick in surprise.

Such bubbling cries as she would have otherwise made were now muted by the surging of my prick backward and forward over her tongue, the sensation being made all the more enervating by the sight of her squirming hips and the chocking sobs that sounded in her throat.

Alas, my own transports were not to remain long so, for in but a moment Helen—who was insistent that Monique should have no final pleasure for a period— ceased her own ministrations and beckoned to me to withdraw my steaming tool. At that, Monique would have leapt up, save for a fierce smack that she received across her thighs from Maude, who thrust her down again.

"How dare you rise without my permission, Monique!" Helen snapped, though she was swift to confess to me afterward that she would fain have fallen upon her as I. Her brown-berried nipples, erected by the excitement she had sustained, poised quivering on the snowy hillocks of her breasts. One leg, slumped down onto the floor, exposed her pussy in its bouquet of dark curls. Her haunted eyes stared at us as Maude stood warningly over her, forbidding her to move by the sternest of looks.

"I tell . . . I tell Mama, I tell Papa!" Monique howled.

"Really? Your Mama will never believe you—I shall see to that. I shall explain to her, Monique, that you are much given to erotic fantasies which find some wicked fulfilment when you lower your drawers for a strapping. You are quick to draw them up again when she appears, are you not? *No!* Do *not* interrupt me, girl, when I am speaking. As to your dear Papa, he will find naught but merit in my methods. What think you of her, Jack?" she asked, turning toward where I stood with lewdly bared prick still.

I shrugged. "Pretty enough, but I doubt if the first who injects that tight-lipped pussy will bother to do so again. There are many enough like her," I countered, knowing well that this was the way Helen wished me to speak.

As for Monique, if her face had been flushed until now, it grew a deeper shade at my words and her eyes blazed. A spluttering of French came from her which caused me to turn to Helen and ask languidly, "What did she say?"

"Something to the effect, my dear, that no young lady should be spoken of in that way and that she could never bring herself to be so wicked before she reaches the marriage bed. *Monique!* Keep your legs *open!* Smack her, Maude, I will not have her behaving in this rebellious fashion."

"Na-ah-aaaah!" bitterly sobbed Monique, who now displayed two red patches on her thighs where Maude's palm had fallen. *"Oh,* I hate, I hate! I make revenge! Papa, he keel you, he keel you!"

"What airs she does put on!" Helen laughed. Slipping one shoe off, she raised her leg and laid her stockinged foot swiftly up between Monique's splayed thighs so that her toes curled over the girl's plump mount. "Do not think, Monique, that you are going to continue in the same vein—*tu comprends?* It is not you, my pet, who will offer your bottom in a mischievous moment in the future, such as you have previously done. You will be taken at will—like medicine!", she laughed and moved her toes, causing Monique to writhe and sob very prettily indeed.

"Supple, is she not?" Helen asked me, maintaining her foothold, so to speak. "That delicious little bottom is going to agitate itself quite deliriously when she is put to the cock."

"Ah! *Non, non, non—c'est défendu!*" Monique howled, though from the screwing up of her eyes I could see that she was gaining a little more pleasure than it seemed from the subtle, curling movements of Helen's toes.

"Forbidden?" Helen mocked, echoing her last word. "You are the last to speak of such things, Monique. Very well, Maude, lift her up. I want her in a sitting position, your hand at the back of her neck."

"Ah! What you do?" came then from the girl, who was promptly hauled up at command, whilst this time it was Helen who pinched her nose tightly and caused her mouth to open like a fish—though I may say a devilishly attractive one with her thighs bared and her breasts lolling free.

"Very well, Jack," Helen declared. The moment then was mine as, steadying Monique's sweet oval face the more, I plunged my yearning prick once more into the warm, moist haven of her mouth whilst Helen whispered to her the selfsame warning that she had done before, therewith releasing her hold on Monique's nose.

Monique's eyes bulged, staring up for an instant at me as if I were truly a fearful apparition, with my cock deep embedded now over her tongue and my balls all but

dangling at her chin. Taking the lobes of her ears, as a
precaution, I squeezed them gently, moving my cock
slowly between her pursed lips whilst Maude assisted
the movement by rocking Monique's head slightly back
and forth. But then there occurred also a whim of Hel-
en's that she was obviously delighted to realise, for
passing around the divan and immediately behind Maude,
she loosed the front of the young woman's dress and
drew out the noble orbs of her white breasts whilst beck-
oning me to lean forward and kiss her.

I did so to a gobbling, choking sound from Monique,
who thus absorbed the last two inches of my fleshy
rammer whilst Maude's mouth, obediently meeting
mine, opened to inject the flickering of her tongue in
my mouth. None of this, of course, Monique could see
or be aware of, nor that Helen had raised Maude's
gown and was fondling her naked bottom at the same
time. Indeed, I suspected that her fingers were becoming ever busier, for Maude's tongue commenced swirling hungrily in my mouth as the suction of Monique's
increased.

Whether or not Monique knew what she was about
to be given, I could not guess, though I suspected now
that mine was the first cock to which she had been
brought. Drawing Maude's mouth from mine, Helen
leaned forward in turn and applied her own sultry lips
to my own whilst delicately twiddling her companion's
slit and bottomhole. Then, nudging Maude to follow
suit, I had in a moment both their tongues working
together about my own whilst Helen's bottom was
freely bared in turn.

A frenzied glugging came from Monique as my cock
flashed faster, whilst, with their mouths passionately
open, Helen and Maude whirled their tongues about
mine until with a myriad of electric thrills coursing
through me I pulsed out the rapid jets of my sperm,
cloying Monique's tongue and spurting down her

throat. Maude, maintaining faithful hold on the nape of her neck, ensured that not a droplet was missed before I withdrew the shaft that had expended all its treasures in Monique's adorable mouth.

Thereupon order behind the girl was quickly restored. Maude's hold released, she slumped back, blubbering the froth of my sprem around her lips, and sobbing as if she had just been whipped. Helen had not yet finished with her, however, and was about to produce her *piéce de résistance* and one of considerable surprise to myself. Raised to her feet and held anew by Maude, the fevered eyes of Monique watched as if hypnotised by Helen's short journey to a cupboard and back, for now she held in her hand a metal object such as I had never laid eyes on before.

Nor, would I wager, had Monique, but by the deepest of instincts she divined its meaning and purpose full seconds before myself.

"Madame! Madame! No! I forbid! I will not! I tell Mama! I die first!"

So she shrieked and howled unendingly whilst I, to my bemused fascination, realized that Helen intended no less than to gird her in a chastity belt. Of light metal and prettily chased with several highly erotic figures about its waistband, it was slid up Monique's legs despite all her wailings and struggles until it was at last secured. Forming a broad cup around and beneath her pussy, and from thence to her hips, its front and rear apertures were sufficient only for the natural functions.

"*Mon Dieu! Mon Dieu!* You cannot!" Monique howled, wrenching in vain with her hands at that which now veiled her dark-furred pussy.

"Take her to bed, Maude," instructed Helen sharply, whereat the erstwhile sophisticated young Monique was led sobbing from the study whilst Helen surveyed my look of wonderment with amusement.

"'Tis not to frustrate *you*, my pet," she laughed. "We

can have it off very quickly when it comes to breaching her bottom. I trust not all the girls, you see. The various teasings and titillations we afford them may give one or two a taste for nighttime activities with other girls. Monique would lend herself to pussy tonguing, I feel sure, but the minx is now well frustrated, for scarce the tip of a finger will get through that small hole in front."

That I gazed at her in admiring surprise is not to be doubted. "Have you any more such inventions?" I asked.

"None to rival yours, Jack, but I have a problem. We must be serious for a moment. A letter from Samantha's father arrived by special messenger this morning. It appears that his wife has caught some scent of our activities and has insisted that he bring her here to form her own judgements. From such hints as I can gather in his letter, she may be a problem."

"Which you will well know how to divert or dispose of," I said gallantly.

"Perhaps. Or you may know even better, Jack. You remember what you told me about Lady Betty and her daughter and how you dealt with them both so scrumptiously?"

"That I certainly do. What a voluptuous pair they made in the end! But the devil of it, there is a complication in this case since the husband will be here also."

"Where there's a will there's a way, Jack. Do I really need to tell you my thoughts on that?"

For a moment, the scene in the stable with Amelia and her guardian flashed before my eyes. Then Helen came and wound her arms seductively about my neck, pressing her gloriously curved form invitingly against my own.

"Two males and two females, Jack," she murmured. "I'm sure that you can find ways to satisfy all concerned!"

Chapter 13

THE REMEMBRANCE of how I had treated Lady Betty and her daughter, bringing them by divine tortures of fingers and feathers to lick one another's slits, came back to me again and again in the ensuing days that preceded the visit of Sir Charles and Lady Edwardes, the parents of the proud Samantha.

I observed the lovely girl frequently and lusted for her all the more now that I sensed her eventual fate. Helen, however, proved once more the counsellor in this.

"She is as hard a one to break in as any we have, Jack. I quite adore her imperiousness, in fact. She will make quite a divine bedmate for me when we have her fully tutored, for like most girls of her kind—and you must not take this amiss—she responds more amourously to the female tongue than to the male finger. I have caned her twice now—yes, caned her, Jack—and felt her cunny afterward whilst Maude has held her. It is the sweetest fruit you ever did lay a touch upon—tight but elastic, puckered, and yet ready to open like a flower to the seeking phallus."

"As her bottom must be," I murmured.

"You will enjoy it even more than Victoria's—or Clarissa's," Helen observed, mentioning a girl whom I had successfully "cornered" and put to my cock the afternoon before. "Samantha's bottom shall be yours, Jack, but she must be put otherwise to her sire first."

"While Lady Edwardes watches?" I asked.

"Maude and I will be dealing in great part with Lady Edwardes, dearest. By the time we have finished with her—and, naturally, with your help—she will be in quite a delirious state. Was not Lady Betty? Did you really have to use violent force when you laid her upon her daughter—both naked as the day?"

I had to confess that even with the help of my lovely assistants at the time, that had not really been so. In great part, the voluptuous pair had been overwhelmed by the circumstances, their patent capture, and all that we had done to them to agitate their juices.

"Did you not tell Molly to lick you balls whild you fucked her Mama, and did she not obey?" Helen reminded me, recapturing the moment I have already described in my first volume. "What a challenge for us to bring Lady Edwardes to lick her husband's balls—and yours—whilst in your turns you are possessing the exquisite girl. But to your peephole now, for I am about to have her in and you shall see such progress as she has made."

I was within my den in a trice and no sooner had settled comfortably than the door opened to admit Samantha, who for once was not accompanied by Maude. In place of a dress she wore a Grecian gown of white translucent material, girded at the waist by a golden cord which ended in a broad double tassel dangling at her hip. White sandals adorned her feet, but she was otherwise naked beneath, her rich, slender curves scarcely veiled by the gown which clung lovingly to her bottom, breasts, and thighs. The vision was breathtaking, for there are moments when such frail adornment is more enticing than nudity, and this simple form of attire was of the utmost eroticism. Not only was the cleft of her glorious bottom offered to view, but with each forward step there showed the alluring haze of her pubic curls, which formed a sensuous padding around her mound.

Helen smiled at her gently, as if in greeting. "In what a bloom of health you look, Samantha. Are you not enjoying your stay here after all?"

Approaching her, the young woman's head tossed slightly. "You are going to cane me, Madame?" she asked in a tone almost devoid of expression.

"It may come to that. Be seated with me here on the divan a moment, Samantha. Aren't we friends? You look perfectly delicious, my dear, in the gown—virginal and sweet. I shall have an excellent report to write on you, I believe."

"Really, Madame?" Samantha's lips curled slightly, seated as she now was in a prim position with her hands neatly folded in her lap.

"You think it is my wish to break you?" Helen asked softly, running her hand up Samantha's back and to her swanlike neck, where her fingers nestled beneath the soft fall of hair. "I have no wish to do so, my dear. Your proud bearing pleases me, though it may surprise you to hear it. Such a lovely mouth, such high, firm breasts, such elegant thighs. Stand up again a moment before me that I may look at you properly. Yes, so—close to me. Now part your gown back from your tummy and sweep it behind you. It will hold there."

Compressing her lips, the girl obeyed, a light flush sweeping over her beautiful features as she was thus brought to expose her well-bushed pussy to Helen's closed gaze. The faintest of tremors swept through her as Helen now picked up a thin whippy cane and gently stroked Samantha's thighs with it.

"Next time you are attired so fetchingly in this, you

shall wear black silk stockings, my pet. The combination will be quite marvellous, in particular with your long legs. Ease them apart a little now—just a trifle. Come, Samantha, do not be difficult."

A murmur escaped the girl's lips as the tip of the cane then inserted itself between the tops of her thighs, gliding between the silky columns so that the polished surface of the cane rubbed visibly between the lips of her slit, which by the lightest of pressures it parted slightly.

"Move your hips back and forth a little now, Samantha," Helen urged whilst the girl's breath was withdrawn sharply. "Come, dear, we are women together, are we not? I know what you like, despite all your attempts to conceal your hidden passions beneath a screen of haughtiness. Move now, or I shall bring it more bitingly to your bottom than you have experienced yet. No! Not such a timid movement, girl! Bend your knees slightly . . . *Now,* urge your hips!"

Samantha's mouth jerked open, and then a faint whimper came from her lips. Increasing the upward pressure of the cane, Helen was forcing the young woman to both pleasure and humiliate herself as the polished cane rode along the mouth of her cunny, making her blush deeply.

"M . . . Ma'am, I cannot! To behave like this— oh, it is wicked!" Samantha cried. Despite Helen's warning, she would have straightened her knees and stilled the urging movement of her hips had not an intervention suddenly come. The door had opened silently and Maude had entered. Her hand held a cane that was much like Helen's, save that it was shorter. By some instinct, Samantha made to turn her head, but it was too late. With several strides forward, Maude was upon her, and a tearing shriek burst from Samantha's throat as Maude's cane seared scross her marble buttocks, leaving a distinct pink streak.

Therewith the young woman's hips were impelled

forward anew, forcing her cuntlips to part again over the cane that Helen held pointing forward between her thighs.

"No-OH!" Samantha shrieked, but now there was no escape, for she could either bump her navel into Helen's nose or, in endeavouring to retreat, meet the cutting kiss of the cane, which now crisscrossed her bottom with two lightning strokes from left and right. The howl that came from her throat might well have sounded out over the grounds, had the room not been well padded to muffle all sounds.

"Do-on't! Oh, don't please! I can't b . . . b . . . bear it!" she sobbed, for in its blistering trail, Maude's cane had now laid three fine parallel strokes across her white hemispheres, as if they had been drawn in red ink. All pride seemed to have melted away from her. Never, it seemed, had even Helen accorded her the cane so bitingly. Her back arched, mouth open in anguish, tears pearling down her cheeks Rising then, Helen embraced her with almost motherly tenderness, so that Samantha sagged against her in her sobbing.

"There, dear, there, I have no wish to be harsh with you, but you must be taught. Maude, the leg restrainer, please!"

"My God, no!" Samantha screeched, but clasped tight as she was in Helen's embrace, her struggles were but futile. Maude, fetching from the desk the stout wooden rod with ankle straps, knelt and thrust it quickly between Samantha's thighs and there secured it so that her feet were held wide apart. In a flash, Helen stepped back, leaving her swaying.

"Stop it! What are you *doing?* I can't stand like this!" Samantha howled.

"You are perfectly able to do so, my dear, if you stand still," Helen declared, "though you may need support in a moment or two. A chair, Maude, please— place it with its back to her so that she can lean forward and hold it. Yes—just there. Now, Samantha, if you care to . . ."

"*Ow!*" Samantha screeched in alarm, for, by giving her a light prod in the back, Helen had made her fall forward so that whilst her splayed legs remained as they were, her hands were flung forward wildly to grap the top of the plain wooden chair. "If you cane me again— if you do—I shall die!" she sobbed.

"Your back dipped a little, Samantha, please. I want it well up, or by heavens you *shall* get the cane again well enough. Good. Excellent. What a perfect moon, or shall I better describe it as a split peach? What do you think, Maude?"

"Superb, yes. Quite the most perfect globe in the establishment, Principal. A tickler, perhaps? She responded quite well to the feather last time."

"*No!* Not *that!* Oh, I beg you! It tortured me!" came Samantha's cry. Stretched forward as she was from the hips, the gourds of her breasts hung ripe and full whilst from the rear the slit of her softly pursed vagina plumped sweetly under the adorable bulge of her bottom. "Please . . . please let me go," she whimpered. Her arms strained in that moment, and she made as if to attempt to rise, but the effort was impossible. A bubbling cry broke from her lips as Maude then stepped to her side, her hip firmly into Samantha's waist. Facing away from her, Maude gently prised open the springy cheeks of her bottom and drew from the neckline of her own dress what I immediately recognised as a dildo. It was some seven inches long, moderate in diameter, and sheathed in black velvet. The crest was shaped precisely in the fashion of the male knob, and a horrified wail broke from Samantha as it was gently inserted in her bottomhole.

"*Na-aaah!*" she shrieked, quite unable to jerk up as she wanted to. Helen had but commenced, however, and reaching to the edge of her desk took up what I thought was a perfume spray of cut glass. Instead, as I learned later, it contained a fine oil wherewith she sprayed Samantha's rosette into which only the knob was inserted, and misted a film of oil also along the dildo.

"*Mama—Mama!*" came then from Samantha, whose neck jerked and strained to the ensuing urging of the hand-held imitation penis within her. "*Whooo-hooo-hoooo!*" she chattered through her teeth. "Oh! *Wow-ow!* Do not! How horrid! *Aaaah!*" A visible trembling ran down the shapely lines of her legs as half inch by half inch, the firm but softly covered dildo was impelled within her until just sufficient remained for Helen to obtain a grip on it by virtue of an extending "palm piece," which nestled comfortably in her hand.

"*No-oh-oh!* Don't *Yeee-eeech!*" Samantha squealed. Her torso twisted, her face full flushed, "Oh, my God, why are you doing this!"

"To bring you on, my pet—the feather, please, Maude."

It was then, I noticed, that Samantha's cries took on a different strain whilst Maude, bending, began working the tip of the feather around her slit, seeking out—as I knew she must be—the girl's clitoris. Wilder strains came then into Samantha's tones. The notes were no longer so high-reaching, but resolved into ever-longer moans, whilst both the tickling feather and the urging dildo soothing in and out took their toll of her resistance. Her knees buckled, whimpers bubbling from her lips. Much as she endeavoured to still any answering movements of her hips and bottom, she was unable to. Though her hair clouded down over her face, I could see that her lips remained open, her eyes being half-closed where previously they had been wide open. Her silk-clad ankles quivered against the restraining of the rod twixt her legs.

Helen turned her head in my direction and smiled.

Agitating the dildo faster, she then motioned to Maude to take hold of it, so that her assistant became thus two-handed whilst a stuttering "N . . . n . . . n . . n . . ." came from Samantha's throat that I, as well as they knew, betokened the oncoming of her delicious crisis.

This then was the moment that Helen chose to act in a way I had not expected. Stepping quickly toward my peephole, she beckoned me out so that I stood at a far angle to Samantha and placed her finger to my lips. Samantha herself was too far gone to be conscious of what else was happening and perhaps did not even suspect that Helen was not still immediately behind her. Pressing her lips to my ear, Helen uttered the very words I longed to hear.

"Take her, Jack. She has already come once," she breathed. "But *quietly*—do not speak!"

In a flash I was behind the girl, from whose delicious bottom the dildo then withdrew. Taking her hips whilst she continued to moan, perhaps momentarily thinking that my hands were Maude's or Helen's, I positioned the glowing crest of my knob carefully against her secretive aperture and drove smoothly up to the hilt. At the same time, Maude knelt, the better able in that way to guide the tip of the feather where it was most needed.

"*Wow-ooooh! No! Ah!* Stop! Oh my God, what is it?" Samantha cried. "Take it out!"

Mindful of Helen's instructions, I uttered not a sound. Indeed, it pleased me not to do so, for I was in perfect heaven at being so deeply, warmly, and tightly ensconced in the warm bottom of such an erstwhile proud maiden. She jerked, wriggled, sobbed, and strove as best she could for long, delirious moments whilst I, of a purpose kept her fully plugged.

"*Aha! Aha! Aha!*" Samantha sobbed endlessly, feeling my large prick all but withdraw, plunge in again,

and then begin its steady pistoning movements. Her
hips swivelled as sensuously as I ever knew any woman's to, bumping and squirming until her velvety cheeks
smacked against my belly. A mewing sound came from
her which Helen judged more quickly than I signalled
her onrushing of pleasure. Passing her hand down, as
she stood at the girl's side, she cupped one silken gourd
and rubbed the nipple delicately between thumb and
forefinger.

"Mamamamama!" Samantha moaned insensibly.
The backs of her luscious thighs quivered against mine.
Her back sagged. Knowing as I did that her very en-
trails must be melting, I empelled my sperm into her in
great gobs, flashing my cock back and forth as I did so.
The suction of her bottom drew every drop until my
very balls felt drained. Drawing my prick out slowly, I
observed scarce a pearl of come seeping from her rosehole, which seemed to have puckered itself tightly
around its liquid prize. Unable to prevent myself, I caressed her bulbous cheeks, her thighs, and the bubbling
lips of her quim. Momentarily depleted of my forces,
then, my expression must even so have told of another
hunger, for Helen quickly bid me retire before Samantha should espy me. That I did so immediately pleased
Helen, who smiled and blew me a fond kiss.

From my cubbyhole again, I watched the limp, sobbing figure of Samantha being released from her leg
bonds. Half-collapsing, she was guided quickly to the
couch and there laid.

"Oh my God, what have you *done* to me!" she
moaned. Seemingly unable to struggle again, she waved
her arms but limply whilst Helen, at the end of the
couch, pressed her knees up and applied the slow
sweeping of her tongue to her pussy. At that, Samantha
did strive to rise, but with the lightest of efforts was
pushed down again by Maude, who set to sucking the
quivering tips of her breasts. Samantha's eyes rolled.

Her legs made as if to straighten and then drew back again. Her fingers clenched and unclenched.

"Oh! Oh . . . M . . . M . . . Madame!" she whined. Whether she had come again so quickly I know not, but Helen seemed as one possessed. Rising with wet mouth and lolling tongue, she drew up her gown and threw herself full upon the girl, who received her with a moan. The lips of their slits rubbed together in a veritable anguish. The sucking of lips came to my ears, though Samantha's face was now hidden beneath that of Helen.

"Ah, my love, how well you are going to take the cock now!" I heard Helen whisper.

Chapter 14

THE VOLUPTUOUS orgy that lasted then for some twenty minutes threw me into a high state of spermatic excitement, but I prided myself still on not bursting out upon them and so interfering with Helen's ways.

"Had you but known it, you could have had my bottom, Jack, whilst I was upon her," she laughed afterwards. "What a delicious girl she truly is. She will never fully be broken in by a man—that is what I adore about her. She will take the cock often in imperious silence once we have ceased to tease her. She is a girl's girl at heart," Helen sparkled at me with all the pride of her femininity.

"So? Then what will you do with her next?" I asked. "Before her Mama and Papa arrive, I mean."

"Cane her, of course," Helen replied crisply and with a slight air of surprise as if I should have known that. "At heart she wishes me to be the stronger one, for she will succumb more willingly to me than to the male."

Disbelief evidently showed on my face, for she cuddled up to me beguilingly.

"There are such women, Jack, beloved of and by both the sexes, yet always veering to their own, for our ways are more subtle—and besides, we last longer at the sport."

"Are you really telling me that Samantha will not enjoy a good sturdy fuck?" I asked.

"Oh, you silly boy, of course she will but she may not show it as I do, for she believes that her spirit would be broken. That won't prevent her hips and bottom waggling amorously to your cock or to another's, I can promise you, but she will surrender neither with words nor promises, nor by any flirtatious flashing of her eyes. You will see. Very shortly you will see." Helen laughed and went on. "As to most of the other girls, they will respond eventually with silly giggles and will be quite enamoured of having cuddles before or after. Some will not need to be strapped or birched or anything else once the term is done. They will become simple pleasure maidens, though I doubt that they will be so much fun in the end. Victoria will need the strap occasionally, for I believe in truth she likes it. She considers it a symbol of authority, though she would give in also without it. Monique is probably the same, for she likes to consider serself a little devil at heart, and once she is put to the cock will continue to squeal for that reason. The Samanthas of this world are comparatively rare. You may strap her for the pure pleasure of it provided you are aware that her own pleasure is also there. Whatever her future cries or whimpers, you will get little out of her vocally otherwise; yet, if you are strong enough, she will so expect you to treat her before you ram her. She quite adores the struggle that goes on inside her twixt her submissiveness and her desire to remain imperious and aloof, but comforts herself that the latter trait will always prevail."

"Good heavens, you are quite a psychologist!" I burst out admiringly.

"Am I not?" Helen laughed, for she was always exceedingly pleased at my compliments. "But, Jack, I do not wish to rule the roost completely, as I fear I have been doing. What is your wish for the evening? And do not say it is to fuck me, for I know that already."

"Then I shall tell you no lie, Helen. I want to try out my new device which you have not yet seen. It stands in The Snuggery now, together with its twin."

"Really? How mysterious, Jack! A twin, indeed, and therefore you want two girls?"

"Exactly, and for all we know it will be a rehearsal also for Samantha and her Mama. Now let me think a moment. Yes—I will have Victoria and Monique. They will make a nice combination, don't you think?"

"Perhaps they might, you wicked man. At what hour will milord require these damels for his lewd pleasure? Shall we say at nine-thirty, after dinner? Then we can tuck the two up quite contented for the night, I do hope. But, Jack, you must still not attempt their pussies yet. After all, you have Lucy and Maude and myself for that pleasure."

"Very well—I shall pass up that honour," I declared gallantly, "but what say you if some of them do not return after the end of the first term with their splits already then spermed?"

"Then I say that you will have a dozen replacements, Jack! But seriously, I see what you mean, and indeed I have thought on it. Perhaps I have been a little too cautious? Knowing girls can always feign virginity, of course, by wriggling, by tightening themselves up, and by crying out, and no doubt they would do so on receiving advice from me, for I am sure they are all sly enough at heart. Why, yes, Jack, I have decided—you may fuck them!"

"Samantha, too?" I asked cunningly, though I little suspected what effect such a question would have on Helen, who immediately wound her arms tighter around my neck.

"Oh, I feared this!" she declared. "Do you so love her and want her, then?"

Her tone of voice, such as I had never encountered before, brought a smile to my lips.

I replied fervently, "I adore her, of all the girls. . . ."

"Oh, no, Jack, please! Do you not love me?" she burst out.

Her tone was so petulant, girlish, and anxious that I smothered her face in kisses. At last it seemed I had cracked her facade, yet with Helen one never knew.

"Helen, I love you to distraction. Did you believe me? The girl is perfect of figure and wondrous to observe in all her movements. I want nothing better than to quell her finally under my cock, to flood her tight quim with my come. But, as to comparing her with you, what a nonsense! Has she your wit, your wisdom, your wickedness, your inventiveness, your adorableness?"

"No, of course she hasn't—I was but teasing you", came her reply, though she could not hide a certain light of relief in her eyes. "Well, now, I will tell Maude to bring the girls this evening. Do you want me in attendance?"

"No," I said bluntly, but then, seeing the look in her eyes I added, with a twinkle, "but you may remain in your study and peer through the peephole. It is my turn now!"

Clapping her hands and laughing, she agreed. Maude would be sent packing. It would be our own little *"théâtre érotique,"* as she called it. So all was arranged. Intrigued as she was at my mention of a dual device, Helen decided not to view it "before the curtain rose," as she said. Dinner was thus a special event, for we were both keyed up for the occasion, only Maude being a little put out that she was not also to enjoy whatever mysterious events were to occur. Comforted by Helen that she could, as a consolation prize, take one of the other girls to a private bedroom for the evening, she departed, having deposited the two comely maidens with me.

Helen absented herself from her study during their entrance, and thus they thought themselves completely alone with me. Both, I had no doubt, were overawed at finding themselves so and were plainly dying to ask what the purpose of their summons was.

In the study itself, I poured them each a liqueur, which they were glad to accept, being additionally tense by virtue of the fact that I had not asked them to sit. Both were bubbling to ask questions, but were too timid to do so. At last Victoria broke the silence and asked whether Madame was to attend on them.

"No," I answered curtly, "Victoria, you will accompany me first into my own study, which is through that door. Monique, you will remain here until called. Do you understand?"

I was not beguiled by the French girl's fluttering eyelashes or the appealing, liquid pools of her large dark eyes, much as she wished me to be for the purpose of effecting her escape. I offered her no view inside my den, but slipped Victoria quickly within. The four oil lamps I had arranged cast their lambent glow over all. Her eyes widened at what she saw and she stepped back. In a flash I had seized her wrist and drawn her against me.

"You will make no sound, Victoria, or I shall treat your bottom far more so than I intend to at the moment. Remove all but your shoes and stockings and go to the board, girl!"

"Oh, sir!"

With what apprehensive glances had she seen the device which I had had made in London by my chairmaker! I must therefore now describe it. In principle, it consisted of a large "board" some seven feet wide by six feet high. Handbuilt as it was in smooth and closely fitting pine planks, its base stood upon stout feet which were shaped in the manner of a claw. These, for a further purpose, which will be seen, stood upon casters. Just above the centre of the board and in line with each other were cut two perfectly round holes, each comfortably padded by horsehair within collars of leather.

In its horizontal dimension, the board was actually made in two halves, which could be made to part by turning a handle at either end. When the upper half was raised to its fullest extent, it enabled a girl's shoulders to be thrust through it. On being lowered, the two halves of the circles met again, thus imprisoning the intended victims by the waist. The centre of the board, from top to bottom, was hinged between the two circles. Thus the casters—for by using the hinge, the two halves could be made to form a large V and thereby two captive females would be facing one another.

"Oh, sir, what do you intend to do with me?" Victoria asked pleadingly. I passed my hand around her thinly veiled bottom, causing her hips to stir uneasily.

"Be a good girl and you may receive the same as you did in the stable. Come—display yourself as you have been taught to do!"

"Oh!" she gasped and blushed. Casting her eyes slyly all about as if in some last hope of escape, she raised her hands and commenced unbuttoning her dress. It was—under Maude's tuition—her only garment. Her black silk stockings were new, as were her strap-over shoes, whose low heels gave her thighs a deliciously plumpish look. Biting her lip, her face suffused and gazing ceilingward, Vitcoria waited whilst I walked slowly round her.

"Open your legs, Victoria—feet straddled—hands behind your neck!" I barked.

She jumped but obetyed, though moving her ankles so little from one another that I—facing her then—groped her pussy and cupped it. How soft and tickly the bunched curls were, and how luscious her slit! I felt its warmth and pulsing on my palm whilst I growled to her to improve her posture. Shuffling her toes uneasily and seeming almost too scared to breathe, she obeyed at last. Too easy a prize, I thought, but the image of the sport before me and the vision of her milky nudity and young curves had aroused my cock fiercely. Whilst she closed her eyes and trembled, I parted the lips of her quim with my forefinger and felt a slight mist of excitement there. Then ensued a brief conversation that I recall as if yesterday.

"What is the purpose of your strappings and birchings, Victoria?"

"Oh, sir, ooooh! To m . . . m . . . make me show my b . . . bottom better."

"And what else, pray?"

"S . . sir! Ah! Oh, your f . . . f . . . finger . . . I must k . . . keep my bottom up afterward and n . . . not move until I am told."

"And you will offer it then to the cock, Victoria?"

"Oh, sir, no, I could not—not as you did—oh, 'tis naughty—*Oh!* Oh, stop, please, no!"

Victoria's last cry came as I swung her off her feet and carried her struggling, to the board, the upper half of which was already raised. Kicking and crying as she was, I had her head and shoulders through the farther hole in a trice, then rapidly lowered the top half so that she was securely held. Her hips, bottom, and legs now displayed themselves on my side whilst the upper half of her body was hid from me. She would have collapsed, limp and doubled over had there not been a wooden bar, extended forward, for her to grip on the farther side. Thus was she held captive, her hips and bottom wriggling divinely beneath my eyes and her howls resounding.

Not hesitating any longer then, I threw open the door and espied Monique cowering by Helen's desk.

"Non, monsieur, non!" she screeched as I lifted her bodily and carried her within. *"Ah, que c'est horrible!"* sounded her cry then as she saw the jutting derriere and stockinged legs of Victoria, whose wails sounded with her own.

I dallied not with Monique, but by sheer force denuded her of her dress while her warm, sleek body wriggled like an eel. What a treasure she was! Victoria was herself superbly fuckable and cuddly, but the French girl had a figure infinitely more subtle in its blending of curves. Her high, polished breasts were as firm as melons—the berries of her brown nipples seeming ever stiff on the gelatinous mounds that were already sufficiently weighty to lure the palm. Her skin was as satin and flawless, her waist a mere twenty inches, yielding to the sensuous curving of her hips. The impudent bubbling of her tight round bottom seemed even more alluring than Samantha's.

"I tell all to Mama!—I tell all to Papa!" Monique shrieked whilst I yanked her, kicking and swinging under my arm, to the hole adjoining Victoria, whose sobs of anticipation ever came on. A flashing of sleek limbs, and Monique in turn was secured so that I now had the blissful spectacle of their naked bottoms side by side.

Lightly clad as I was, I stripped naked and took down from the wall a tawse. Then a further refinement struck me, which I put into immediate effect. Taking a broad leather cuff which I had fashioned for such a purpose, I squatted down and secured Monique's left ankle to Victoria's right one, thus ensuring that they were virtually unable to kick back.

"Non, non, non, non, monsieur!" came Monique's howl, for in rising I had brought the split ends of the tawse sharply across her perfect nether cheeks. Victoria screeched in echo with her on hearing a sound so familiar and one which, but two seconds later, resounded with as sharp a *Cra-aaaaack!* cross her own chubby

cheeks, which contracted so deliciously that I all but inserted my cock between them on the instant.

"*Yeeee-ooooh!*" came from Victoria.

"Don't do *eeeeet!*" came in an equally higher shriek from Monique, both their bottoms receiving stroke after stroke from the bottom-burning *sweeee-issssh!* of the tawse. A dull sheen of pink rose upon the impudent cheeks of both in no time, their bound ankles jerking together, whichever next received the leather forcing the other to kick as well.

My enthusiasm, however, must have overtaken me, for both had received a good dozen before the door opened and Helen entered. Walking swiftly and silently toward me, her fingers to her lips and on the blind side of the sobbing, hip-twisting pair, she stilled my hand whilst running her eyes mischievously up my straining prick.

"Permit me?" she whispered. I nodded, wondering what she was at as her feet next took her around the board so that she was able to confront the delectable pair. I, peeling round, saw her lift their chins one by one as they clung still to the extension bar.

"Now, girls, stop your silly crying," Helen declared. "Your bottoms have been well-warmed, but no more than they deserve to be. They look quite adorable wriggling as they are, and I'm perfectly sure you know it."

"Oh, Ma'am, p . . . p . . . please let us go!" Victoria sobbed, whilst Monique uttered her own pleas just as heartbrokenly.

"Do you know what I think you are?" Helen said by way of response. "I think you are two dreadful little flirts who adore taking men to the brink and then refusing them the satisfaction you appear to have offered. You have both had your drawers down often enough, so don't deny it, and I'm perfectly sure that you are both aware of the effect your unveiled pussies and bottom cheeks have in bringing the cock up. Well, you are both about to enjoy the effects of that, and Victoria shall be first."

"M . . . M . . . Madame, *no!*" came the wailing cry from Victoria, whom one would have thought a perfect innocent of a cherub who had not already entertained my corker in her bottom.

I needed no second bidding and was to the rear of her again in the instant, her hips waggling even more strenuously as she heard my footfalls. Her pretty quim, nestling in its bed of curls, was already sufficiently moist after her exertions to offer its cleft juicily to my knob. Settling it at the entrance and gripping her hips tightly whilst Helen remained for the moment on the other side, I spread Victoria's free leg wider and nosed my crest up slowly within the warm, spongy haven.

What spellbinding bliss it was! Truly I believe I enjoyed that first succulent moment more than I had done in entering her bottom in the stable.

"Wha-ooooh!" came her shriek. Lodged but two inches within, I exerted deeper pressure, felt the delicate membrane within yield and, to her piercing cry, rammed slowly full within until the warm butterball of her nether cheeks were couched into my belly, where they squirmed so enticingly that I almost came. In the same instant, groping Monique's furry cunt with my fingers I brought an echoing squeal from her.

A veritable pandemonium of sobs and moans then resounded as the steady sluicing of my cock and urging of my fingers under Monique's glossy hot bottom brought twittering cries from their hidden mouths. Helen reappeared then, her face glowing.

"Ooh-ah! Oooh-ah!" came now from Victoria, who was clearly taking some pleasure from the reaming of my stiff prober in her tightly gripping slit. Her cherry had been popped easily enough, it seemed, and evidently gave her little pain as the gentle grinding of her bottom cheeks against my belly evinced.

"Steady, my pet, you have to grind them both," Helen uttered for both to hear. "They know well enough they are to be put to the cock at the end of term. Let us hear them declare it—but first give Monique a taster!"

No sooner then had I withdrawn my flaming charger from its inviting dell than it presented itself in turn to Monique's figlike slit, which had already been well-lubricated by the ministrations of my fingers. Cupping the sleek, apple-round heaven of her tight bottom, I expected resistance within to the probing of my knob, such as I had encountered with Victoria. Instead, my stiff shaft slid as easily within as a warm knife into butter, bringing a bubbling moan from the girl and a faint look of surprise from Helen, who had observed well enough the ease of my passage. The bulbous bliss of Monique's bottom was held firm into me. My cock throbbed deliciously in her sleek nest, upon which she squeezed in fervent invitation.

My eyes blurred with the sensation of being so warmly ensconced in that velvety channel.

"M . . . M . . . *Mama!*" Monique howled, for all the good effect that such an utterance could produce, though I doubted not its fervour. Having stayed for a good four or five seconds within her, I withdrew my plunger and pistoned it yet again within whilst Helen, quite beside herself with the voluptuousness of the spectacle, knelt behind Victoria and applied the *"feuille de rose"* of her pointed tongue to her bottom whilst soothing her forefinger back and forth under her pouting slit.

The result of all this was to make me come rather sooner than I had expected. Realising a trifle too late that she had taken my cock all too easily, the artful Monique applied the nutcracker action by virtue of squeezing her vaginal muscles around my stiff pounder as if to assert a virginity long flown. For response, I rammed her faster, though finding her internal titillations such a delight that within a few seconds my sperm was squirting up within her in such long, thick shoots as made her oily passage work frenetically on my tool.

"Ah, you are coming, my love—pump her well, she has had it before!" Helen declared, roguishly reaching up to squeeze my balls very gently whilst they expended the last of their essence which rilled out around the lips of Monique's quim as I finally withdrew.

"Into the drawing room with them next," Helen then declared. Maude, having absented herself, the coast was clear, for all the girls were abed.

"Oh, what you *do* to me!" Monique howled, being the first to be released.

"No more than you have already had done to you, little minx," Helen replied, giving her a swift smack on her bottom. "Come! out with you—both of you! I will have no nonsense—and more, I will have the truth out of you. Bring the tawse, Jack, for I think they may need another taste of it."

This declaration brought forth further wails as the nubile pair were bustled along the corridor and into the greater comfort of Helen's drawing room, where the curtains were drawn and a small, cosy fire already lit. Sternly advising the two girls that neither was to utter a sound, she seated them side by side sobbing on the sofa while coolly pouring two glasses of liqueur, one of which she passed to me. Speculatively, she surveyed the "miscreants," who hid their eyes and looked for all the world like two lost angels.

"P . . . p . . . please, Madame, may I have a drink, I'm so thirsty!" Victoria uttered, uncovering her eyes and then veiling them again.

"Indeed you may in a moment, Victoria. Stand up, girl, and you too, Monique—face to face—*closer!* I want the tips of your noses touching. Heavens! Can you not move faster!" *Sweee-isssh!* sounded the teasewhip first across one luscious bottom and then another, until they leapt to obey with tiny shrieks and so stood, quivering in every limb, and presenting a most enervating spectacle with not only the tips of their noses touching, but their flat, glossy bellies and their nipples, too.

"You will speak first, Monique. I had thought you but a cock-teaser. Instead I find you to be a cock-taster. Is that not so?"

"Aaaah!" shrieked Monique as the thongs bit into her bottom once more. The deep pink flare left by the tawse had almost died away, leaving a translucent glow.

"Oh, *Madame!*"

"I am waiting, Monique. No, Victoria, do *not* move—not a muscle or you shall feel the tawse again. Place her hands on her hips, Monique, and press those naughty pussies together. Ah, how sweet! Do they not look so, Jack?"

I agreed fervently. With their naked bodies pressed together, their bottoms bulbing out on either side, their black stockings and schoolgirlish shoes, they made an extremely erotic picture.

"D . . . d . . . do not make me say, Madame!" Monique pleaded.

"Oh! I am thirsty!" wailed her companion, her thighs quivering gently against the other girl's.

"Very well. Monique—throw your head back. I will fill your mouth with wine. You will *not* swallow it. You will pass every drop into Victoria's mouth, and then she in turn will do the same. Perhaps then I may let you off your naughty confession. Mouth open, girl!"

I watched entranced, my pego lifting up anew. With cheeks puffed out with a full glassful of wine that Helen had poured in, Monique held Victoria's hips a little tighter and pressed her lips to hers. A soft bubbling sound came from both as the wine transmitted itself between their mouths. Then, at a word from Helen, Victoria raised her face in turn and the operation was performed to what I perceived as much excited working of their tongues.

"They are coming more on heat, Jack," Helen whispered to me. "You will fuck Victoria next. Two more glasses, and then . . ."

I could scarce wait. Wine trickled from the corners of their pretty mouths as they were brought to absorb, one from the other, the additional libations which left both so heady that Victoria but uttered a moan as they were separated and I swiftly laid her upon the rug.

"Knees drawn up, hands behind your head!" commanded Helen, whilst taking hold on the waist of Monique, who swayed hip to hip against her. Victoria obeyed as in a daze, but the eager little movements of her bottom showed well enough her desire as I lowered myself between her spread thighs.

"Reach down and rub my prick gently—then insert it," I murmured. Her hot-flushed face, wine-scented lips, the stiffness of her nipples on her firm tits and the delicious feeling of her stockinged thighs grazing mine was a delicate ecstasy as she obeyed. Fumbling blindly and finding at last my rigid stander, she soothed it so gently that I well suspected her to have handled a prick other than mine before the stable incident.

Murmuring incomprehensibly and with her head undoubtedly swimming as much as my own was under the silent excited gaze of the pair who stood beside us, she grazed my swollen knob briefly against her pouting cuntlips and then fumbled it within.

"Your tongue, Victoria! Slip it into his mouth, then return your hands behind your head," came Helen's voice. With that, the warm slithering of her tongue came upon my own. I cupped her round bottom, drawing it up clear of the rug and felt her belly give an answering quiver as I sheathed myself slowly in her spongy dell. With her hands at the back of her neck and her knees drawn widely up, she presented a perfect picture of voluptuous pleasure. Mingling our moans together, I rodded her smoothly until my balls hung beneath her bottom.

Victoria bubbled softly into my mouth, her tongue more greedily working while I allowed the full nine inches of my pego to throb its pleasure in her. A murmuring of voices came to me from above as our pubic hairs meshed.

"Only once, Monique, and you have teased him ever since?"

"Oui, Madame—oh! do not tell, I could not help, Mama she go crazy. Now he strap and kiss me—he feel me—I am naughty—I feel his thing, so big, but then I must not—I pull my drawers up quick."

"You bad, naughty girl, Monique!"

A slap and a squeal came to my ears, but I was blind to all but the luscious squirming of Victoria beneath me as now I began to sleek my pestle back and forth, her breasts forming two perfect elastic mounds under my chest. Her bottom wriggled amourously on my palms.

"You know better now, Monique?"

"*Whoooo!* Oh, Madame, your f . . . f . . . finger! Oui! I obey now, I give! *Oooh,* Madame!"

Victoria's rushing breath cascaded into my mouth. My cock, flashing ever faster, was sucked in at every forward stroke. Unable to control herself any longer, she threw her arms about my neck and hung literally beneath me, I cradled her slim form in my grasp as I fucked her ever more vigourously. A thump, and Helen fell beside us. Her hand, grasping Monique's hair, thrust her face between her open thighs.

"Lick, Monique! *Ah! lêches-moi!*"

A gurgling and a lapping sounded. Helen's arm reached for my neck, dragging my face over upon hers. Her hips bucked, bumping her bottom on the carpet at the edge of the rug. Slewed sideways now upon Victoria, I felt her stockinged legs jerk down stiffly, her belly rising and knew that she was coming. A soft rattling cry burst from her throat. In that instant, Helen's long tongue entered my mouth. I groped her bared breasts. With a quivering groan, I expelled my strings of sperm within Victoria's clinging cunt as the answering heaves of her bottom signalled her own attainment of bliss.

Chapter 15

SUCH an explosion of lust I had not expected, nor perhaps had Helen, who confessed that she had gone farther than she meant. But at least, as she said, both girls were more thoroughly prepared now, albeit a trifle prematurely.

The next morning brought news of the impending arrival of Samantha's parents, two days hence. Samantha was not to be apprised of the visit, as we agreed. Maude was told and so, too, was Lucy. She had been kept in purdah by Helen for such an event and was plainly bubbling over with frustration, for Helen made no bones about talking of our conquests in front of her. Several times Lucy had been set to the peephole to see how young ladies were best subdued and seduced, but Helen had not allowed her upon my cock.

Helen's spirits now were plainly higher than ever. The restrictive attitudes she had applied relaxed more after our little orgy with Victoria and Monique.

"What is done is done," she said philosophically. "I am minded to have several other of the girls fucked now for good measure. It is such a perfect delight to see it, Jack. You may deal with Belinda after lunch. I have no doubt of her virginity, but in the circumstances that I also know of, naught will dare be said about the loss of it. Indeed, it might he thought an improvement!"

Belinda, the daughter of a wealthy curate, was a comely, well-built girl with a splendid pair of legs and a plump bottom. She had the most modest and innocent air of all our incumbents. She would scarce uncross her legs save to sit down, Helen told me, and whinnied like a filly under the birch, which hitherto had been applied only through her drawers.

"You may tease her to distraction, Jack. She has been neither feathered nor fingered yet and will cause a great to-do about it, I am sure. When she is brought under, she will prove as lusty a fuck as she is intended to be. The passions of Priapus are yet to be aroused in her. Her breasts have been fondled—in the seclusion of the church vestry, as I gather—and she is exceedingly sensitive in that area. Her mouth opens, her eyes glaze, and she can do naught but whimper. Her bottom, thighs and all are as statuesque as you could ever wish. Her cunny needs a good creaming before we send her back to the vicarage, where she will then receive regular doses."

"Leave all to me, my love," I declared happily, "but pray, what will you do?"

"I shall observe from The Snuggery, Jack, with Lucy. It will work her up perfectly and have her in good prime for Lady Edwardes."

Hence, at three-thirty precisely, the sacrificial maiden was led within by Maude. Upon seeing me waiting alone, she started back, but received only a push forward for her pains. Her dress was of brown silk, buttoned from neck to waist, her lush brown hair piled and pinned up. Rouge had been applied to her lips, which apparently she resented. The size of her breasts were those of a matron, rather than a twenty-one-year-old. Of middle height, and with small feet that twinkled out from below the hem of her dress, she had a round face that in time would grow podgy, but for the present was pretty in a sulky way.

"Wh . . . whaaaat?" she began, looking round wildly for Helen.

"Belinda—come here!" I snapped. She advanced several feet toward me, hesitated, and received another push in the back from Maude, which sent her thrusting against me, her titties bumping heavily onto my chest. It was exactly the opportunity I wanted. I clasped her waist immediately and held her as a look of perfect horror passed over her features.

"Sir! Let me go!"

Her hands beat feebly at my shoulders. Maude divined my purpose immediately and, drawing out the wooden leg-restrainer from beneath the divan, forced the girl's legs apart and clipped one end to her left ankle. Such shrieks and alarums came then from Belinda that I was hard put to hold her, but increasing my bearhug did so. By virtue of pushing upon the end of the rod she had already secured, Maude was enabled to prevent her from kicking. In a trice both her legs were secured and held wide apart.

"Oh! I shall die of this!" Belinda howled, for in rising Maude gathered up the girl's dress, gliding the hem up the backs of her calves, into the bends of her knees, and above until the ivory columns of her thighs were exposed and—above them, to my amusement—brown silk drawers.

"If you do not *stop!* Oh! I can't bear the shame of this!" Belinda wailed as her dress was firmly tucked up about her tummy, leaving the white skin around and above her whorled navel exposed.

"*Ah!* Don't you *dare!*"

Belinda's shriek rose almost in anticipation of the busy hands of Maude, who then thrust fingers and thumbs into the waistband of her drawers and drew

them down with ceremonial majesty until they were
wreathed tightly just below the maiden's stocking tops,
which themselves were of brown lisle. Unable to stretch
back from me lest she fall fully onto her back, Belinda
beat again at my chest till I, having enough of this
sport, took both wrists and—cautioning her sharply to
remain upright—moved behind her and fastened them
securely.

"The authorities! I shall inform the authorities!"
came Belinda's wild wailing cry as I was now able to
perceive her treasures more closely whilst she stood
sobbing and swaying with her legs forcibly spraddled.

Her bottom was large for her age—noble indeed in
aspect—but perfectly round, glossy, and flawless save
for a dimple on either protruding cheek. Her thighs
would in time become majestic, but now were exceedingly voluptuous and made to look the more so by the
tight bands of her stockings. Her bush, darker in colour
than her coiffure, was superb. The bunching of curls
was luxuriant, making her pubic mound look appetis-
ingly plump. A howl of total disbelief came from her as
I, standing sideways to her, reached beneath and fondled the rolled petals of the lips of her cunt.

"Let me go-oh-*Oh!*"

"The first fondling of your delicious cunt, my pet?" I
asked ironically. "You shall take my cock there first,
Belinda, before you are mounted in the vestry. The
feather, Maude! Tickle her bottom up a little whilst I
expose her tits."

"You beasts! You horrid, filthy beasts! Ah God, if
you do not stop . . . *Wha-aaah!*"

No sooner had the tip of the feather sought between
her bottom cheeks than I unbuttoned her dress at the
front. From the sagging folds of silk on either side there
loomed into my hand the wondrous globes of her—
each large milk-white melon crowned with a thick berry
of a nipple.

"Oh, what a lovely fat bottom she has. You will have to inject it as well," chortled Maude, who was in fine fettle in the physical absence of Helen, whose eye, I knew, must be glued to the peephole.

Belinda, sobbing, howling, and uttering occasional imprecations, dared not sway in any direction as I weighed her luscious mammaries in my palms. My thumb brushed first one stublike nipple and then the other. Immediately they rose, extending themselves to a full half-inch and coursing their points into the skin of my palm. Causing her tits to wobble about so, I caressed them with a fervency that I sensed she had previously experienced, for her louder cries petered away and the selfsame glazed look of which Helen had spoken began to appear in her eyes. With my free hand I cupped the plump bulge of her bottom at its lowest curve, beneath Maude's hand.

"Jack, hold her cheeks open. Heavens, she has such a deep groove I can hardly get it in," Maude jerked.

To a high-pitched squeal from Belinda, I obeyed. The weightiness of her bottom was superb and was heightened by the surprising slimness of her waist. Making to rock forward as she did, I was forced to fling one arm backward about her waist, by which time, having fully exposed her crinkled rosette, the feather was well inserted.

"No-no-no-*No!* I can't bear it! Oh, the horror of this!"

I confronted her again in a flash and calmly lifted both hands to weigh her glossy tits again, once more titillating her sharpened nipples so that her howl broke into moans, her mouth petulant, eyelashes fluttering.

"More, Jack—I want to get more in!" Maude uttered from below. Leaving Belinda's tits, I released my straining cock swiftly and reached behind her, so pressing it against the tickling of her thick bush whilst once more I prised her bottom cheeks apart. Her screech all but shattered my ear.

"I cant bear it, I can't bear it, oh, I can't *bear* it!"

Undulating her hips between us, she bounced her belly madly whilst the insidious feather pursued its course up within her tight rosehole and twirled with all the expertise that Maude now commanded. I, reaching in my pocket for a length of cord, then wound it about her waist and tied it to her left wrist whilst releasing her other hand. I doubt now that it would have raised itself to strike me had I not seized it.

"Play with my cock, girl, for that is what you were sent here to learn," I growled.

"No! I will never, I will *never!*"

"Maude—insert the feather to its fullest and fetch the whip!"

Maude was up in a flash, leaving the end of the feather protruding lewdly from between the plump cheeks. Within but three seconds she had brought the thongs swishing up beneath the bulge of them, causing the wildest sobs and howls to come from the girl who, in endeavouring to retreat from the stings of the thong-tips only succeeded in squirming her silken belly against my throbber.

"Yee-eee-eee-eeeek!"

"Hold my prick, girl!"

"No, no, I cannot, dare not—stop it—*Ow!* I can't bear it, I can't bear it!"

"Harder, Maude!"

I stepped back, my prick jutting up, reaching my hand forward to cup one of her superb tits so that she would not overbalance. *Sweee-isssh! Sweee-ish!* the thongs hissed, making Belinda throw her head back, her heels of her shoes coming off the floor so that she was poised too delicately even to sway her hips.

"I won't, I won't, I wo-oh-on't!" she shrieked anew, her breasts juddering against my fondling palm.

"No more, Maude! To the couch with her!"

Dear God, I admired Belinda's stubbornness as, with wildly kicking legs, she was carried bodily to the narrower of the two divans which I had modified slightly. While narrow enough to ensure that the victim's legs normally flopped down wide apart, with the heels hanging over both edges, I had affixed beneath it two rods which drew out from sockets and held ankle straps at the ends. To these, Belinda's silk-clad ankles were promptly secured whilst Maude held her shoulders. It being impossible for her then to rise even into a sitting position, I stepped back and surveyed her.

Such was the position of the rods, some little distance up from the end of the divan, that her knees were held flexed, her thighs being open in a wide V. This, exposing her cunny, showed the gleaming of its lips and the salmon-pink interior beyond. Such long pubic hairs as strayed into the inner surfaces of her thighs at the tops gave her an even more sensuous air of abándonment. A moan of despair escaped her, head twisting from side to side as I lifted her hips as Maude withdrew the almost-buried feather from her bottom by groping beneath her.

"Oh! I beg you-ooh-ooooh!" Belinda sobbed, perceiving me take up another with an even finer feathery tip. Well-spread as she was, I had no need to touch her other than to graze her further thigh with my knuckles as I passed the seeking feather upward and brushed it against the small pink nub of her clitty. Her reaction was immediate, her bottom rising a clear inch off the divan. Her back arched.

"No-oh! No-oh!—No-*Oh!*" Her free hand beat the air and fell. The other, being captive behind her, Maude released it and then set to tonguing and sucking her nipples.

"Na-ah-ah-aaaah!" Belinda moaned. Her hips rotated as the insidious tip of the feather worked about her little exciter. Her eyes rolled upward until all but the rims of her pupils showed. Her belly tightened and then shimmered. The blissful crisis was approaching. The moment need no longer be delayed.

My trousers were off in a flash. A wild shriek from Belinda, and I was upon her. Gaping slightly as was her succulent slit under the constant titillation she had received, my knob sank in to a softness and moisture as sweet as that of a split pumpkin. My arms wound about her hips. A low, moaning cry sounded from her. Her hands clawed at my shoulders. With a single lunge, I buried my shaft and held it throbbing within her enticing nest.

The sounds that came from her then were truly inexpressible. Her hips bucked as if to dislodge me, but instead succeeded only in affording me the most voluptuous quivers. Then, with her lips parted and the prettiest of tears on her cheeks, she lay suddenly quiescent. Passing my hands down under her I palmed the superb hemispheres of her bottom and whispered coaxingly at her ear, working my lips about her soft cheek.

Belinda's hands strained and clawed at me.

"Is this not better than merely having your titties felt?" I asked. The thick brush of hairs on her mound made a voluptuous pad on which to press my own. Keeping my cock still full within her, I felt her strain her plump bottom full onto my palms. Then, as if by some legerdemain, the clamping of her cuntlips around the root of my pulsing weapon tightened and I knew her to be coming. Her lips compressed and then parted again in an expression of wonder.

"Work your bottom, my pet—you are coming," I breathed.

"Oh, yes!" she gasped. I withdrew my cock almost to the knob and pistoned it slowly up again even as a fine misty rain sprinkled upon it. Her thighs trembled and pressed silkily against my own. Her bottom shifted gently. With head hung back and her eyes now wide open, she appeared to be in a total daze or, as I suspected, the arisen dream of some long-quenched lust.

Within the study now, whilst Maude sat upon the floor watching with fascination, was total silence, save for the faint creaking of the divan and our deep breathing as I measured the length and power of my strokes, nibbling at one moment upon her stark nipples and at the other upon her cherry mouth.

"You are being fucked, Belinda—is it not what you needed?" I asked.

"Oh, yes! Oh, kiss me!"

So girlish, sweet, and innocent was her voice, yet her hips and bottom worked now as sensuously as any woman's. Absorbing my tongue, she licked the tip of it as delicately as a butterfly hovering about a flower, her breath flowing warmly within my mouth as I commenced reaming her in earnest. Truly, she was a luscious fuck, her cunt as juicy and clinging as any I have known. My balls smacked against the lower bulge of her bottom in our rising passion.

"Fuck, Belinda, fuck! Say the word!" I ground out.

"F . . . f . . fuck! Oh, fuck!" she moaned. "Oh, I want to!"

How long she had repressed herself, I know not, but she became now as a veritable fireball, churning her hips violently so that her slit mouthed back and forth of its own accord along my straining tool. Our bellies smacked together. Our mouths meshed in a fury of desire.

"Come over my cock, Belinda!"

"Yes! Ah! *Ooooh!*"

The fine liquid essence spurted from within her, trickling, burning, and itching over my balls and impelling from my sheathed penis the celebratory jets of sperm which Belinda received with wriggling pleasure, her nails digging into my shoulders in the urgency of her pleasure.

Tremoring and quivering, she sucked upon me to the last and then lay soft and quiet, her stiff nipples stinging into my chest like thorns. Affording her a last salutory kiss upon the mouth, I withdrew my steaming organ and arose, leaving Maude to lavish kisses upon her in turn. Retreating quietly whilst the pair lay in a tender embrace, I entered The Snuggery, where Helen immediately threw herself into my arms.

"Ah, Jack, how she was fucked! What a lustful mount she proved—did I not tell you? As for Lucy—oh, the wicked girl—raise your skirt, dear, and let Jack feel you."

The wanton maid uncovered herself to her belly with scarce a blush and parted her shapely legs to my palm which, gliding under her bush, found the lips puffy and wet. Lucy quivered and would have sagged against me had her Mistress not given her a light smack on her bottom.

"No, Lucy, not yet! You will have full pleasure in a day or two. Have I not promised you?"

"Yes, Ma'am."

Even so, her hips gave an impudent little twist, squishing her cuntlips over my cupping hand before she stepped back and dropped her skirt, her eyes hot with longing.

"Now, Jack, you may prove your virility," Helen said, nodding toward the adjoining room. "I will have her bottom breached, for I suspect she will take particular pleasure from it at the moment, and that, no doubt, is the first route that her fond Papa will wish to take, so we must ensure she is not over-tight there. Can you manage that little chore, d'you think?"

"I believe it to be possible," I answered gravely, "but upon one promise—that Sir Edwardes and I shall pleasure pretty Lucy in turn after we have concluded matters with Samantha."

A squeal came from Lucy and a laugh from Helen, who put her arm about the girl's waist.

"So be it—she will be in a fine froth for it by then. Go, my dear, and breach the portcullis!"

By the time I re-entered the study, Belinda was sitting with Maude beside her, both partaking of a strengthening liqueur. The greater flow of passion being passed from her, Belinda cast her eyes down and blushed at the sight of my cock again. That she would need to be inducted rudely into the new path of pleasure, I did not doubt. My penis already stirred again at the thought of the rich hemispheres between which it would soon be buried. Reading my intention well, Maude took their empty glasses and laid them to one side, whereat Belinda gave a start and made to jump up.

"You must show your bottom now, Belinda," Maude said gently.

"Oh no!" Her hands covered her face. She would have bent forward over her knees had I not taken her chin firmly and raised it.

"The lessons of obedience must be instilled in you, Belinda, until you have learned to offer yourself," I said sternly. Forced to look up at me, her eyes flooded with tears, but I knew the wiles of woman well. Such tears would undoubtedly be one of her attractions. Her lips worked as if she were about to speak, but no sound came.

"I will fetch the strap, Jack," Maude declared and rose.

"No, please!" Belinda quavered. "Oh, if you will just let me get up. Please release my legs!"

"Stand, then," I said and drew her up, the awkwardness of her position showing itself as she was forced to shuffle into position with my cock stirring thickly against her white belly. In order to turn her I would have to lift her, as she well knew. Her eyes widened in anticipation of my clasping arms, her hands beat feebly against my shoulders.

"No!" she shrieked.

Her hips swivelled madly beneath the clamping of my arms about her waist. Bared flesh bumped against my prick, stinging it further into life as at last I had her spun full round so that she had no recourse but to slump forward and support herself on her hands, which rested on the edge of the couch. I, gripping the ribbons of her dress around her waist, restrained her from falling just as one reins a horse. Maude thereupon sat quickly next to her and, passing her right hand under her sticky quim, cupped it fondly.

"I believe she knows already what you intend, Jack!" she laughed.

"I do *not!*" Belinda wailed, though there was little enough conviction in her tone.

"No doubt she has been felt up here already," I teased, rolling the ball of my thumb about the rosy orifice which nestled between the glorious cheeks.

"No-*oh!*"

"Oh, what a story!" Maude uttered, moving her fingers meanwhile in a rolling motion about Belinda's clitty which, sensitive and swollen as it was, made her churn her hips exactly as I wanted. The bulging of her bottom rubbed sensuously against my cock.

"Are you not fibbing. Belinda? Have you not had a hand in your drawers at this very spot before?" I asked, pressing my thumb more firmly against her rosehole.

"*No!* Oh! Do not put it in! I beg you, no!"

"You are in the confessional now, Belinda. Lest you tell all, I shall have my cock full in your bottom."

"Belinda, what a naughty tease you are! Oh, how you are wriggling! Is it nice? Put your prick in, Jack!" Maude cried.

"No! don't! *Ah!* Yes, once. He w . . . w . . . was feeling my breasts and put his hand down my knickers."

"Like this?"

I inserted the tip of my forefinger at the words, making her squirm violently.

"Yes—*Ah!*"

"Go on, Belinda."

"It m . . . m . . . made me feel faint. I cried to him to stop—he . . . he . . . he had his hand on my breasts. Oh, I feeel dizzy! No! do not do it! *Aaaaargh!* Take it out!"

Too late! My knob was at her portal. The insidious working of Maude's fingers around her slit made her knees sag, hence bulbing her bottom out perfectly for my purpose. Tight as the rim of her bottomhole was, it yielded. Amid all her moans and cries, the rubbery ring gave, absorbing the crest of my penis and thereby allowing it to slip within the oily channel. Flexing my knees and holding her wavering hips firmly, I inserted the long, thick peg slowly to a gritting screech from Belinda that died away into a febrile moan. With four inches inserted, I held there for a long second and then drew her hips back powerfully toward me, so that the movement served to cork her to the full.

"*Wha-ah-ah-aaaah!*" Belinda howled, her round silken cheeks nestling firmly into my stomach.

"Wait, Jack!" Maude uttered. Sliding back on the divan, she brought her legs together and then eased them between Belinda's and my own, so sinking down and forward that her mouth came perfectly under the girl's hairy quim.

"*Whooooo!*" Belinda moaned, her cunny now as deeply invaded by Maude's flickering tongue as was her bottom by my prick. A lecherous little movement of her hips made itself felt. The signs of her oncoming pleasure were undeniable. Bending full over her back, I cupped her wobbling tits and commenced moving my cock slowly back and forth in her heavenly tightness.

"Your tongue, Belinda!" I croaked.

Her neck turned. Face flushed, mouth open, she lolled her tongue cowlike into my mouth whilst the steady lapping of Maude's sounded beneath. Breath rushing out warmly over my own, Belinda commenced responding ever more eagerly by rolling and surging her bottom cheeks to my thrusts.

"Little bitch, how frequently he will bugger you now, will he not?" I mouthed.

"Yes!" she confessed hotly. Her lust was well up, her bottom gripping upon me like a clam. "Ah! *Oooh!* Do it! I want it!"

I felt Maude's legs kick between my own, her hand working busily between her thighs, where she had drawn up her skirt. Her gentle spluttering announced the salty libation that was spurting upon her lips from Belinda's quim. Unable to hold back any longer, I corked the delicious girl to the full and squirted the powerful jets of my warm essence into her very bowels as her tongue worked avariciously in my mouth.

Had not Maude had the mind to escape in that moment by drawing herself quickly up again, Belinda would have smothered her in her falling, still gripping my pulsing cock as she was. Her arms floundered, a vibration shook her, and then she lay still. Couched upon the velvet cheeks I held my prick inserted for yet a long, blissful moment until I slowly uncorked.

Maude threw herself down on the farther end of the divan, wiping her sodden mouth.

"Oh, what a lovely do!" she laughed "If only Madame could have seen it!"

These words being but to disarm Belinda, I kissed her quivering nether cheeks and released her legs from the restrainer. Rolled over onto her back, she flung her arm over her eyes.

"How wicked I have been!" she murmured in wonderment. I moved her stockinged legs wide apart, giving her thigh a tap as she made for a moment to close them and then sighed and relaxed. The thick curls around her mound shone wet with the spurting of her essences and the labours of Maude's tongue.

"You have restrained yourself too long, Belinda," I chided her. "You will scarce need to be birched in future—or perhaps just a touch of it."

She laughed shyly, choking upon the laugh as if she should not have let it escape.

"Yes, just a touch," she whispered and hid her face.

Chapter 16

HELEN had set her plans concerning Samantha so well and with such precision that it was as if we were about to act out a well-rehearsed play. How the unknowing "artistes" would react was another matter, but we had few doubts about our prowess in that direction.

That Lady Edwardes and her husband should be first separated on arrival was essential to the scheme. To this end Lucy was to provide a diversion and was attired as if she were a Mistress, which is to say fairly primly and in black. Another "innocent" to be brought into the scheme was Victoria. Helen made sure that she was coddled and spoilt during the days preceding the visit, so that the charming girl quite preened herself. However, her eyes dimmed uncertainly when Helen instructed her as to her role—though she knew it not to be that.

Sir Humphrey Edwardes, it was explained to her, was an institutional inspector of the highest rank. He would expect to see the manner in which the girls were disciplined. Victoria, of course, started at these words and looked fairly apprehensive.

"We have chosen you, Victoria, because we quite

consider you our star pupil," Helen told her glibly and
went on. "I shall be a trifle occupied at the time, and
hence Lucy will be deputed to deal with you. Fear not,
however, that your pretty bottom will really suffer
thereby. Lucy has strict instructions to strap you gently.
However, I do wish you to howl and wriggle exceedingly as if you were really under it. The gentleman in
question will then surely be perfectly satisfied that we
know how to keep things in order. You will do that for
me, I know."

"Oh, well, Madame . . . ," began Victoria nervously and twisted her hands together.

"Really, Victoria, do you not trust me? Think what a
splendid report I shall be able to write upon you at the
end of term. Much better than that of any other girl, I
do assure you."

"Well, Ma'am, all right, Ma'am. You promise she
won't strap me hard?"

Helen thereupon smiled and whispered something in
her ear which caused Victoria to giggle and blush. Afterward, having asked Helen what was said, she apprised me that she had simply told Victoria that she was
well aware that the girl had a secret taste for her
bottom-warmings and more so for what came after, and
that plenty of that would follow if she obeyed.

Thus our little scene was set, though Victoria knew
not the real purpose of it all and, not daring to address
Sir Humphrey, would never know.

The sun shone upon our venture, wicked as it was.
At three precisely on the appointed day, the dull blue-
and gold-striped carriage of the aristocratic pair arrived. I, being of a purpose attired as a footman,
gravely descended the steps at its approach and assisted
Lady Edwardes down. She was not, I was pleased to
see, gross of figure, being in her early forties and possessing a figure neither plump nor thin and seemingly
firm in all the appropriate areas.

Upon taking my hand, she gave me a small but disdainful smile, for which I inwardly swore that she would pay as equally as ever had Lady Betty. Descending from the carriage, she immediately loosened her fingers and waited upon the gravel drive for her husband to join her. He was, as I suspected he might be, a man of military aspect with a finely twirled moustache and somewhat sunburnt from a sojourn in India. Nodding gravely to me, he nevertheless looked a trifle apprehensive. I doubted not the reasons for this since he, far better than Lady Edwardes, knew the purpose of the establishment.

"I take it that the Principal is ready to see us?" asked Lady Edwardes haughtily.

"She is waiting in great expectancy," I replied. We had neared the steps and were mounting them. With rising nervousness, Sir Humphrey fell back a little, which was perfect for our design, since Lucy then appeared from within and sidled against him as we made our entrance.

"Sir, may I speak to you for a moment?" she asked in a hushed voice.

Great wonderments no doubt arose in his mind, believing it perhaps to concern Samantha. He nodded, for she succeeded in drawing him aside whilst with perfect timing, Maude appeared and greeted Lady Edwardes with a smile, declaring her great pleasure at her arrival. Before the dear lady knew it, she found herself being whisked along to the study, quite unconscious of the fact that her husband was not in her wake.

As to that gentleman's initial adventures, I must recount them as if I had been present—the play being performed on two stages in its commencement.

"Is it Semantha?" he asked Lucy, who replied that it was not, though he would see her soon enough. Curiosity then drew him on, having learned that it was "another of the girls." He was then led to a private bedroom, the door being swiftly opened and closed upon them. There, to his profound astonishment—and obvious pleasure—he spied Victoria kneeling, sobbing on a bed, in great pretence of having been strapped. For good purpose, Lucy had smacked her several times on her bottom, so leaving a faint rosy glow upon the refulgent cheeks which saucily faced Sir Humphrey on his entrance.

I will dwell not on this episode, however, which was intended solely to placate and arouse him. That it did so in double-quick time was obvious from Lucy's later description. Attired as Victoria was in but a flimsy chemise and best silk stockings, she presented an ardent offering which wriggled enticingly whilst Lucy demonstrated briefly "our method of strapping."

Sir Humphrey's erection was plainly visible under his trousers in no time at all, and very willingly indeed did he inspect Victoria's flushed bottom more closely at the invitation of Lucy, who chanced to pass her hand as if accidentally across his trousers at the same time.

"The purpose, of course, is discipline, sir—to make the pupils keep it up," she explained whilst Victoria hid her face and plumped her bottom up to show her fig and Lucy quite entranced him by feeling his hidden cock more boldly. "As an *inspector*, sir," Lucy went on, giving him a nudge, "you are permitted to feel the girls to make sure that all is in order. You will find this one quite moist from her exertions."

"An inspector, eh what? Ah, yes, of course, I say!" burbled the gentleman who thought he had the whole thing thoroughly twigged.

Suffice to say that within a minute or two, urged silently on by Lucy, he had his knob well in between the succulent lips of Victoria's quim—she receiving him with a squeal of surprise and a prompt jerk forward that dislodged him.

"Your pardon, sir," said Lucy, putting herself then

between them and grasping his cock at the same time, "the girl is backward still, I fear, but there are others who are not so. Shall we try another. Such as Samantha," she whispered so that Victoria could not hear.

"By Jove, yes, but I fear she may be with my wife," responded Sir Humphrey, who must have found himself in a highly mixed state of frustration and excitement.

"Your wife, sir? Ah, yes, she is inspecting also?" responded Lucy smoothly—or so she would have had us believe afterward. "I will take you to her—come."

"I say, but hold on, it might be a trifle, well—you know—embarrassing what?"

"Not at all, we have all things perfectly under control here, as you will see," he was assured, being led out with his cock still jutting rudely up from his trouser gap. "I beg you, sir, only to make no sound during the proceedings. You will see the reason for it soon enough," he was told and thereupon led along to a small room, normally unused, which abutted on to the study and in the wall of which I had drilled two peepholes.

In the meantime, the proceedings in Helen's study had already commenced and, in order not to have to move the stage around too much, I had placed my boarding device at the very door of my Snuggery, so that it could be wheeled in when required. On entering, Lady Edwardes had found Helen quietly seated at her desk, making a great do of studying papers. This scene of calm was not to obtain for long, however.

Lady Edwardes appeared quite piqued that Helen had not at least bowed to her and, seating herself, addressed her quite rudely on the subject of the establishment.

"I wish to know—and I wish to know plainly—what is the nature of your so-called correctional exercises," she declared and crossed her legs. I, watching from The Snuggery, viewed this simple change of posture with pleasure for it would keep her off balance when I approached from behind.

"We strap their bottoms, Madame. They are bared first, of course. The birch is sometimes applied. The cane is also used as a correctional instrument," replied Helen without batting an eyelid.

"The st . . . st . . . strap? On their bare bottoms?" echoed the dame in great indignation.

"Does not Samantha have her knickers removed at home for disciplinary purposes? I trust that she does. Heavens, she is old enough for it," Helen answered. No flicker of her expression betrayed the fact that I—having stripped myself down to shirt and trousers—had now entered silently behind Lady Edwardes and was approaching her stealthily.

"My God, how dare you, you frightful woman! Never would I permit my husband to do such an unspeakable thing! I shall have her out of here on the instant! *Pmfffff!*"

This last exclamation was occasioned by the fact that in that instant I lowered a black velvet bag over her head which enveloped the whole of her face and neck. A muffled screech of surprise and anger sounded from beneath it, and her hands would have clawed it off had I not whipped my arms beneath her armpits, bending her head forward with my hands and—dragging her bodily off her chair—hauled her with many muffled screams to the divan. There, whilst I held her shoulders, Helen quickly forced her legs apart and secured her ankles to the restraining rods which—as shall be seen—I had adapted.

Thus made as helpless as Belinda or any other of the divan's occupants had been, Lady Edwardes had her hood removed.

"Ah! you beasts! You filthy beasts!" she screamed, for I then was already in process of raising her dress.

"Be *quiet*, woman!" snapped Helen, who, having

swiftly changed places with me, was now poised on the side of the couch and had dampened any further cries for the moment by clamping her hand firmly over Lady Edwardes's mouth. "Your daughter is in an adjoining room. She will well hear your cries. Do you wish her to listen to anything so humiliating!"

Lady Edwardes's eyes bulged, her cheeks becoming florid. Not only had she heard clearly enough, but I had by now raised her dress and underskirt to her waist, uncovering thereby a noble pair of thighs —plump and well-fleshed—gartered stockings and a pair of Directoire drawers of purple hue.

Seeing that our prey was all but ready, Helen removed her hand from Lady Edwardes's mouth and just as promptly pinched her nose, bringing a perfect squawk from the lady's throat. Soothing her other hand about her throat, whereon shone a fine necklace of pearls, Helen then began with feminine delicacy to unfasten one by one the buttons of a bodice which was considerably thrust up by the breasts beneath.

"For God's sa-ay-ay-ake!" squealed Lady Edwardes, despite all warnings, whilst I loosed the silk ties of her drawers and, reaching beneath her big bottom, commenced rolling them down.

Helen immediately clapped her free hand over her mouth again whilst continuing to pinch her nostrils. "Hush now!" she declared in a tone one might use to a wailing infant. "We intend to remove your drawers, my dear, to inspect your treasures—as I hope they may be called—and then to tickle you up a little whereby to extract a few of your naughty secrets. I'm sure you have some. Be sure, however, that you whisper them to me or Samantha will hear. Ah, Jack, you've got her!" she exclaimed as I drew down Lady Edwardes's most intimate garment to her knees, clipped the fine cotton in twain with a pair of scissors, and drew the two halves off.

What bubblings and hissings of breath came then from the prostrate lady, whose cunny was now revealed together with all else! For, whilst she strove furiously to prevent me, I utilised my adjustment of the securing rods to which her ankles were held splayed apart. I had them now in runners beneath the divan and, by forcing them in the direction of her shoulders, as it were, made her knees bend sharply. Held thus in the most lewd of postures, Lady Edwardes displayed not only her well-furred quim, but sufficient of her bottom to ensure that its rosette could be reached by a mere touch of the finger.

The divan creaked as she struggled in vain against this further outrage, though my own expression remained hopefully as calm as Helen's.

"At least she is not fat. You will enjoy her, Jack. The feather first, of course."

The unearthly shriek that would have arisen then from Lady Edwardes's throat was fortunately dimmed by the pressure of Helen's hand. It emerged only as a shrill gurgle as I parted the rolled lips of her quim and traced with the feather's tip upward until, amid the soft folds of flesh, it alighted upon her clitoris. Her bottom being able to move slightly, she bucked at the first touch, her eyes rolling. Sweeping the feather down again I twiddled it about her cuntlips, delved it under her bottom to titillate her bottomhole, and then brought it up maddeningly again and much more lingeringly to her spot.

"Oh, my Go-oh-oh-od!" cried our voluptuous victim as Helen smoothly removed her hand from Lady Edwardes's mouth.

"I am sure that your daughter will enjoy your vulgar screechings," Helen observed. "We will let her scream her head off, Jack, and let her make a fool of herself."

"Please no, please no! Oh, the torture of this!" Lady Edwardes sobbed, her breasts now fully revealed by

Helen's nimble fingers. And noble orbs they were indeed—full, fleshy, and succulent.

"You have been unfaithful to your husband, of
course—I can tell that by the ardent movements of
your bottom. How many cocks have you entertained,
my dear?" Helen asked in the most matter-of-fact tone
whilst I, picking up another feather, deftly attended to
both her cunt and her bottomhole at the same time,
causing her face to crease up, her lips to purse, and her
eyes to tighten.

"You be-ee-ee-easts!" she sobbed. "Oh, if you do
not cease this outrage—"

"You will come," Helen laughed. "All right, Jack, do
you fancy fucking her bottom now?"

"Never!" screeched Lady Edwardes, who apparently
did not care whether the whole establishment heard her,
though in fact all the other girls had been sent off on a
picnic with Cook.

"Speak, then, you silly woman!" I snapped.

"Oh, wh . . . wh . . . what . . . *Ah!* . . . what
would you have me sa . . . s . . . say? V . . . v
. . . very well, yes, I have b . . . b . . . b . . .
been unfaithful!"

"With whom?" Helen asked in a clipped tone, very
well aware that Sir Humphrey could hear all. With both
features well inserted into the dame, I had her hips
writhing madly. Tears streamed down her plump, rouged
cheeks.

"L . . . L . . . Lord Melkin and . . . and . . .
and . . . his brother!"

"Aha! Not together, though, I trust!" Helen chortled. "Very well, Jack, give her a taster!"

Such a prime target was Lady Edwardes that I had
but to strip off my few garments quickly and slip onto
her between her splayed thighs. Her eyes opened in
horror, for she had had plenty of time to perceive the
state of my cock and a howl of despair rose from her as

I entered my knob between the slippery lips of her cunt.
Her bottom reared. She endeavoured to unmount me. I
ignored her efforts and began sucking upon her thick
nipples while urging my cock to its full extent in her
quim, which I found a little tighter and more succulent
than I expected.

Tossing her head from side to side, her expression
florid, Lady Edwardes began to moan. Helen, seizing
her head, held it still, thus permitting me to peck upon
her full lower lip.

"Kiss him prettily, dear lady, for you are to be well
fucked today," chortled my lovely companion. "Bring
her on, Jack, and then I will untie her legs so that we
may see her mettle."

"No! Oh, *no!"* moaned Lady Edwardes, whose cunt
nevertheless was beginning to draw on my cock in a
way that evinced her internal excitement. Her mouth, at
first lax, responded hesitantly to the seekings of my
tongue. Her thighs quivered at every thrust of my powerful cock.

"Oh! Oh!" she sobbed, little aware that in her enforced passion Helen was now loosing her ankles. They,
of course, would have flopped to the floor on either
side of the narrow divan had Helen not raised them and
crossed them quickly around my waist, where she secured them tightly with a piece of cord.

"Aha," Lady Edwardes screeched, for, by pre-
arranged design, I now cupped her big bottom, raised it
clear of the surface and—parting my own legs and
lodging my fervent prick in her to the full—so allowed
Helen to delve beneath and glide her velvet dildo slowly
up into Lady Edwardes's bottom.

A blistering sob sounded under my mouth, for I cap-
tured the lady's lips in the same moment and writhed
my mouth savagely about hers whilst she now haplessly
entertained both the real pestle and the imitation one.
Jerking her plump stockinged legs violently, she was

nevertheless quite unable to slide them down from their locked position around my hips.

"You will have him fuck you, Lady Edwardes?" came Helen's voice.

"Oh, my God! Sto-o-o-op! It is too much! Ah, you are k . . . killing me!"

"With pleasure no doubt!" I croaked, working my cock back and forth while Helen imitated the movement with the buried dildo. "Come, say you will be fucked, and the other shall be removed!"

"*Wha-ah!* Yes, yes, yes . . . *Ah!* I w . . . w . . . will be fucked!"

"Off, her, Jack—the woman is lewd beyond all belief, but I suspected it of her the moment I saw her," Helen said coolly, drawing out the dildo from Lady Edwardes's bottom whilst I, in a fair lust to conclude the bout, forced myself to remember my role and eased my steaming cock from her nest. Her legs, then released, flopped heavily down on either side of the divan, feet resting on the floor. Her belly twitching, she rolled her head from side to side and moaned insensately, her eyes closed.

"I will never, never live through this!" she sobbed, quite unaware that Helen had moved behind her, removed her dress and—sleekly naked except for her stockings and shoes—knelt from the rear upon her. Clipping Lady Edwardes's arms to her sides with her knees, she plumped her bottom and pussy full over the aristocratic lady's nose and mouth whilst leaning forward to lay her palms flat on her thighs.

"Blub!" came the sudden outraged splutter from beneath whilst I, opening the door to The Snuggery, wheeled in my board which I arranged in such a manner, by virtue of the centre hinge, that one-half concealed the study door from inside view whilst the other stood at an angle. The half of the board facing the outer door stood some six feet from it, which allowed now in this instant ample room for Maude to lead Samantha within.

The girl, faced by the contrivance which she had not been privileged to see before, made to step back. Through the waist hole she could see a pair of plump stockinged thighs and Helen's hands, laid upon them. Her dear Mama's splutterings must have come also to her ears, but she was given little enough time to absorb what might be happening before Maude and I between us bent her swiftly, raised the upper half of the contrivance, and thrust her through it.

The upper half of Samantha's body now lay on the side of the study where her mother was engaged with Helen. Doubtless not recognising the former at first, she nevertheless let forth a horrified shriek at finding herself so held with her already bared bottom protruding toward the door that led to the corridor.

Of a purpose, Helen had attired her in the manner in which we had first seen her in her photograph. A green velvet riding dress was her sole outer attire, the top being fully unbuttoned so that her lovely breasts hung free from it in her bent-over position with her hands madly clasping at the projecting rod. To the rear, the soft velvet was piled up about her gleaming hips. Her stockings were of green silk and gartered tightly, her laced boots brown and brought up to a high polish. A perfect symphony of woodland colours, I thought, which most decoratively framed the luscious naked sphere of her snow-white bottom.

Most wickedly rolling the lips of her quim over Lady Edwardes's mouth, Helen was joined by Maude, who, throwing off a gauzy robe, presented herself in a state of Nature. Throwing herself down at the other end of the divan, she began to lick luxuriously around and within Lady Edwardes's slit, which, because of her wide-open legs, was most plumply displayed.

"What a delicious taste—I vow Jack's cock has been

in here!" Maude murmured, licking the inner surfaces of the lady's thighs at the same time so that she quivered and jerked, her moans muffled beneath Helen's bottom. It was time, however, to entertain Samantha properly, and so Helen lifted her hips sufficiently to permit the girl to see Lady Edwardes's hot-flushed face.

"Mama!" shrieked Samantha in perfect horror, which, in turn, caused her mother to cry out her name in echo, though her scream lasted not long before it was muffled again beneath the descending globe whose cleft was apparently pleasantly tickled by Lady Edwardes's nose. Maude's tongue, continuing to lick and slurp, meanwhile, the lady was fast losing her senses, for the tip of that tongue was infinitely more luring than the feather she had recently entertained around her clitty and was causing Lady Edwardes's heels to drum upon the floor.

Unheard by either of the female victims, then, the door behind Samantha opened and a distraught Sir Humphrey was led in by Lucy, who had a firm hold on his upstanding cock. I tactfully absented myself from his view on the other side of the board and listened.

"We have endeavoured to bring Samantha to a pitch, sir, where but six strokes of the leather have her in fine fettle for it—perhaps you would care to try?" came Lucy's voice.

This, being perfectly well heard by Samantha, despite her shrieks, caused her to utter them more loudly since she could have been in no doubt as to the owner of the voice that uttered an astounded *"Ah!"* The luring fingers of Lucy about Sir Humphrey's distended cock, however, did the trick, for there came then as fine a *cra-aaaack!* As I have ever heard. Samantha's eyes bulged, a loud *"Whaaaaaah!"* leapt from her throat, and amidst all this cacophony was heard the wail of Lady Edwardes, who, being freed at last from the sumptuous weight of Helen's bottom, uttered her husband's name in a tone that would have been of despair had Maude not been nearing her goal.

"H . . . H . . . H . . . Humphree-ee-ee-eee!" came the sobbing cry.

"Jack! She is about to come!" Maude uttered, and, with Helen, drew aside to allow me to plunge upon the voluptuous victim, my cock entering her cunt again in one long stroke. It was plain she could no longer resist. Her belly rippled under mine. I sought her mouth, plunging my tongue within. Levering her heels upon the floor, she began to work her bottom, moaning insensately. A velvety gripping of her slit about my prick, and I knew her to be lost in a fervour of lust from which she could no longer withdraw. Her arms winding about me, I sought her bottomhole with my finger and eased it within, causing her to buck even more amourously.

Cra-aaaack! Cra-aaack! had sounded meanwhile as Samantha's bottom writhed on the hidden side of the board to the descending strap.

"One more, sir, and she is ready," Lucy's voice came.

"Pa-pa-pa-pa, *no!*"

Lady Edwardes's petulant sobs sounded meanwhile in my ear as I reamed her. Twice now she had spattered my indriving prick with her effusions. Maude, throwing herself beside us, seized upon Lady Edwardes's mouth, the lady heaving and blubbering between us, her jellied breasts rolling under me.

Striding toward the board, Helen swiftly removed the bar to which Samantha's hands clung and, kneeling before her, took her tear-streaked face in her hands.

"You are to be put to the cock now, Samantha, as long ago you should have been. Give me your tongue, my sweet."

"*Nooo-oooh! Mama!*" Samantha wailed, but all was lost in that moment in a perfect symphony of cries and issuing groans of lust. Unable to hold back any longer amidst such a lubricious scene, I commenced pumping my sperm into Lady Edwardes, whose sparkling libation sprinkled at the same time upon my spouting knob, her mouth avidly receiving the tongue-thrusts of Maude.

Sir Humphrey, meanwhile, had clearly inserted himself, as the shrill choking cry from Samantha announced. No longer supported by her hands, she was forced to cling to Helen's shoulder's, such a babbling and sobbing issuing from her as was finally quenched by the insistence of Helen's mouth against her own.

A rattling moan came from Lady Edwardes, as our slippery loins sank down together and remained stickily enmeshed. Soothed still by Maude's mouth, she appeared to be in an unknowing daze, her face pale, eyelashes fluttering. My cock, remaining embedded in her, stiffened anew at the sight of Samantha's falling tears that glittered even upon Helen's cheeks as her mouth moved gently over the girl's.

"Come, dear, he is well at you now, work your bottom," Helen urged.

"Oh-oh-oh-oooh!" from Samantha. Her knuckles whitened in their grip.

"She is moving to him now, Ma'am," came from the hidden Lucy. "Faster now, sir, I believe she is coming."

"Mama! Ah! Oh-oooooh!"

A last wild cry from Samantha, and her shoulders slumped. She would have fallen full down had Helen not been holding her. Stinging sweetly in the tight clutching of Lady Edwardes's slit, my prick had begun to move again. A hollow groan sounded from Sir Humphrey behind the board. Samantha's mouth opened, a soft *"whoooooo!"* issued from her throat, and then her head sank upon the shoulders of Helen, who stroked her hair, regarding me with a quick look of triumph over her shoulder. I, working my loins anew, commenced awarding Lady Edwardes her second injection as the matted hairs around her plump quim rubbed beneath my own.

Had I but had her on my own, I might have rested from my labours a moment, but the ever-practical Helen would not have it so. Raising the upper half of the board, she presented the combatants full to view, Sir Humphrey's limp cock being nestled in Lucy's palm like a stricken bird. Moving quickly around the partition, Helen took up the limp and sobbing Samantha, who, being urged toward her Mama, from whose supine and quivering form I arose, fell upon her.

"Oh, Mama!"

"Oh, Samantha!"

Such an idyllic scene of reunion did not last for long, however. Taking up a cane, Helen awarded Samantha's fiushed bottom a quick *sweeee-isssh!* which, bringing a shriek from her, caused her also to roll backward onto the floor. Her dress, being well wreathed up still about her waist, displayed her glistening quim, her noble young tits, and the splendour of her long, curving legs.

"Go to the armchair, Samantha—sit! Lady Edwardes, up with you!"

"Yee-aaaah!" Samantha's Mama squealed, being awarded a quick flick of the cane across her thighs. In a moment, she sat upon the edge of the divan, head bowed, murmuring and moaning, "Oh, God, what will happen to us!" Such feeble attempts as she made to cover herself were forestalled by Maude.

"Some wine, Lucy!" ordered Helen to the maid, who, divested of her dress also and looking exquisite in shimmering black stockings and black knee boots, offered her impudent bottom, dark bush and bouncy tits to our view. Sir Humphrey, being attired in only his shirt—in which condition Lucy had first led him in— sank on to a pouffe and gazed about him as dazed as his wife. Helen, whilst the wine was being poured, settled

herself on the arm of Samantha's chair and placed her
arm around the shoulders of the girl who sat blushing
with her gaze fixed on the ceiling.

"Drink!" Helen commanded her sharply when Lucy
brought round the tray. Taking the glass blindly, Samantha raised it to her lips, spluttered, choked, and
then, with an inane giggle, emptied her glass at a gulp.
Maude, taking Lady Edwardes's chin and lifting it,
manoeuvred the rim of the glass between her quivering
lips and so held it whilst she drank.

"Sir Humphrey, I believe you will have no further
problems," Helen said crisply," but to ensure that you
do not, I have arranged a private bedroom for you.
You will have heard your wife's lewd confessions. I
have no doubt that you will deem her fit for discipline
henceforth as well. Lucy will conduct you upstairs in a
moment. I shall require your report upon the pair in the
morning."

"H . . . Hu . . . Humphrey!" came a single wail
from his wife. Maude, holding her fast, she watched as
Lucy—having handed him the last glass—then sank to
the floor and took the knob of his cock in her mouth.

"I say, I . . . *aaaargh!*" he groaned. His prick began to stiffen perceptibly. In a moment, the thick shaft
moved smoothly in and out of Lucy's pursed lips. Having so quickly effected her purpose, she then got up,
and, with swaying hips, advanced toward me for her
prize.

Helen sprang up. "Here, Sir Humphrey is what you
will best need in addition to that wicked weapon," she
declared, handing him the cane.

"Well! I say!" he replied all of a fluster, spilling his
drink as he rose to take it. Samantha giggled again and
hid her face at the sight of his hairy thighs and stiff
prick which she had vainly avoided trying to look at.
All the proud demeanour which she had previously possessed appeared to have deserted her. Her quavering

cry of "No! Oh, I can't!" was cut off abruptly by Helen's awarding her a sharp smack on the bottom as she pulled her up.

"No, Humphrey, you dare not!" sobbed Lady Edwardes in turn. But doubtless, to her amazement as much as Samantha's, it was his voice now that cracked across the room.

"You dare oppose me, woman, after your wicked confessions? Up with you. Come here Samantha, you too!"

"Oh, Papa!"

"Oh, Hu . . . Hu . . . Humphrey. *Yeee*-ow!"

This last exclamation being caused by the stinging palm of Maude across Lady Edwardes's bare bottom, she leapt up with a howl, her waist being seized by her husband, who looped his other around the blushing Samantha. The cane, gripped with some authority in his hand, tapped at her silken thigh. Lucy now had lowered her mouth to my cock, drawing sweetly upon the knob, as Maude opened the door. The empty corridor and the curving staircase loomed before the trio.

"I will conduct you, Sir Humphrey. You have no need to keep a hold on them. I will ensure that they follow," Maude declared. A cry from Samantha and a wail from her mother, and they were gone. In but three minutes, a flushed Maude returned, displaying the key.

"I fear that Lady Edwardes is getting the cane first," she laughed. "Oh! And you should see the look on Samantha's face!".

"I would prefer to see it when she gets the cock next," Helen responded with a chuckle. And then, turning to me where I sat with my prick still being juicily sucked by Lucy, murmured, "Come, darling, you have three luscious pussies to entertain, and you will give us all a little poke first before we intrude on the scene upstairs!"

Chapter 17

"WHAT A NIGHT, JACK!" Helen murmured to me fondly the next morning upon the departure of Sir Humphrey and Lady Edwardes—and Samantha.

I had to confess that it had surpassed all expectations and—more—that all of Helen's intutions about the girl had been correct. Apart from the small lapse of her nervous giggling in the study, she had afterward disported herself exactly as Helen had forecast. Committed to her fate, she had that previous evening taken both offered cocks in her bottom one after the other, whilst Maude and Lucy between them had teased and feathered her Mama into a more abject and panting surrender. Apart from a slight hissing of breath through her nostrils and little impetuous movements of her bottom as her excitement rose, Samantha had neither surrendered vocally or by her facial expressions.

"She behaved like a perfect machine of desire—her heart cold, her bottom warm," I exclaimed, not without a little wonderment and a certain admiration for the beauteous girl. "Yet, on the first occasion—" I made to continue when Helen halted me by placing her finger against my lips.

"We must allow her that, Jack—the physical surprise of her initiation—but how she recovered from it! She will draw men by the score, for all will wish to conquer her heart as easily as they appear to bring her to the cock . . . if they do. I quite adore her. She will never be broken in."

"A marble Venus and no more," said I. "I would sooner have the more responsive charms of a Victoria or a Monique—or, indeed, a Belinda—any day."

"But she charmed you, did she not? Come, confess it, Jack. Such young women always will, though such as Samantha are a rare enough breed. Your board is a lovely invention, for it held her the first time exactly as pleased me. Little do you know how luringly she was tipping her tongue into my mouth whilst he was up her! I shall have her yet," Helen said almost wistfully, adding quickly, "but in private, Jack. You won't deny me that?"

"I deny you nothing, my sweet," I assured her, "provided you are not as cautious henceforth in maintaining the girls' virginities."

"I have been wrong about that, Jack, yes. I give you my pledge that you shall have them by every aperture henceforth. This will not prevent me from giving them preliminary training, of course. In some cases, though, that may be shorter than others. After last night I have been reflecting about the matter and believe we may reduce each term in some cases to a period as short as a month. Take, for instance, the case of Sally."

"Who?" I interjected, bringing a silvery laugh from Helen as we strode at morning across the sunbathed lawn.

"The Honourable Sally Wittington, my dear. She is *very* young—a mere sixteen—but quite an intriguing subject. In the last year, as I understand, she has taken moderately well to having her bottom spanked, and has been ringed into the bargain."

"Ringed?" I echoed, though even as I spoke a glimmering of understanding broke upon me.

"I believe, darling," said Helen confidentially, "that it means he has had his knob at least in her bottom. Shall we discover if that is so? She will be here shortly."

I affected to yawn. "Something of a bore, but I think we might manage it," I responded, after a loving nudge from Helen.

"It is you who will do the boring, my pet—into her bottom—and her pussy as well, I trust. You see, she has two sisters, and both are promised to us if we do well with this one. Enough said?"

"Ample. Are they older? I do trust so."

"Oh, really, what a prig! Fifteen would be a perfectly good age for a nubile young thing to be inducted—but have no fear in this case. The other two are her seniors, though not by so much. I think we shall dispense with Maude's assistance on this occasion. I would rather like us to have Sally to ourselves. Agreed? Oh, good. Be a good boy and you shall have what you want. She is too young for the cane, by my standards, but a good spank will bring her up, not to say a touch of fine oil to ease her surrender. I suspect that has been the trouble to date," Helen concluded with mock solemnity so that I could not help but pause and kiss her and fondle her bottom.

"Enough of that, Jack," she exclaimed after an all too brief passionate embrace. Seeing my expression, she laughed and fondled me.

"I believe you do truly like me," she said wistfully, and I—knowing her to be acting, in part—raised her mouth anew to mine and kissed her gently.

"I love you and adore you," I said with a fervency that astonished even myself and caused her to sigh with pleasure as her perfumed breath flowed over mine.

"Then that is settled," Helen declared with a laugh, "for I will continue to keep a close eye on you and you are to know it. Come, let us make ourselves look all solemn and institutional for Sally. I'm sure she will expect it!"

How right she was in all her anticipations! Maude looked quite put out at three that afternoon when, having led Sally in, she departed again immediately upon a nod from Helen. Gazing at me first a trifle wonderingly, Sally stood as any schoolgirl might in front of Helen's desk, though as we gathered she attended no school but had a governess.

"Is your tutor nice, Sally?" Helen asked disarmingly.

"Oh, yes, Miss, she is quite young and pretty and . . ."

"Go on, Sally."

"Well—I don't know if I should say it, but she gets in . . . in . . . indoctrinated, like me . . . well, sometimes."

"Indoc?" Helen began, and then a smile spread over her features. "Oh, yes, I see—and does she have her knickers taken down for it as well?"

"Oh, Miss?" A deep blush spread over the pretty young thing's features. Her mass of golden hair, her cherubic features, her smallish stature, and the promising curves that displayed themselves beneath her grey silk dress all bespoke a perfect angel.

"It does not matter, Sally, you will tell me in due course, I am sure. You have had lunch. Was it nice? Oh, good. Now I am going to give you a little spank just to see what a good girl you are. Come, dear."

Rising at her words, Helen went to the wider of the two divans and, seating herself, extended her hand toward the hesitant girl with a sweet smile. "Come!" she repeated whilst the flush that had already infused Sally's cheeks grew deeper and her eyes darted toward me again where I sat casually in a chair.

"Oh, Miss, but he—" she began, only to receive a tut-tut from Helen.

"It is necessary for him to observe your progress,

Sally. Are you going to come and lie across my lap, as you are perfectly used to doing in other circumstances, or not? Jack—bring her here!"

"Miss, no!" came a panicky squeal from Sally, who thereupon rushed to the door and seized the handle, turning it in vain.

"It will *not* open, Sally, until I wish it. Do you make so much fuss as this at home? I believe not. I am minded to make you take off your drawers yourself, but I think it would be far more pleasurable for you if we do."

A fair chase then ensued around the study, much to the amusement of Helen as the little minx several times escaped me but was finally caught up and carried, legs kicking, to where Helen, with a wink, had already drawn her own dress up to the tops of her thighs, displaying the full length of her elegant silk-sheathed legs.

"What a nonsense!" she chuckled gaily whilst a wriggling and crying Sally was hauled over her lap, and by force of Helen's arm around her waist, held so whilst I drew her dress up, exposing a delightful pair of legs in white stockings and, above, the chubby richness of her bottom which in as quick a time I had uncovered.

"No, Miss! Oh, it is rude! *Ah! Oh! Ooooh!* It stings!"

Smack! Helen's hand had descended immediately, leaving the pink imprint of her palm and fingers on the pert hemispheres beneath which I could espy an enchanting little nest of brown curls.

"Miss! *Ow!* Don't! St . . . st . . . stop it! *Ouch!* Oh, my bottom!"

Smack! Smack! "Yes, my little pet, it is your bottom that most needs attention, though I suspect that your bubbies get fondled, too, do they not? Jack, I think we'll have her dress off. What a pretty one she is!"

Smack! With her bottom already flushed full pink now, Sally sobbed and struggled as between us we brought her to her feet and—Helen standing—got off her dress and chemise, so bringing her to a state of Nature, save for her stockings and pink frilly garters. The fuzz on her belly was light and soft. Beneath it, two delicious lips pouted as well I saw, when, in pretence of holding her legs, I knelt to observe her.

"Oh! It's so naughtee-ee-eee!" howled Sally, whose bottom projected so impertinently.

"Yes, dear, of course it is, and we mean you to be naughty. In fact, we shall make you even naughtier than you have been. Jack, have a little taste first before I warm her up further. Lay her on her back!"

"No! Oh, I won't! I shall tell Mama!" Sally shrieked, her legs prevented from kicking by Helen who, seating herself, held them well enough apart for me to finger her adorable little slit. Her exertions had already brought about a certain moisture there, and my finger slipped easily enough in, making her arch her back and squeal louder, "Mama, Mama!"

"Hush, you silly girl! Your Mama would have heard these silly yelps long ere this had you been minded to let her. Spin her over, Jack, and feel her bottom. What a chubby one!"

To an apparently outraged *"Yee-*ow!" from Sally, spun over she was, her ankles gripped anew by my wicked accomplice. I laid my hand in the small of her back and prevented her from wriggling whilst I bent down and passed my tongue deeply into her groove.

*"Whoooo-*oooh!" Sally squealed. Her hips twisting madly, I then gripped them, holding her so tight that she could no longer jerk the delicious cheeks which my tongue invaded anew. Feeling the tip at her puckered rosehole, she squeaked madly and beat upon the divan with her fists. Imitating Helen, I dipped my tongue a full inch within the warm orifice and felt her quiver throughout her being.

"Allow me, Jack," interjected Helen. Swiftly enough,

whilst Sally made the most frantic efforts to rise, we changed places, I holding her stockinged legs wide apart whilst she was forced still to lie on her belly as Helen parted her bottom cheeks wide and better exposed the rubbery ring to her caresses.

"Now, my little love, we shall see what you like. You have had his knob in, have you not?"

"No! Oh, how horrible you are! Stop it! *Ow!* Oh, I can't st . . . stand it!"

Helen's pointed tongue was now full at work, making Sally's hips squirm sensuously. Her orifice then distinctly wetted, Helen sat up, threw her hair back, and dipped the index finger of her left hand within, bringing a high-pitched squeal and a further beating of fists.

"Hold her firmly, Jack!"

Gliding her free hand under Sally's silky tummy, Helen cupped her plump quim and, curling her index finger within, tickled her gently whilst beginning to move her other in and out of the girl's bottom.

"No-oooh! Ah! Oh, no, you can't! Don't! I don't *want* to!"

Strong as my wrists are, I confess to having had a job to keep the little minx still whilst Helen thus attended to her, her elbow frequently bumped by Sally's heaving back, yet not a flicker of expression save perhaps a tinge of curiosity passed over her lovely features as she relentlessly went on with her sensuous "twiddling."

Sally's cries grew noticeably lower then, I noticed. Her yells changed to sobs and her sobs to muffled burblings. Weepily she continued to try and distort her exquisite young form still, though with less energy than before. Finally, withdrawing both her fingers, Helen gave her a playful little smack and stood up.

"Yes, I think we can make you very naughty, Sally," she declared quietly. "Let her go, Jack, I want her to stand up!"

"Oh, Miss, no! Let me dress! Oh, I want to go *home!*"

"Get *up,* Sally! All right, you won't? Jack, fetch the cane!"

"No!" Such a screech of utter dismay came from Sally, who literally leapt up with a haunted expression in her eyes and covered her pussy shyly with one hand, which Helen as promptly smacked away.

"Stand properly, Sally! Oh, really, what a great to-do with you! Hands at your sides, girl, or you shall have the cane! Now, what is the truth of this? You have had the cane? I suspect as much."

"Oh-oh-oh!" Sally sobbed, looking deliciously eatable as she did, with her firm young tits as proud as pomegranites displaying their cherry nipples.

"All right, Jack, she will not speak. Hand me the cane."

"I will, I will! I did once—I did have the cane. Oh, it was awful! I let myself be spanked now, I do, I do." Sally sobbed so much that Helen gathered her in her arms, cunningly soothing her palm about her proud young bottom.

"Yes, dear, I know, I know. Such a good girl," Helen said softly, giving me a sly nod so that I immediately divested myself of my light attire and stood in avid waiting behind the girl. You have been a little naughty, too, haven't you, Sally? Come, tell me. You can tell me, you know. What do you have after your spankings? Cuddles and kisses for not making too much noise? Yes? Oh, I thought you did. And what else, a finger in your pussy? Come, whisper, darling, he can't hear. Ooooh, that's nice! But what goes in your bottom—his knob? Come, tell me, I *do* know. What? Oh! Three times only? And did you wriggle a lot?"

"T . . . t . . . t . . . too big!" I heard Sally whisper then, for all her other words had been lost to me.

Cuddled as she was in Helen's arms, she appeared to have forgotten my presence.

"Too big? Oh, they are all big, darling, but they do go in, Sally. Now, will you do one thing for me? Turn round now and look at this gentleman's cock."

"Miss, no!"

Sally's shriek seemed to bring her back to earth, which by no means prevented her from being spun round on it by Helen, who continued to clasp her firmly, her arms gripped to her sides.

"There—is it as big, Sally?"

"Oh!" Unable to cover her face, Sally could do naught but stare at my upstanding penis, which quivered in full erection. The fact that I still had the cane in my hand no doubt caused her to lick her lips.

"Speak, Sally!" Helen commanded.

"No, Miss—yes, Miss! Oh, I mean, yes, it is—but I don't want to, please!"

"Very well, Sally."

To my surprise, then, Helen simply let go of her, doing it so suddenly that with a squeal the girl bumped her tummy full against my stiff, springy cock and then ran to the farther corner by the door, huddling there.

Ignoring her, Helen slipped off her dress and cuddled amorously into my arms, kissing me and rubbing my prick. "What a silly little girl she is, Jack, isn't she? Come, let us have a drink or two, and then I will have it instead. Pour me some wine, dear."

Seating herself on the divan and crossing her black-stockinged legs, Helen hummed gently to herself, not looking at all in the direction of Sally, as I also avoided doing, being much taken with the game. My prick stemming up lewdly, I sat with her, her warm thigh pressed to mine. Acting as if the girl were not there, Helen became to chatter away to me about all number of things, referring, whilst she did so, to "all the other girls we have had, and none made this silly fuss, did they?" I, of course, agreed with her solemnly. For a full fifteen minutes we sat thus, Helen lovingly caressing my tool and kissing me fondly from time to time. I had in fact replenished our wine glasses and was about to sit down again when a small voice from the corner said, "Miss..."

Helen turned her head casually and asked, "Yes, Sally?"

"M . . . Miss, if I do . . . c . . . may I go?"

"Do what, Sally?" came Helen's cool reply.

"Well . . . if . . . if I'm naughty, I . . . as you wish me to be."

"Come here, Sally. No—don't sit down and don't cover that pretty pussy of yours. I shall recommend no more spankings for you, but an occasional strapping until you are properly obedient. Show her the tawse, Jack."

I got up and produced the instrument, noticing as I did so that the little minx had her eyes on my stiff cock as much as on the thick supple leather. A sound somewhere between a giggle and a gasp came from her.

"Ooh, Miss, it will hurt me!"

"Of course it won't *hurt* you, girl. It will sting you, yes, for it is intended to do so, but it will warm you up nicely and help to keep your bottom well up for your 'afters,' as I call them. Do you know what they are?"

Putting her finger in her mouth in a manner that I felt sure was intended to beguile us, Sally looked quickly at my longing erection again, blushed, and stared at the ground. "It's what . . . it's what . . . oh! I can't say it!"

Helen gave a light laugh and, rising, whispered something in the girl's ear. Hesitating but at last obeying her, Sally knelt then upon the divan on all fours with her bottom forming the most enticing little peach. "P . . . p . . . please not hard!" she stammered and closed her eyes tightly as her hair clouded down over her face.

"Two dozen light ones, Jack," Helen whispered to me.

Two dozen seemed to present an eternity to me, then, for I was longing to get into the adorable little thing. Neither Helen nor I had any doubts about her willingness to take the cock if she was brought to it properly. At the first *thwack!* the luscious apple of her bottom jerked and squirmed with surprise, bringing a sharp "Oh, *Miss!*"

"Dip your back—bottom well up—legs apart, Sally—come on!" Helen snapped.

Thwack! "Wow-ow! Ooooh! It stings! *Thwack! Yeee-ouch!*"

"A little harder on the last three, Jack," Helen whispered to me as a radiant sheen of pink spread over Sally's pert, wriggling globe. To panting *"Oooh-aaah's"* from the girl, Helen prepared herself for the event by sliding onto the divan immediately in front of the girl's head. Slithering her own naked botton on the seat, she raised her legs up under Sally's armpits and quickly wound her calves around the girl's shoulders, thus bringing her face down onto her belly, where she was held secured.

Thwack! Thwack! Thwack!

Scarce had the last *"Yeee-owch!"* ripped from Sally that I was up on the divan behind her. Taking her madly weaving hips, I nosed the swollen crest of my prodder under the pursed lips of her quim and, rubbing it gently back and forth in the succulent groove, urged in with a groan.

"Neee-ow!" from Sally.

"Yes, Sally! Hold her tight, Jack!"

"St . . st . . . stop him! Oh, it's big! Oh! *Ah!"*

Squirming crazily as she was, Sally could do naught now but accept the slow invasion of my stiff cock within the silky, clinging depths of her cunny, whose walls yielded inch by inch to the valiant invasion. Her sobs resounded whilst Helen stroked her corn-gold hair.

"Ooooh! Miss! *Oooh-Hooooo!"*

With a last quivering lunge, I was rammed in her to the full, my balls dangling heavily at her bottom, which burned to my flesh. Reaching beneath her and feeling every quiver of her divine young body, I cupped her sweet tits whose rubbery-stiff nipples tickled amourously to my palms. The suction of her cunt was so tight that for a moment I feared not to be able to get it in again as I slewed out almost to the knob and then began to piston her.

Her sobs quieted as her bottom bulbed once more into my belly in the inward strokes, the juicy interior of her quim clamping about my straining rod like a small deep mouth. Defensively, as it seemed, her arms wound themselves about Helen's hips, little bubbling sobs issuing from her lips. Grinding myself full into her, I began to fuck her in short little jabs, bringing breathless gasps from her.

"All right, Jack—I want to see her willing now. Slip it out and we'll turn her over," declared Helen. Twisting out from under Sally whilst I grooved out my now-well-moistened cock, she turned her upon her back, causing her to squeak and cup her hands over her face.

"No, Sally, not like that! Uncover your face, girl, draw your knees up, and spread your legs well. Get hold of his cock and tell him you want to be fucked. Come on, now, or I'll bring the cane to you myself!"

Sally's attempts to squeeze forth tears were all too transparent now. Her obedience came slowly whilst I knelt in avid waiting between her legs. At the first moist touch of her petal mouth to mine and the sly groping of her hand to my throbbing cock, she was lost as surely as was I. In the instant I was lodged full up her again. Winding her stockinged legs tightly about my hips, she beat a veritable tattoo with her heels upon my buttocks.

"I want to be . . . I want to be . . . I want to be f . . . f . . . fucked!" she blathered.

Ah, what a juicy little fuck she proved as, clinging beneath me and sobbing her pleasure divinely in my mouth, I reamed her strongly and steadily, feeling the tight ringing of her demanding little cuntlips with every burning stroke whilst my balls smacked back and forth under her bottom. Clawing her nails into my back, she uttered a tremulous *"Oooooh!"* The little witch was coming! Sprinkling the nose of my cock with her pleasure fountain, she received in turn the thick, shooting leaps of my own libation whilst her bottom bumped and bounced on my palms with eager pleasure.

Calm being restored at last, Helen awarded the sweetly flushed girl a loving kiss, caressing her everywhere and telling her what a perfect pupil she was.

"You will come down again this evening to have another lesson," she soothed as she helped her dress. Sally, being in such a trembling of wonder, knew not where to look.

"Yes, Miss," she replied at last whilst Helen gave me a knowing wink and rang for Maude, who appeared so quickly that neither of us were in any doubt that she had been longing to be called in. No sooner, however, than she had led Sally off than Lucy appeared.

"It's that young lady's two sisters," she declared. "The gentleman said he had decided not to wait after all."

"Oh!" Helen responded with a pretty laugh and turned to me with a smile.

"Well, Jack, it's going to be a busy day!"